the girl
that he
marries

Also by Rhoda Lerman

*Call Me Ishtar*

# the girl that he marries

a novel by

## rhoda lerman

**holt, rinehart and winston**

**new york**

Published simultaneously in Canada by Holt,
Rinehart and Winston of Canada, Limited.

Library of Congress Cataloging in Publication Data

Lerman, Rhoda.
  The girl that he marries.

  I. Title.
PZ4.L613Gi    [PS3562.E68]    813'.5'4    75-29908
ISBN 0-03-015336-0

Excerpts from the lyrics of "The Girl That I Marry"
by Irving Berlin, on pp. 48, 62, and 211, copyright 1946
by Irving Berlin, © copyright renewed 1974 by Irving
Berlin. Reprinted by permission of Irving Berlin
Music Corporation.

Excerpts from the lyrics of "One Alone," words by
Harbach and Hamerstein II, music by Sigmund
Romberg, copyright 1926 by Harms Inc. Copyright
renewed. All rights reserved. Reprinted by permission
of Warner Bros. Music.

First Edition
Printed in the United States of America
10 9 8 7 6 5 4 3 2 1

To Barbara McCrory and Margie Roth

with special gratitude to Julia Coopersmith
and Marian Wood.

the girl
that he
marries

The Lanivet Cross Number One has on it, incised into the ancient Cornish stone, a simple sketch of a man with a tail. On the end of the tail is an appendage which looks like a heart. It also looks like the rear end of a turkey. The Christian legend is that the wicked men of Cornwall were cursed by St. Augustine to grow tails. Whatever the pagan significance of that heart-shaped appendage on the end of the tail, what is significant for me is that the man's heart is directly related to his asshole.

We decided one night in someone's den, at a party raging beyond us, that we would be perfect friends as long as we could. We had just met. Standing over an Arabian dip, tearing crusts of bread, I felt his finger pressing instinctively into the fine scar line along my throat. "I have to talk to you. I mean really."

"Talk," I invited over the table.

"I really want to talk to you. Seriously." And seriously he lifted an invisible flute from the same basket which held only bread crusts for me, ran his polished moon-pink nails along the silver sides of the flute, turned and walked away, looking once, over his shoulder, eyes dancing, at me. So I followed him, whoever he was, into a pink, carrot, plum den in the eclectic cliché which includes at any cost a mounted Nautilus, I. F. Stone, *The Way of the Pilgrim*, and something, at least one, of Alan D'Arcangelo. I followed him past a waist-high digital calendar clock flipping its large minute pages at us, whirring, whizzing, and wasting, the letters and number the size of hands, fluorescent and plugged in. Everything was plugged in, on time, set, ready. The couch he led me to faced a built-in plugged-in movie screen, backed up against a gleaming ebony desk with its own sets of plugs for projectors and anchored on either side with a telephone, a fresh, scented pile of notepaper, and a pewter mug of newly sharpened pencils. He laid his flute on the arm of the couch, addressed my attention to the screen, the telephones, the notepapers. Then, with courtliness, it could be described no other way, presented me with a fresh pencil and pad. We laughed. I gave him a fresh pencil and pad. We wrote, exchanged sheets, he sniffed my hair, murmured "delicious," and read my name aloud.

"Stephanie."

I had written my last name also. He didn't read that.

Along with his first name was a phone number. "Richard," I returned.

"My office."

Something of the purity of the situation, the way what should be happening seemed to be happening, became entangled with his office number. I didn't know why. His eyes were gray-flecked, his grin incorporated a convincing percentage of his orthodontic teeth, fleetingly crooked, a dimple in a strong chin, slightly uneven nostrils, a lovely soft dusting of downy hair spread between his nostrils and his cheeks, creature hair. Interesting. Not fascinating. But interesting. I put his note in my pocket.

He offered me the couch. I sat next to him as he took my hands, looked deep into my eyes, just like the movies, while I tried not to flutter or flush. "Stephanie, it would be *so* easy to make love to a girl like you."

Yes? No? The perfect dilemma. Keep your mouth shut; let him think he's in control of the situation. How to relate to a man. How to find a man to marry. This is it. Is this IT? Don't say, "That's a hell of a line."

"Do you understand me?"

"I think so, Richard." I tried to sound serious, just as he sounded, but actually I wanted to laugh.

"Good. Because what I *need* is a friend. A *real* friend, Stephanie."

2

I nodded for space.

"And I want you to be my *friend*. Really."

If I had thought or perhaps understood then, I would not have reached up to the pale sea-creature blond hairs, waving like cilia along his cheeks. I didn't think. A page buzzed, preparing itself to flip over, clicked, flipped, and another page began to buzz. He reached up to feel the cheek I had touched.

"Anything wrong with my skin?"

"You left some hairs, that's all."

"Oh." He hadn't liked my touching him.

"Anything wrong with my touching your cheek?"

"Nope. As long as you understand, Stephanie."

He spoke my name as my piano teacher had when I couldn't lift the fourth finger of my left hand. "You'll never play the piano with a lazy finger like that, Stephanie," he would grumble behind me while I struggled with that utterly paralyzed extension of myself. Later my mother told me it was my ring finger which wouldn't move.

"Stephanie, do you understand?" Richard's face was close to mine.

"Maybe I don't really know what you mean, Richard."

He loosed my hands and I folded them in my lap. I thought he might kiss me. He leaned an elbow on the couch arm and chewed lightly on his manicured thumb, lips pressed together. The calendar clock never gave up. We would sit here forever, the month ending, the year ending, and I, stupidly, happy with anticipation and thoroughly discontent as if there were two of myself, waiting to be kissed and wanting to scream.

He spoke at last from his reverie. "I've never had a good friend since Steve. I'll tell you about Steve sometime. I want you to be my friend. Will you?"

"I'd be glad to."

"There are rules, of course."

"Of course."

He didn't tell me the rules. He laid his hand on my

wrist. "I won't talk to you any more tonight. You have to think about being my friend. We'll go out and enjoy the party and do whatever we expected to do if this hadn't happened. I won't take you home. But I do want you to go home and really think about being my friend. Seriously."

The calendar clock seemed to speed up. He said nothing, rocking his head to the tick of the clock, tapping his feet into the depth of the Rya. I waited until the blood danced around his hand, up and down my arm. His rule was that we wouldn't speak. I had no idea what he wanted. Once a man had turned to me in terror in the lobby of a hotel and said, in true pain, "Meet me in Room 414. I've had a terrible accident." His face was ribbed in agony.

It could have been a brilliant pickup and I laughed until something motherly clicked and reminded me that he was an utter stranger who might truly need someone to help him. I followed him to his room and as I came in past the bellboy, he was screaming from the bathroom, "I haven't been laid since my colostomy. Since *June!*" Only a woman like you so intelligent would understand." I ducked out past the bellboy who held a vested suit reeking of fresh excrement, beyond the naked screaming man and flushing toilet and running bathwater and out, racing away. I could still hear the echo down the corridor, "Who needs you anyway? You look like an aging Pepsi ad."

"Stephanie, when can I call you to know what you've decided?"

"Listen, are you crazy?"

"I'm *not* trying to make a pass at you, Stephanie. I love you. I just have to know if you're going to be my friend. When can I call you?"

His hand tightened over my wrist.

"How about Sunday at two? Can I call you Sunday at two?"

"Sure." He handed me my notepaper for my phone number.

4

"Let me walk out first. You count to one hundred. Sunday at two?" I was into the eighties when I asked myself what the hell I was doing. By one hundred, I was free to come out and I saw him sitting at an ebony piano on a deep white swath of Flokati. A young girl with rich thick henna hair and buckteeth that were almost predatory leaned against him. A very young girl, in something patchy and poor from India. He riffed on the piano badly and then slid into a familiar tune from *Show Boat*, anachronistic, not even camp, unlike the girl, the Flokati, the scene. I didn't recognize the song until the girl began to sing it in a wonderful high voice. It wasn't *Show Boat*, it was *Annie Get Your Gun*. It was "The Girl That I Marry." I realized they knew each other well. He had just told me he loved me. I held a glass of soda water at eye level and peered over the icy lip for his eyes to catch mine in the significance I thought I had just become deserving of. He never looked at me. He kissed the girl often on the head. Too often. And then she burst into "I'm Just a Girl Who Can't Say No," which he picked up on the keyboard as if they had rehearsed before the party. I had never wished to be younger or to sing badly in church-choir soprano or to be in love with a man who plays a bad piano and knows only show tunes. Nevertheless I considered shoving her off the piano bench. I felt a challenge and a surge of jealousy so rare in my life that I welcomed with surprise the richness of the emotion although I knew even then it was too soon to feel it.

Actually though, I thought in the cab home, I was much better looking than the girl at the piano. I did look like an aging Pepsi ad but that only indicated I was reaching the age when I could sell Lincoln Continentals and oven cleaners. Flash of white tooth, Sassoon-cut hair, a little flat-chested but leaner, longer, cleaner, athletic. I wouldn't, for instance, look out of place with a pair of afghans. Wholesome. I liked being wholesome. I had integrity, inside and out. Men like Richard always like me, and I'm attracted to them because they play games. I also know if you get hooked on their game as real, or their secret as truth, or their dream as possible, or their potential as hero, then it's suicide and you're stuck with the prize. Sometimes my lesser self, although it might be my higher self, says yes to the Richards just to see how far along into the game I can go and still survive. And even if the Richards aren't as interesting as I think they are, their interest in me always kindles my interest in them. This Richard was interested. With some kind of psychic economy, this Richard fit right into my movie.

He didn't call on Sunday at two. The phone rang at ten-thirty that night, after I had cleaned the entire apartment, washed my hair, slipped into new Pucci bikinis, blue and seascape silk, which I had been saving for an occasion, and read Campbell's *Myths to Live By*. It didn't quite have the scenario for my movie. After an aesthetic supper of yogurt, maple sugar, and wheat germ, I had given up waiting, that catlike awareness, and I was outraged at myself for having waited. Which of course was when the phone rang and as I waited for it to ring itself out, I answered from the couch the last intelligent words of a good-looking gentile from the Midwest with a Ph D in art history and the beginning of a good collection of Sumerian fragments: "Can't dance. Don't ask me." On the eleventh ring I lifted the receiver.

"Can't talk," my nemesis said. "Just wanted you to know I haven't forgotten. I love you. Catch you later."

I love you? Catch you later? I didn't know what either meant. Calmly and rhythmically I tore a package of dinner napkins into feathery shreds. And then, because I couldn't decide on an emotional response appropriate to an intelligent good-looking et cetera, I cleaned out my refrigerator. There were a good half dozen salad dressings, four kinds of relish, a terrible relic of mozzarella, my soybean collection for Lent, what had been a natural-food raisin kelp loaf, smoked brook trout from Zabar's, instant

6

tea, white-appliquéd brie, and gray Carnation milk. I threw everything out. Thinking back, it was an odd response. He had one hell of a nerve to keep me hanging. And I was pretty stupid to keep hanging. On Monday I would call him and tell him to throw out my phone number. That's integrity.

My friends, who all live on commuter routes in Connecticut, have four-wheel drives and reversible fur-lined canvas coats, admire my integrity. My friends have all sold out. They come into the city dressed alike, their fur-lined storm coats canvas side out, their canvas-lined storm coats fur side out, jersey snoods, jewelry. They made those decisions: which side should I wear out. And they tell me, I who slip in and out of gray and black and beige things that I know are mine because the cleaner in my building has put my name inside them, that I always look so city.

They admire me because, they say, I could be what I wanted to be. I always wanted to be a dancer, I would say silently because they would be very disappointed in me to hear that. Am I still on vegetables? Who am I sleeping with? What happened to Harry Hardhat? Where do I get my energy? Are men really more interested in anal sex these days? Would I recommend the pecan pie from Amanda's? Isn't it overpriced? Do you know your vegetables are fresher in Gristedes than they are in New Canaan? Where am I getting my hair cut? Does he have a good brush? Should we get tickets for . . . is it any good? Should we make reservations at . . . is it any good? What's your next trip, Stephanie? God, if I could only get away like you and *live*.

"She really lives," they tell each other about me.

"You only live once," they answer each other.

"What do you mean?" I would ask them.

"For one thing you get to sleep with lots of men."

"And you're free," they add, knowing the first answer won't suffice.

7

Nor will the second. "Terrific," I answer. They need me to be what I am more than I need to be what I am. Whatever that is. I have no idea what I am. If tomorrow I were no longer an art historian at the Cloisters, I would have a serious problem. I would be free, but I would have a serious problem.

They at least have made a choice. They chose Pound Ridge, Ridgefield, New Canaan. They chose four-wheel drives, birch trees, reversible coats and stone fences. I have wandered along amiably making no choice at all except not to choose.

That's fairly avant-garde as a statement but sometimes it can be worth a double session. "That's very avant-garde," my best friend Miriam would assure me. "And it's definitely worth a double session. Bring yogurt and your wheat germ and meet me in the park."

My family doesn't believe in shrinks, the New Deal, or God. I didn't have a shrink to help me figure out what Richard's "catch you later" meant. It meant Wednesday. I never did figure out what his "I love you" meant.

He called Wednesday for lunch Thursday. He told me he'd been up to his neck in the wards and at lunch I asked him if he were a psychiatrist.

"A lawyer."

"What are the wards?"

"Se hable espanol?" he asked. He didn't pronounce the tilde.

I offered him an un poco. I should have offered him a Spanish lesson. He said, "When the right girl comes along, the right girl comes along." I was impressed by his ability to make a decision but not with the decision. We were at the Four Seasons and nine out of the ten waiters listening to us and watching us eat spoke Spanish with tildes. It wasn't an unusual gift.

Richard was a wee ipso facto for me and in response I shoved velvet chocolate cake into my pretty little mouth. Actually it was a large slice of chocolate icing. I don't remember what else we had for lunch because I didn't know what we had for lunch. The chains were moving across the windows and something was awry in the wiring or the overhead lighting so that there was a severe ringing in my ears every few minutes. Our ten waiters didn't seem to hear it. I toyed with the idea of asking Richard if he heard it also but decided not to just in case it was psychosomatic. No one else around me was holding their ears. In fact, as I examined the room, except for the waiters, everyone around me looked like Richard.

"That's why I'm so busy. I'm being 'groomed.' You'll meet my mother. It's very funny. She calls me 'The Governor.'"

"Is that what you're being groomed for? Governor?"

"Well, ultimately, but you never know what happens. Let's say I'm in the bullpen, right office, right backing. I leave the big decisions to the professionals."

I never eat dessert but I spooned whipped cream onto the chocolate icing, a nice self-destructive act. I heard a waiter say, "Thank you, Mr. Doubleday" to a man with a blue plaid suit, a blue plaid tie and blue plaid eyes who was probably the best tennis player in Sneden's Landing. Richard didn't yet seem to have a last name although the waiters acknowledged his presence. Everyone looked as if he were being groomed or had been groomed for something.

The waiter had said to Richard, "Yes, Sir?"

And Richard had answered: "The usual."

And the waiter brought the usual in a covered dish. God knows if Richard had ever eaten there before. That's what grooming is. And he was well-groomed. The one finger swishing through the martini I could have lived without. His tan was deeper than the blue plaid man's tan but the blue plaid man was older and didn't have to work so hard at being groomed. A Richard would have a limousine if he could. A blue plaid man would have his chauffeur-driven Land Rover. Richard ate the usual carefully. I, of course, had said, to be amusing, "Make it two." Richard's eyes kept moving beyond mine. He had jockeyed with me for the window seat. And since I had not been able to pull it away from the wall for him, he pulled a chair out for me so that I faced 52nd Street and he faced his constituency. Now his eyes lit up as he nodded at people passing us. The problem with men like Richard, in fact with Richard in particular, is whether I want to go to bed with him or to the Democratic National Convention. I didn't know. I couldn't tell if I were getting hooked on him or his potential. If he hadn't taken me here, if he hadn't swished his pinky around in his martini just once, if he hadn't been so smooth and so bursting with possibility which I couldn't read as sexual or political, I might decide what I wanted from him.

Richard also knew how to slide his cream along the rim of his coffee cup. And he knew how to involve me with a swift expedience.

"Stephanie, does there always have to be pain and suffering when people love?" He was equally solemn about the cream and the question.

I allowed the question to float between us, trying not to laugh at him.

"You see, Stephanie, I'm disillusioned."

Disillusioned means I want love. They usually say jaded when they want sex. I smiled Delphically.

He smiled crookedly, attentively still. "You might say jaded."

Aah. It was delightfully pornographic. I licked my lips over the cream. He licked his lips over the cream. I tasted the promise of him as he was watching me. You don't get to walk arm-in-arm into the Executive Mansion together and lick lips. You never get both. I was pleased to consider the licking of lips but I had a strong feeling then as I would later that if he had sat facing the window he would be watching himself and not my lips. I should have known then I was buying into the Democratic National Convention.

"I've even considered . . ." He looked at me seriously. I couldn't fill in the blank. "Well, let's talk about you."

*11*

"What are you grooming for, Richard, at present?"

"Councilman, probably, next election. But these things are years away. Right now I'm grooming for you."

I lifted my coffee cup and murmured, "Sweet." Delphi was empty. I truly could not read Richard. "Well, I'm the wrong girl, Spanish-speaking or not. My family's midwestern Republican, they tend toward reactionary. They send money to the Liberty League and the only reason my mother quit the Birchers was because she thought some of the little ladies were Lesbian."

"Really?" He was casually interested. I couldn't offend him.

"No. Not really. They don't even vote. My father thinks politics is too pushy. He's a general—minor, but heavy career. I mean *he* is *Army*."

Richard laughed. "Do you think he'd let his daughter marry a Jewish Democrat?"

"Only if he's governor."

"I'm serious."

It was a surprise shot and I had no return except not to take him seriously and so I laughed. The whipped cream dribbled from the corner of my mouth. I wiped it, blushing. Somewhere, I'd overheard men joking about making love to shiksas. When they come, creamed chipped beef dribbles out of the corner of their mouths.

I was suddenly uncomfortably aware of how unlike Richard I was. He was wiping the side of my mouth with his large napkin. As he leaned toward me he saw someone he knew and stood to talk to him, dropping the napkin on the table. I sipped my coffee. The power had shifted to him. And I had to recoup. He began to talk above me, animated, behind me, about ward politics. It was absolutely fascinating and he made great sense. I closed my eyes. I could imagine him on a podium; he became FDR waving from the open car; he became Jack Kennedy. He became Adlai, and I loved him. I stood beside him smiling to applause, shaking hands at street rallies. I had a breast removed. I changed my mind. He sat down and picked up his napkin.

"Unless it's an advantage to the woman, I don't believe in introductions," he explained impressively.

I sipped my coffee coolly now, knowing he was a mistake and quite relieved with my decision.

He sipped his coffee coolly also. I wondered if he'd made a decision. "Stephanie," he broke our summit silence, "tell me something."

"Mmmm."

"Tell me something you've never told anyone before in your life. Tell me your secret." How did he know I had secrets?

"Why?"

"Because we have to start someplace and life is too short to wait."

"And you're a busy man."

"You're not being fair."

"I don't know you. I have no reason to trust you or not to trust you." I had made an error. I had let him sniff the faint spoor of hostility. I hadn't meant to. With me and with men like Richard the faint spoor of hostility worked better than musk.

"Listen," his hand covered mine. He was leaning forward. "You and I have to believe in something. That's the kind of people we are. We can start believing in each other."

"Oh, Richard . . ." I don't know what I meant.

"We can, can't we?"

He was so sincere that day. He meant everything he said. Then. They always do as they're saying it. I removed my hand from under his. I had time either to recoup or to take my vote and leave the hall. His eyes swam before me. You have to trust someone, sometime. It might have been the time. I decided it was the time. There had been other times that hadn't been the time. And I did so like the interaction.

*13*

Girlishly, I smoothed my well-cut hair from the sides of my well-born face. Girlishly, I pulled at a lovely earlobe. Girlishly, I looked into my bowl of whipped cream as if it held tea leaves. Girlishly and sincerely, I said at last, "Well, I've always wanted to be a dancer." Girlishly, I sighed. Victoriously, he smiled. Little did he know. I never had quite defined integrity. I had just assumed it among midwestern WASPs.

He took my hand again.

"You know," I continued. "Free, floating."

Sometimes that secret worked but sometimes it didn't work. It was, though, my truth. I thought perhaps this time it might work because Richard seemed like the kind of man it might work on. They all seemed like the kind of man it would work on and I had never given up the hope that if they weren't, I could change them into the kind of man it would work on: a man to share my dreams.

I think it must have worked. He held my hand between both of his and said huskily, "Yo te amo, Stephanie." I nodded. The waiters, who were probably going to imitate him in the kitchen later, had to move away from the table. "That's what we have to believe in." How had the waiters managed not to laugh?

God, the lines were wonderful. He was pure cliché and yet I liked to hear him except I hoped that if he were going to leave out the tilde his professionals would put him in Dutchess County and not the South Bronx. His hands were warm and silky. I preferred the jaded to the fumbling.

But before I could respond or not respond with something terrific and jaded like "mi casa es su casa what are you doing this afternoon," he had motioned a waiter, flashed his gold American Express card, which I tried to read upside down, flourished his signature as if it were the Brest-Litovsk Treaty, and then we were leaving, his elbow steering me very firmly between the tables as he nodded and greeted a lot of men eating the usual. He seemed known, quite known. Maybe the usual was really the usual. The power was exciting, the potential of his power even more so, but I would have to keep the two separate. Perhaps that's what kept ringing in my ears—the charges of power he was giving out. Maybe I could help him with his accent. Maybe I could be his transformer. Maybe that was the lure. At the checkroom, he lifted my hair to help me on with my raincoat and as he did, he blew hot breath against the back of my neck. "I want you. I want to love you. Very much," he said as he smoothed my shoulders under my coat. "I want to feel you come." I shuddered involuntarily. I was so damned suggestible. Hypnotists were always after me too.

Although I had strong doubts about him as a. governor, b. husband, c. trustworthy, d. sharer of secrets, I had no doubts about sharing my shuddering with his jaded propensities.

"I wish," he whispered as he guided me past the palms, "I wish you didn't have to go back to work this afternoon, Stephanie. We could get close somewhere."

"I don't have to," I said softly. He opened the doors to the street. I wasn't sure he'd heard me. On the sidewalk he closed my eyelids with his fingers and explored my face. I could feel my eyelids quivering like moth wings.

"So?" he said or asked. "Are you ready, Stephanie?"

I didn't know what he meant. But I knew what Mona Lisa was up to. You just smile. You don't expect to understand them. He hailed a cab as I stood smiling beatifically, as I told him my address. He told the cabbie. All the women the masters did were whores anyway. A palmist told me once you can tell by their hands. I smiled. I climbed into the cab. And then he closed the door. He was on the street. He smiled.

I had no time to heal my face. I pressed it against the window as he motioned me to roll the window down. I did so while he looked at his watch.

"Stephanie, darling, not this time. Not this time. This time I don't want to make any mistakes." And then he patted the cab and it drove off. I went home because I couldn't have faced work anyway. I didn't scream until I was home. I had, for all my manipulative girlishlies, deserved exactly what I got. And I still didn't know his last name.

The next day, at work, my desk piled with shipping notices, bills of lading, scale drawings of Celtic crosses, wires from the Board Failte and catalogues from Trinity at Dublin, I shoved the pile aside, flattened his slip of notepaper in the empty space and dialed Richard's number. I was, I considered, almost thirty, a grown-up. I was on loan to the Cloisters to arrange purchase and display of a score of marvelous Celtic crosses from the British Isles to be placed in the gardens here. Eventually my exhibit, shipped, catalogued, landscaped, would be a tremendous contribution and terrific for my career. But Richard's slip was on my desk. A receptionist answered with an impossible list of names, partners I imagined in a mushrooming law firm. I could not say, "Which one is Richard?"

I said lightly instead, "Let me talk to Dick."

"Just one minute, Madam."

And then I was connected to another woman who asked me if she could help.

"I'd like to speak to Dick? Richard?" My cheeks burned. My fingers itched to tear the bills of lading into tiny pieces. I controlled them.

"Is this a personal call, Madam?"

"No, uh, yes, as a matter of fact," I stammered.

"Mr. Richard Grossberger is not taking personal calls this morning. Mr. Richard Slentz is not taking personal calls this morning and will be in court this afternoon and Mr. Richard Braithwaite is out of town. I will be happy to take your name and number, however."

I pressed with an icy forefinger the ugly final buttons of the phone rest. I felt weak and burned with shame. I dialed Miriam's number at the Jewish Memorial. "Help. I've got yogurt."

And in that quiet perfect sanctuary over the sound of bubbling fountains and Gregorian chants and the distant hoots of boats along the Hudson far below, I was prepared to scream and rush through the Cloisters tearing tapestries with my long fingernails, tearing until I reached the essence of the Unicorn and asked him my question, which I will ask Miriam at lunch. "Unicorn, Miriam, what the hell is it with men?"

"Sissy," I shouted at my secretary in the room beyond, unnecessarily and sharply, "I'm going out. I'm not taking any personal calls."

"Which?" she called back. She was a few years younger than I. I thought she was the Cloisters' spy in residence. She also wanted my job. When Sissy's mornings were filled with personal calls from a vast amorphous network of Lesbians and/or lovers, I ground my teeth. When she worked she was invaluable. Once I said to her that she would find her days easier if she kept her social life out of the office. "So would you," she rejoindered and went away daubing at her tears until after noon at which time she handed me a neatly printed note of calls which included two ex-boyfriends, my mother, and Miriam, twice.

"Both!" I snapped as I walked past her desk.

"Is anything wrong? Did I do something wrong?"

I tore my coat from the closet and left the office. Sissy sniffled loud and juicy behind me.

The problem was, I think, although I only harbored

the suspicion, which Miriam had planted, that Sissy was attracted to me. Miriam was as many years older than I, as I was older than Sissy. It is still so. But I listened to Miriam and Sissy didn't listen to me. She imitated me faultlessly as a role model until I was driven mad by my own inadequacies, in vitro, behind our glass dividers. I knew she smiled crookedly and inwardly at my . . . what she calls . . . "problems with men," as if that were a disease common to unenlightened women who had not yet surrendered to the true love of another woman.

I'd never mentioned any of this to Sissy of course. The subject repelled and frightened me. I sensed a lascivious thrill when I watched Sissy examine my women visitors and I tried not to imagine what she was thinking. But her eyes always met mine since I, fascinated, was watching hers. And oddly enough, often, as if she were trying to save me, she would indicate to me: "She's one, at least latent. She'd be good." I was also richly delighted when she fought with her roommate.

Outside, as I walked to my hiding place, I could see through the arched windows that the city swelled with late spring, ripe for summer. The George Washington Bridge rose and lifted against a periwinkle blue sky, cloudless and perfect. Rich purple clematis climbed the arches and crabgrass poked through the cobblestone paths. On the south slope the flowering crabs were a lush ready magenta. Inside the sun shone, dappling the red tiles of the walks and throwing strong shadows over the worn flat stones of the old chapels and the deep carvings of their doors. Fountains bubbled among crocus gardens and the jasmine overwhelmed everything with its wild sweet spoor. We were all waiting to unfold, caught between promise and blossom, blossom and fruit. I would have been happy crying softly anyplace in the Cloisters . . . a simple announcement, not of sorrow, but that I was connected to every molecule of it. Pippa Passes and all's right with the world, morning's at seven et cetera.

The rooms I love at the Cloisters are filled with arcane symbols, rooted, waiting as I am for someone to unfold their histories. Grotesque and laughing acrobats support beamed roofs, snakes entwine column shafts, lions devoured themselves above doorways, spirals, triangles, the magic lines of the Pythagoreans and the musky mysteries of Sheba and Solomon, all of them rebuilt, woven in the supports of early Christendom and carried to Upper Manhattan by the Rockefellers.

Down the road, below Fort Tryon, poor Mother Cabrini, our first American saint, lies in a Cinderella coffin, wax-faced and decorated with plastic roses. I have tried to love her wax head and hands, but she doesn't offer me the kind of peace that would allow me to cry before her. For me, most corners in the Cloisters, unlike poor Mother Cabrini's nouveau arches in the cathedral, are so privileged with silence and beauty that my soul opens as a bloom on their signals.

So I walked through the jasmine, through the Cuxa Cloister, and thought of men I'd loved and men I wanted to love. The guard turned on the sound system for me and taped Gregorian chants filled the rooms gently, distantly, from another time, following me to my rare and special place. Another guard nodded and walked away.

Enveloped by streaming sunshine through stained glass, surrounded by stone coffins, I stood before the peaceful statues of Doña Dulcia and Armengol, lying above their sarcophagi in the tiny chapel. The guidebook explained that Doña Dulcia and Armengol were Spanish nobility of different generations but still history, fortune and oil had placed them together as husband and wife, her stone coffin resting below his, with peace carved on the planes of their broad and elegant faces. It was the same peace I sought. The same belonging. I sniffled a bit and dug for the Kleenex I never remember to bring with me.

An angel held the pillow under Doña Dulcia's head. A

dog lay below Armengol's feet. The guidebook said the dog represents fidelity and domesticity. Not a lion for bravery in battle. But a pleasant dog. That's all I wanted. I didn't want a hero. I wanted a man who wasn't crazy. I wanted a man who wouldn't drive me mad. Someone to keep my bed warm. Someone to bring me aspirins. Someone I would bring aspirins. Someone who cared. Someone who was my . . . friend? Perhaps it was time to do something permanent, rock solid and lasting. To make my imprint on the world with something more than Celtic crosses at the Cloisters. Perhaps I wanted to have a child who would build me a chapel and worship my effigy and remember my words. No, I didn't even want that. I wanted something meaningful in my life.

In another corner of the sun-dappled chapel a young Armengol lay inside his sarcophagus with, the guidebook explained, a note pinned to the 500-year-old linens covering his bones: "His spirit sought the stars in 1299." That's what I wanted. Something meaningful in my life so when my spirit sought the stars, my face would have the same peace, the repose of a life led simply, kindly, decently, sanely. Of a life led having loved and been loved. The faith in that: the body has dissolved, the oriental silks are dust, the parchment of the note yellowed, but know forever that the man inside has gone to seek the stars. Better than plastic roses. Better than sainthood. That faith. Would Richard pin a note to my breast when I died? He was the first man I had met who I thought might really share my dreams. But it was spring and the oak branches waved at me through the leaded glass window of the chapel and it might have been only that it was spring and my goddamn sap was running. Like the centaur in the Bestiary: half man, half horse, of superior intelligence but ruled by animal passion.

All I really wanted was a nice safe rational relationship. I didn't want pornysex. I didn't want sportscars and country weekends or a man who wears his jeans with his

Guccis. I didn't want status or hysteria. I lived on my own fine line. My worst, my last, my really serious relationship was with a compact, curly-headed psycholinguist who lived in the Village and chewed on a pipe, constantly.

The last time I saw him, almost a year ago, I took his compact shoulders in his wide-wale corduroy suit, this man whom I thought I would love forever, for whom I squeezed fresh orange juice because I wanted to and ironed his shirts because I enjoyed it, I took that man and shook him and shook him and shook him. He was a psycholinguist. He was psycho but never spoke. Just sucked on his pipe. "Tell me what you're thinking. That's all I ask. For once, tell me what you're thinking."

He removed his pipe, answered very softly and calmly, "Nothing."

I watched as he placed the pipe between his teeth again and I shook him and shook him and shook him. He stood still, unshaken. I never even dislodged the pipe. I screamed, I shrieked. I told him there were thirty-five women to every man in madhouses and thirty-five men to every woman in jails. He nodded.

"What do you think of *that*?"

He said nothing. I tore down every drape in the living room and the den. He left as I ripped the kitchen curtains into rags.

And there had been Michael who was my teacher at Wellesley, who taught Bible history, with whom I grew up, who was fifty-five to my twenty, with a wild pornographic streak that matched my willing, somewhat virginal experiences. He yelled at me and I adored him for a summer on the Cape. He died in the fall suddenly and there had been no way to go to his funeral without his wife and children and academics knowing who I was. The last thing he'd said to me was "I was reading Hegel before you had hair on your pussy." That line, long after he died, always turned me on. I had mourned for Michael in the little Chapel, half sorrowful, half excited, not for my loss really, but for his happiness. Which I had given him. He had died happily and I too would simply like to live normally and die happily. Mother Cabrini's bells tolled noon and I wrapped my coat around me, thanked Doña Dulcia for the moments of silence, wondered if Richard knew Hegel, and left to meet Miriam in the park.

Sissy yelled at me as I walked down the steps to the cobblestone drive.

"Mrs. Slentz called." Sissy flew down the stairs and reached me. "I'm so glad it wasn't Grossberger. But Braithwaite would've been nicer."

"I'd appreciate it if you didn't listen to my conversations. I do not listen to yours."

"Yours are so much better than mine."

I slammed the enormous twelfth-century doors in her face and left. I too would have preferred Richard Braithwaite. My heart paused. Mrs. Slentz? It must be a coincidence. One thing I knew about Richard was that he wasn't married. But with Sissy there is no coincidence; there is only fate.

Miriam ran up the path to the Fort. She had a small capable body, athletic, neat. She was bright with crisp gray-black hair cut short, sensibly attractive. When she ran like that I knew we would share a bloodcurdling Il Duce story. We ate yogurt with plastic spoons, gnawed on natural-food loaves, and talked about men. Miriam was a psychiatric social worker at the Jewish Memorial Hospital. She spent her days reconstructing families, adjusting sibling relationships, curing alcoholic husbands and relocating abused children. For all of her training and her success with The Threatened Family of Upper Manhattan, Miriam seemed irrevocably destined to nurture in her own men a latent criminal insanity which ripened just about when they met Miriam and burst into full bloom within two or three months of living with her. "I get them," she explained, "just when they're coming around the old corner. And finish 'em off fast." The market analyst was doing yard work at a Catholic retreat in Elmira and the doctor was writing a four-volume work on his oversoul during weekends underground in Howe Caverns, a volume for each soul, and weekdays he worked at the Beechnut plant in Canajoharie because he identified with all those little round lifesavers. Number Three was a math teacher she met on a Club Méditerranée week in Marrakech. She wired me: "I am loved. I am worshipped." Madly in love, they decided this was it, bought a house on Staten Island, made promises, commitments, introductions and married within the week they landed at Kennedy.

Within the next week, although he was a gentle pedant somewhere in the wasteland of the Staten Island school system, at home he became, in that second week, a raging maniacal Sicilian who chopped off Miriam's long hair while she was sleeping and tore out the hems of her short skirts while she was cooking. Among other acts. Miriam was not wholly convinced it was her doing but she felt she developed a certain entropy somewhere.

"Stephanie," she began, paces away, as we neared our bench. "Have I got a story for you. You won't believe what Il Duce pulled last night. You won't believe it." She popped open prune yogurt, I strawberry, and tore corners off my loaf for her. "Mud driveway. I tried to back out, right? And he was in front of me waving his arms, shouting, so I turned off the ignition so I could hear him, right?"

"Right."

"Here, take from my loaf. Yours is stale. He pounds on the hood. He pulls open the door. 'Why the hell did you turn it off? Now you don't have momentum.' That's what he'd been yelling: 'momentum, momentum.' Okay. So I try to back up again. He kicks at the tires. He kicks at the fenders. He is beating his fists into the hood of his precious Bonneville. I don't shift, okay? My hands are dripping with sweat. My heart is bursting. Right? The car slides forward into the house but nothing happens. A chip in the aluminum siding, a dent, nothing. Nothing compared to what he did with his fists to the hood. So he opens the door to the car where I'm sitting. He grabs me by the neck, me, the marriage counselor. And pulls me out. Fortunately I have on my John Kloss satin nightgown so I slide out easy. And tosses me on the ground. Then he

25

drives the car and it slides and smash smash and bends the entire side of the house under the kitchen window. And then he backs it out, parks it on the street and walks by me."

"Are you still on the ground?"

"You think I'm going to move around and be a living target? And he says, 'From now on, I drive the car.'"

"Did he hurt you?"

"Only when I laughed."

"Did you laugh?"

"Are you kidding?" She wrapped her loaf back in its foil and slipped the lunch remains into her shopping bag. "If I laughed at him, he'd kill me." And then Miriam began to giggle and laugh and roar, wiping her eyes, weeping with laughter, the sound spreading like the old cannons over Fort Tryon. When she was finished, I asked her my question.

"Miriam, what the hell is it with men?"

"I can't leave him," she said very quietly. "He was perfectly calm and sweet and loving and giving when I met him. I have to help him out of this."

"I think he's brain damaged."

She shrugged. "Him? Il Duce? If he's brain damaged, they all are. It's genetic." She took my loaf and distributed crust and crumbs and hard raisins to avaricious pigeons. "You shouldn't eat it stale. All the radiance goes out after a while. Well, Stephanie, your turn. Sissy finally make a pass at you?"

"Miriam, I think I may be getting ready to fall in love."

"Hah!" She tossed the bread crumbs over her shoulder, like rice. "Honey, I'm so happy for you. What's his name?"

"Grossberger, Slentz or Braithwaite."

"I hope it's Braithwaite. Another one doesn't give out the last name, it's such a commitment."

"It could be Slentz because a Mrs. Slentz called me this morning. But he's not married. That I know. Although there is somebody else he's involved with, I'm sure."

"How do you know?"

"He had a date at the party when I met him and things he said, things he didn't say."

"Is he good in bed?"

"I don't know. I just met him."

"As long as you can stay out of bed, that's good."

"Good?"

"Believe me, old-fashioned as it may seem, it's good."

"Frankly, I think it's lousy. But Miriam, I don't want to make any mistakes. I really need your advice."

"Well, a clean apartment is conducive to clear thinking and gracious living even if he doesn't come over right away. It's healthier. You have to do it for yourself too. That's my first day's advice for The Threatened Family of Upper Manhattan. Did you fill your fridge yet? That's the next step."

"Not yet, but I emptied it. And I bought a lot of cheese."

"Very significant. I should do a paper. 'Food and The Threatened Family of Upper Manhattan.' When you get your fridge filled then come back and tell me you're in love."

"Miriam, I think I want to get married."

"A few kinds of cheese, an assortment of crackers, lots of Smucker's, crunchy peanut butter, plenty of chocolate pudding. And tapioca pudding. Always cookies. A cookie jar is like a venus flytrap. Throw out the nuts and the lecithin and the smoked brook trout and the Sicilian walnuts and the fertilized eggs . . . all the health crap. Beer, freeze some eclairs and delmonicos. At least four kinds of greens in the salad and garlic croutons. Always croutons. And little tomatoes, Hebrew National salami, pumpernickel bread, bagels. Get ready. You have to set

27

the scene. Buy some Scarsdale clothes. Stop wearing black. Get into pinks, blues, more beige. Soft, expensive stuff. Don't look museumy."

"Well, it's not that I *really* want to get married, but you know—just in case, I should leave the option open. I've always seemed to close off that option with the other men I've known. I want to leave it open this time and I'm not sure I know how. And I don't want to make any mistakes." God, where had I heard that line before?

Miriam looked at me, squinting just a little, as if debating whether she should help me or not. I didn't think she was concerned with the immorality of controlling another human being's behavior which I should have been concerned with. I think she was remembering something unsharable about Il Duce. "You look for the patterns. Tell me the patterns as you figure them out. Even if you really aren't sure, but if it looks a little like a pattern of behavior, tell me. Then we'll find out you know where to attack, where to smooth, what parts to buoy up, what parts to ignore. Really get into his head. But sweetheart, don't forget, once you got him, you're stuck with him."

"I don't like the way that sounds."

"I know. But it works." Miriam powdered her nose, twisted her lips for lipstick, and stood. "And that Mrs. Slentz?"

"Coincidence."

"You want to be sure. Let Sissy call her and ask what it's in reference to. For an executive, you act like a filing clerk. Then if it sounds like the woman he's—what did you say? involved with—ignore her. She probably wants a hysterical scene and she's lying about being a wife. She's probably nuts. But, she could be anybody . . . like a contributor or want to bake bread for the Fair or get seeds for a medieval garden. Who knows."

"It worries me. I don't want to deal with another woman."

"A gorgeous kid like you? You've got nothing to

worry about. *You're* the other woman. *She* should be scared."

Miriam pulled out Kleenex for me and I tore her Kleenex into puffy shreds which the pigeons chased along the sidewalk. "I don't like being called the other woman."

"Jesus, you're so damned medieval. So don't be. Let him go. Be honorable. You couldn't do it to a sister. If the one who called is the one he's involved with, she's doing a number on you, baby. But if you want to be honorable, conduct your little crusade, forget him." Miriam patted my shoulder. "Stephanie, you act very strange for such a happy woman. Maybe you should rethink this."

"There's nothing to rethink. Look, I'll just let it happen, you know. It's so much easier."

"Sometimes yes, sometimes no. Just remember the rule: if you catch him, you're stuck with him."

I still didn't like the way that sounded.

She sat down beside me again. "Honey, sometimes when The Threatened et cetera comes to me I don't tell them what to put in the cookie jars. When I get back today I'm counseling a beautiful kid, a brilliant kid, a Ph D candidate in Tibetan Buddhism. Right? Her loving, supportive husband who is a Ph D candidate in early German literature, came home one afternoon when she was at a long seminar. At suppertime, he took all her thesis notes and cooked them at four hundred degrees for an hour and a half. And all he said to her when she asked why was that she hadn't been home to make his dinner. Don't be in such a hurry to fall in love in time for summer in the Hamptons. Go. Go back and be a brilliant curator and let happen what is meant to happen."

She pushed me up the path until she was certain I was committed to that direction at least. "And invite him for dinner. Feed him," she called after me.

There was no way for me to know if Miriam was a lousy social worker or a great Zen master. Miriam Cohen and her koan, except her name was now Natali and she had no answers for herself. Feed him; don't feed him. Make plans; let happen what happens. Sometimes yes; sometimes no. An odd dozen of blue-gray pigeons left their posts at a trash can and followed me back to work, hoping for more of my loaf and less of my Kleenex. I should have told Miriam about the cab. I shouldn't have gone back to work.

Sissy had one conversation that afternoon. With a friend. About me. Except for a package of carbon paper which I reduced to ribbons, I didn't react. My code name is She. "She's here. Yes. Can't talk. No. Of course, it's spring. No. No. Probably. You know the losers she gets involved with. You know how she gets. The vibrations . . . God."

By three in the afternoon my baskets were filled and emptied as labeled. I took my filled basket to Sissy's desk. She had been working also. There was a calm in the office.

"Good, we're really getting somewhere. Good." I looked over the mail she had answered, the prints ready to ship and the fund requests in triplicate. She was accurate and efficient. I signed a few letters at her desk and as I leaned over her shoulder to sign them, I noticed a small stack of pink Called While You Were Out messages.

"Are those today's?"

"Oh, there were some phone calls while you worked. I didn't think you wanted to be bothered."

I kept my voice soft. She had after all worked well that afternoon. "Sissy, that is not your decision although I appreciate your trying to protect me."

"Well, after you slammed the door in my face . . . which I understand when you have problems with men so don't apologize . . . I knew you were upset and I didn't want to upset you any more. An apology isn't necessary." She swiveled her chair away from me to face her typewriter.

I resisted screaming. I screamed anyway. "I am not having problems with men. I am having problems with secretaries. Nosy secretaries. Is that clear? If I were a man, Sissy, you wouldn't bite my sandwiches or finish my coffee or take corners from my organic loaves. I'm sick and tired of you spying on me and involving yourself with my life. Do you understand?" I was waving the stack of phone messages in her face as she backed her chair against the wall. She could go no farther and I relished her fear.

She answered in a small tremulous voice. "And that Mrs. Slentz."

"What?" Walls meant nothing. She could go farther.

"And that Mrs. Slentz called. I didn't write that down."

"And may I ask why you didn't tell me that? Just for openers."

"I don't think it's necessary for you to be sarcastic. I knew it would upset you and I get upset when you get upset and I can't work and I had a terrible fight with Monica this morning and I'm just trying to help." Sissy began to sniffle.

"All right," I said through my clenched teeth, almost hissing. "Sissy, what did Mrs. Slentz have to say?"

Sissy was suddenly relaxed. Perhaps she only seemed relaxed in relation to myself. Perhaps she seemed relaxed because in the deep dark reaches of her mind she was standing with her foot on my throat and a flint dagger raised over my heart. "Mrs. Slentz was very pleasant. It's nice to hear someone pleasant for a change. She said if you weren't busy she would like to see you. I told her you were tied up and she said she had free time anyway and it was such a lovely afternoon and since she hadn't ever been . . ." Her voice trailed off as she watched my face.

By the time she had finished speaking I had a large handful of the front of her sweater in my fist and had pulled her up from her seat. "When?"

"Just . . . a couple of . . . I don't *know*. You're *stretching* my new Shetland." I released her and ran into my office to call Miriam. Through the glass I saw Sissy crying and pulling at her sweater to smooth it out. If she could only just be a secretary and stay out of my life she wouldn't get dragged into the turmoil.

Miriam answered the phone in her "I'm with a client" voice.

"She's coming here. She may even *be* here. Miriam!"

"Darling, Steph. What synchronicity. In your travels, Steph, among men, have you ever heard that meat eaters have larger sex organs than vegetarians?"

"Miriam, she's probably hysterical. I don't like being the other woman."

"My client who is with me now is trying to . . ." I could hear a low voice in the background ". . . convince her husband of vegetarianism as a peaceful life style and he thinks she is trying to shrink his testicles. What would you say, Stephanie?"

"Miriam, I'm too close to it to handle someone else's trip."

"That's very illuminating. Nothing to fear but fear itself. I'll share that with my client." Miriam buzzed off. It hadn't been fair to call her when she was counseling. That was, I knew, the Ph D whose husband had cooked her thesis notes. I called Sissy, who came into my space red-eyed but composed.

"Sissy, about your sweater, I'm sorry."

"It was my fault. I should have given you the messages."

"Yes, you should have. Now that you have led me

into this situation, I would appreciate it if you would go downstairs and tell me what she looks like and what she is doing and tell whomever is at the desk that if anyone inquires after me, I've left for the week. I'll pay the cleaning. If I've ruined it, I'll buy you a new Shetland."

"I don't know what she looks like."

"Buckteeth, funny clothes, maybe, long dress, maybe, hippy, small, chunky, henna hair, long."

"All maybe?"

"Maybe looking a little crazy. Just look around. But go fast before someone sends her up here." While I go hide under my desk.

"Actually," Sissy was shuffling her feet, "I was waiting for a phone call. An important one."

"Please hurry before she comes up." With a gun, stepping off the elevator, and snapshots of Richard's six mongoloid children.

"If Monica calls, tell her I'm sorry about the laundry."

"No."

"So you go downstairs." Sissy sat back at her desk.

"Don't you have a conscience?" I yelled across our space.

She popped her head into my office once again. "And tell her that I love her and I'll see her when I get home."

Sissy left as I buzzed the front desk. "When Sissy gets down there, tell her if she isn't back here in ten minutes, she's fired."

I used my time wisely. I tore a bill of lading from Newcastle announcing the first shipment of Cornish crosses to New York City. I tore a Xerox copy of the Lanivet Cross Number One into two, four, eight, sixteen, thirty-two ragged little pieces until I had a thumbnail section of a heart-shaped tip of a tail. Sweeping all the other thirty-one pieces into a corner of my desk, I studied the tail of the man on the Lanivet Cross. There was no question that the appendage on the end of the tail was a heart. Definitely organic, clearly incised. I planned to print an entire catalogue for my show on the legends of the tailed men of Cornwall. The Christian legend that Saint Augustine cursed the Cornish men for their wickedness is not sufficient. The stone was older than Christian times and the curse, when true curses were possible, goes deep into pagan times. How I would have loved to have cursed like that, finally and terribly. I would paralyze Sissy from nine to five except for her typing fingers and her eardrums. I would cast a spell on Richard so that he would fall madly and irrevocably in love with me forever. Just knowing I had the power would bring serenity to my soul.

But I wasn't serene. I had no power. I was really afraid. Sitting at the desk, daydreaming about curses, I was most afraid. I wasn't afraid of being accused of philandering. Unfortunately, so far, for whatever reasons, I had done nothing with Richard. And I wasn't afraid of another woman, as such. What frightened me was the possibility that someone Richard loved or once loved or said he'd loved would face me, ravaged and mad, pathetic, tortured and desperately in love with him. Someone he had destroyed. A ghost of what I might be. Someone who was insane enough to call, pretend to be his wife, come here. That someone was led, driven, to maniacal motion, mad enough to blame Richard's unfaithfulness not on Richard, but on me. And she'd say: "How'd you like to see what you'll be like in a couple of years, honey?" And maybe she'd show me scars or tell me horror stories about vaginal herpes or his fear of round things. He thinks women are all diseased and he's always washing his hands and will never touch lips, that kind of thing. Or every Saturday night he goes to his mother's apartment to shave her legs and clip her toenails and shave her armpits. Or, he can't have an orgasm unless the woman wears Dr. Dentons. The kind of story which will be true or untrue but will fester and drain the little precious bit of trust and belief and hope I am so desperately trying to hold. And it will be something I can't ask him about, a nightmare. That's why I'm afraid of whomever it is calling herself Mrs. Slentz, another one who thought she might be the governor's wife, another one who thought she could share dreams, who thought she could save him, could save herself through him. And it just may be that I am entirely incorrect. It may be that Richard is really the right man and I'm so scared of that fact that I'm driving myself into corners to avoid the knowledge. It might be that his name is one of the others—Braithwaite, Grossberger—and that my created Mrs. Slentz is probably a harmless museum member who wants to donate a set of stained glass from Strasbourg in my name because she liked my last newsletter. I hope I don't witness another woman's hysteria because it will be a mirror of my own and that's what I'm afraid of. I don't want to look too closely at myself.

The phone rang and I answered as if I were Sissy. "Ms. Boxwell's office."

"Sissy?" It was Monica's deep-pitched voice.

"She's out."

"Who's this?"

"She."

"Oh." The voice sank lower. "Can you take a message?"

I had had a rotten day. In exchange for a short span of joy I sat at my desk in terror of a madwoman accosting me. I had sold my soul once more to my spying secretary. I had cleaned unnecessarily my apartment, emptied unnecessarily my refrigerator, tormented my soul and my head and my body and convinced myself that I was ready to fall in love with someone I knew nothing about. It was a romance à la Kafka. Monica dictated the laundry list to me while I carefully transcribed all their intimacies, the colors of their sheets, the pairs of underwear worn each week, the towels, by design and manufacturer, the very fabric of their strange life together. I didn't like it. They shared the most detailed information about each other and I loved a man . . . whoops . . . and I was thinking of loving a man, an elusive grinning man who was barely evident, who said he loved me and twice called me on the phone and touched me on the arm and once blew on my neck and once bought me lunch, who created despair in my stomach and whose last name I didn't even know. By his elusiveness, he had created this chaos, but it was the same chaos Il Duce created by his violence. Maybe I really didn't like men. Monica at least called Sissy. Monica suffered. She'd feel something. Did men feel anything? Did Richard, except that I was the right girl, an intellectual decision, a vote-getter?

The only real emotion I'd ever seen in a man was anger. And lust. If that's an emotion. Maybe they feigned emotion in order to satisfy lust. And maybe we feigned lust in order to satisfy emotion. Maybe they've just run out of emotion, the way the world runs out of fossil fuels. Fighting might have done it to them. When I considered Miriam's Il Duce, I thought men really did begin with tails and although they had lost them or perhaps turned them into testicles, they still harbored truly bestial characteristics. Not intellectually, not physically, but emotionally; they were still lumbering destructive swamp creatures, unresponsive, autistic. As a Christian, trained and dogmatic, I think they must at one time have had the same given emotional package we women have. As a woman, I think they never had it or never will. But why did I want one so much? I wondered if I really hated men.

If I could only have related to them. There's a story about a muleskinner teaching recruits to train mules. "First you have to get their attention," he told the recruits as he beat the mule over the head with a plank. Is that the answer? Hit them over the head and *then* relate to them? I could relate to history. I could relate to space and design. Except for Sissy and myself, I could relate to women—well, perhaps I couldn't relate to whoever Richard's bucktooth buddy was. But I couldn't relate to men. But then I didn't even know what relate meant. I meant that I couldn't understand one and I wanted one and I didn't know how to get one . . . the right one.

I decided that some wonderful Black Annie witch goddess cursed the Cornwall men with tails as a memory and reminder not of their wickedness but of their lowly origins. I saved the square $\frac{1}{32}$ of the Lanivet Cross with the tracing of the heart on it and slipped it into my wallet behind my Social Security card. Whatever it was with men, I would put the Lanivet Number One in the center of my exhibit. Someone would understand. I heard the elevator begin its climb upward. My blood stopped in response. Sissy stepped from the elevator.

"Seven minutes," she shrugged, showing empty hands.

"God, am I glad it's you, Sissy."

"You are?"

"Instead of her."

Discreetly, I swept my thirty-one shreds into my drawer to hide them. I didn't need her to know about my tearing things. She knew enough about me already and I had always let her think that it was she who lost my papers. Sissy went to sit at her desk and wait, I knew, for Monica's phone call.

I called her away from her desk. "Are you sure, Sissy?"

"Honest, there's no one. There's a German tourist group, a lot of school kids, a couple of old ladies."

"Are you sure?"

"I looked all over. There was a really batty old lady stealing crocus plants and I told the guard and he wrestled her for the plants and she kept screaming: 'Goy, you'll be sorry come Easter!' And then she told me, very rationally, 'You have the crocuses for a little; I have them for a little. What's so bad?' "

"Did you go into the lower areas?"

"Every place." She was waiting for my thank you. I didn't feel it necessary. "Did Monica call?"

Although I might torment her a bit with the timing as she had done with Mrs. Slentz's phone call, in matters like these we could trust each other. We were aware that we would protect each other when it really counted. I handed her the laundry list. Sissy turned the note over. "Wasn't there any message? Nothing else?"

I shook my head.

"I'm very upset about Monica, Stephanie. It seems to be so important who takes care of the laundry. It's just like a man/woman sexist thing." She sat on my desk. "Oh, God, I'm super upset."

"Sissy," I held my hand to my forehead, "don't tell me."

"Do you have any aspirin?"

I had a vast collection of pills left from the time Miriam had prescribed megadoses of vitamins for me. I dumped a handful of them into Sissy's palm. Miriam and I were off chemicals. Sissy put the pills into her pocket and left, closing the door so carefully I understood it as a message of hatred. When she hates me I'm happier because she leaves me alone.

For the last hour of our day, she worked hard, typing nonstop. It might have been my mail. It might have been a long suicide note. I didn't want to know. I wanted to know who Mrs. Slentz was. I wanted to know if she was lurking someplace in the shadows, behind a column, dagger unsheathed. At five, Sissy popped her head in, composed again in that false obedient efficiency which says I've hurt her deeply but she respects my position as She: "I ordered a case of Scotch tape for you. You're going to need it." And then she left for the night. Sissy's good at last tag.

I would have fired her but if she were ever to defend herself to Personnel, I'd have lost my job also.

All because of Richard No-Name, the Governor, not only had the day been totally lousy, but I couldn't leave on time. I read the personal ads in the *Voice* underlining professional men over thirty who want no emotional involvement and like to sail, until I was certain all visitors, buses and cars had left, all daggers were sheathed, all shadows accounted for. Outside, early dusk slid around the columns and clothed the stones for the night. I paused before the Virgin to pray that if I were going to be in love, it wouldn't hurt. Leaves were closing on the trees and the last rush of orange covered the face of the Palisades. I so wanted to meet him here in the moonlight in a medieval garden and make love with the monks chanting the Psalms of David in the background and the jasmine spoor flooding the air. It was spring and I wanted to be loved a little. That, as Miriam would assure me, wasn't such a crime. That, as the crazy lady with the crocuses said, wasn't so bad. So I have him for a little; so the buck-toothed wonder has him for a little. What's so bad?

Although I would have denied it, I really had expected Richard to call over the weekend, which he did not. He did not call on Monday. He did not call on Tuesday. He did not call on Wednesday. I did not realize then that so far all I knew about Richard was a group of nots. Nor did I realize that Richard No-Name's no-calls were a pattern and that the no-calls as well as the cab scene were things I should have mentioned to Miriam. Not realizing I already knew as much as I needed to know at that point and that he was intentionally giving me nots so I would keep asking questions, when he finally did call at eleven-thirty Thursday night, I became so involved with my own dumb superficial questions, which had nothing to do with the issue, which I wasn't ready to define then anyway, I really didn't hear what Richard No-Name was not telling me.

"Steph, can you hold a minute?"

I began to tear Kleenex, sheet by sheet, sitting cross-legged and safe on my bed. I held on. I heard him talking to someone. Where would he be at eleven-thirty? Doesn't he have to work in the morning? Who was he with now? If I were hooked on him, I'd be suffering. I did have questions that usually tear me apart when I am involved. If I were involved I would be asking: Aren't you going to explain who that woman was who called me? Why couldn't you talk on Sunday? What do you mean, be your friend? Just what does that include? Don't you want to sleep with me? Who are you with now? All I want is an explanation, Richard. An explanation from all the Richards of the world. I can condone any kind of behavior. No, I can't. But I just feel as though I deserve an explanation because I am a decent human being. You are free to go. I simply want an explanation before you leave. That's all. And waiting for an explanation, I would rip things in his apartment or mine to pieces. It was never an explanation I really wanted. Receiving an explanation, I would continue to rip things because what I really wanted to know was what was so wrong with me.

Whoever Richard was speaking to giggled. I was down to the yellow sheets. I had enough shreds to stuff a pillow with.

"How would you like an adventure, Stephanie?"

"It's a little late, isn't it?" I hadn't intended the cold edge in my voice.

"Oh, I'm sorry. You answered the phone so fast, I thought you must be awake."

Pause. I didn't know what I ought to say.

"You don't really mind me calling, do you? I mean, we really are friends, Steph?"

"Richard?"

"Yes, Steph?"

"I think I missed a chapter somewhere."

"Should I call back, Steph?"

"No, no, I'm really glad to hear from you." I sounded like a Jewish infection. Who was he to assign me a nickname already?

"Listen, I really want to talk to you. Are you doing anything?"

I measured the levels of filth in my apartment. What

does a free spirit do on such occasions? Would the governor's wife live like this? Do I ignore the clumps of dust, the stacks of garbage, the empty cans of 9-Lives, the torn legs of my scratching-post sofa and the cat piss in the cold-air return? Do I tell him not to come over? Why not? I'm not the governor's wife. I was into nots.

"Steph?"

"Doing nothing." I scooped up the Kleenex from the bed.

"Good. Grab a cab and meet me at 39th and Third. I'll pay the fare."

In the middle of the night? Because he snaps his fingers?

"My friend, are you hesitating? Also, Stephanie, I want to talk to you about my mother. You were very rude to her."

"Your mother?"

"When can you be here? Half an hour?"

"Your mother? Richard?"

"It's very important to me. Please, Stephanie."

"What do you mean your mother? What do you mean your mother?"

"Half an hour, darling? I want so to see you. I realized tonight that I haven't seen you since Thursday. Half an hour. I'll wait on the sidewalk."

"Half an hour." I cradled the receiver. Okay, so I was the free spirit. I'd go. Funny, he had realized tonight that he hadn't seen me. I had just occurred to him. Are men stupid? Genetically immature? This man was a lawyer, wasn't he? I watched my hands begin to shake. The first time is always like that. If I were really involved, my hands would just shake . . . I couldn't take a step back and watch them. What does he mean his mother? The deodorant lost its control and sprayed itself out on the bathroom tiles in a tiny puddle. Maybe it hadn't been Richard. Or it had been Richard and he had called the wrong girl. I watched my hands begin to shake again. Was there time to set my hair fast in hot rollers? Wear a bra? Don't wear a bra? What is the message? His mother? How curious. I was rude to his mother? Oh, for God's sake! Mrs. Slentz. Mrs. Slentz must have been his mother. Of course. He sent his mother to meet me. My God, he *was* serious. But why hadn't he told me? How was I expected to know? I kept feeling as if I'd skipped that chapter someplace. He must really be serious. *They* must really be serious. And his mother must really be nuts.

And I, while I should have thought in the cab that *I* must really be nuts, reflected instead on being cool. I've ruined a lot of relationships by being too cerebral or threatening hysteria or both. Richard was attracted to me because I was a free spirit and free spirits, I told myself, let it flow. That's it. Stand still, be cool, let it flow, I continued to tell myself as I stepped from the cab with icewater sure enough flowing through my trembling legs and my hot little grin ripping my cheeks apart and smiling benignly and walking calmly to the garbage can where Richard stood. I grinned.

But he grinned too and hugged me at the garbage can, kneading my spine with his knuckles. "You knew. You understood. You must have known how important it was and you came. Because you *are* my friend."

"What?"

"You are such an intelligent *woman*. You must have known what kind of a day I had . . . this new campaign, Jesus, it's all a lot of shit." Richard steered me along the sidewalk by holding my elbow. Free spirits don't ask where they're going. Flow, Stephanie, flow. Pick up your feet, Stephanie. Stand up straight, Stephanie. Let the others be clever, Stephanie. Throw back your shoulders, Stephanie. Be intelligent if you can, Stephanie. Be good, Stephanie, if you want. But Stephanie, be beautiful you must, Stephanie, my mother said as she picked up her beautiful little feet one after the other and showed me how to throw my shoulders back, Stephanie.

"Stephanie." Richard tried to whistle something. "Stephanie, there must be some kind of song for that. Stephanie at midnight." We walked by a drugstore, a deli, a shoe repair. Everything was closed. He tried to whistle again as we walked, hesitating over many bars of many tunes. We came to another garbage can. He stopped and pressed his forefinger against the tip of my nose, then we started walking again as he whistled his song. Miriam, when I tell her tomorrow, if there is a tomorrow, won't believe it. We are walking down the sidewalk going someplace and he's whistling "The Girl That I Marry." I swear to God, Miriam. And she'll say, how come you didn't ask where you were going? And I'll shrug and say, I'm learning not to ask questions. We stopped at another garbage can under a streetlight haloed in mist. He rocked his head from side to side at me, a bird listening for my worm, predatory, measuring. My life is measured in garbage cans, I recited to myself.

"I have a question to ask of you, Stephanie." One finger pressed in the space between my eyes.

"Yes?"

"Have you ever been to Atlanta?"

"Atlanta?" I repeated, trying desperately to follow his direction.

"Smell my hair."

I leaned over the garbage can to his hair. I have played chess in tournaments. I have bid smoothly for major acquisitions. I have fought fossilized museum boards for grants. I know many games. But I didn't know Richard's games. I didn't know Richard's rules. The cool spirit is free, though; noncommittal. Goes along till she learns the rules. Then can play. Maybe can win.

"Would you like to go to Atlanta?"

My holding action consisted of repeating the last word of his question. "Atlanta?"

"Do you like it long, Stephanie? I have to go to

Atlanta next week and I wonder if I should have it cut for Atlanta. I've never been to Atlanta myself."

"Myself?" Either he was the most open man or the most manipulative man I'd ever met. If it was manipulation, then he'd gone one step too far and he deserved what he got from me. My armpits were dampening. I hadn't come to fight. Would I fight to come?

"Why don't we go someplace where we can talk? Where there's light? Then you can tell me if you like my hair this length or not."

We walked past closed stores. There was nothing open. I had no idea where we were walking. Richard continued to whistle "The Girl That I Marry." He was so happy with me. I'm just not enough of an existentialist, I thought. I should learn to enjoy the moment now as I'm living it instead of worrying about my destination. Richard is a man of the new age and I'm still old-fashioned, medieval. I wanted to know at half past midnight where I was going and when I'd get home and how I'd get up for work in the morning. I knew I would bother Richard if I were to ask. Also, not that I needed it, but he had promised to pay for the cab fare.

"Well, Stephanie, if I'm going to keep my promise and buy you a cup of coffee, you are going to have to come home with me. You don't mind, do you?"

"Well, Richard," I answered lightly, with a touch of mimicry also unintended, "it was rather what I expected." I'd lost track of the promises.

"Oh?"

"Does that bother you?" I had been too clever. He didn't like it.

"I like to surprise people. I like to be surprised. The only thing we should ever expect of one another is the unexpected. That way we can always keep our relationship exciting and stimulating."

"So, don't take me there. Take me someplace else."

"Actually, I really want to take you there because I want to show you my fish tank. I was rapping with a friend tonight . . . when I called you . . . and in the middle of everything . . . I hit my forehead with my hand and said 'My God, Stephanie hasn't seen the fish tank yet!' So I called you." Rapping was not *his* word: it was a close friend.

"Didn't your friend mind?" I remembered the giggle.

"I suppose so. But if she were really a friend, like you, she wouldn't mind."

"So then she isn't really your friend?"

"Of course not! You are."

"Richard, it may take me a while to really understand you."

"You are such a naturally understanding woman. I'm not worried at all. I don't live far from here. Do you mind walking?" Richard offered me his arm. It was warm and strong. Not answering was becoming comfortable. "We should have some rules, shouldn't we? What kind of rules should Richard and Stephanie have?"

He whistled again. I said the words to myself. The girl that I marry will have to be as soft and as pink as a nursery. The girl I call my own will wear satins and laces and smell of cologne. The girl would have to do something about her apartment. The girl would have to do something about her nails will be polished and in her hair she'll wear a gardenia and slipcovers and curtains, and plants and a real tablecloth and a new toothbrush and towels, great velvety bath towels and flowers. What in God's name was I thinking?

"Richard, I'm not the right girl, not yet. Let's not disillusion ourselves. If I am the right girl it's going to take a little more than a first sighting to know."

"I understand that, Stephanie. I respect that. I have difficulty with commitment myself. Let's look at it this way: will you just for tonight be the right girl? Can you accept that much?"

It didn't seem at the time so pernicious a compromise. "Listen, as far as tonight is concerned, I *better* be the right girl." I thought I was being amusing.

He was still serious. "One night at a time, darling. That's all I ask. That's all I can ask of you now, Stephanie." He pressed his cheek against mine. His cheek was very smooth and his breath was chocolatey. "Believe me, darling, I don't want to press you. My intentions are honorable. I really mean that."

He had meant that. I just didn't know that honorable referred to his honor and not mine. He certainly was going overboard, I thought, to get me into bed. We began to walk again. He was very thoughtful. I was very curious. He came to a decision. About the rules.

"Tonight's rule is that we have to give each other something so precious, something you'd never dream of giving away, something someone you loved gave to you. Stephanie, you do love me, don't you?"

He didn't lose a pace. "I don't think I've ever really been in love," I answered, sincerely, very sincerely. It wasn't the time to play games. I wasn't the girl.

He stopped and faced me, staring at me as if I had forgotten his birthday or his last name. Then he pressed his forefinger into my forehead. "How can we be friends if you aren't in love with me?"

I should never have skipped that chapter. "Okay." I spread my hands. I didn't know what to say.

"Good!" He clapped his hands together at my eyes. "Then we are loving friends and I will give you my chicken stone. Okay?"

"Okay."

Okay, Stephanie, I thought. Just for tonight, you are going to his apartment at half past midnight. You have on new Pucci underwear and your armpits are very very wet and you want to go to bed with him and you will. So enjoy it. But I had heard stories about rats in laboratories before. I had heard the one about rats given a choice of food or a shot of electric pleasure and they starved to death but loaded up with pleasure. I thought the situation with Richard was analogous. I really thought so. I would remember these moments nostalgically. I could almost step out of them and look back upon them already. How his nose just turned up slightly at the end, the good soft gentle lips, the fall of his hair on the collar of his raincoat. I was really mad for him under the streetlight, slightly misty, and, given the choice, I was willing to face the rat's agony as long as I could get the pleasure. Which I supposed I was about to get. I was sure he would be wonderful in bed. I just had to remember not to talk too much. That's what they all wanted. Someone pretty who didn't talk too much. I had never been on a longer walk. I had never looked so dutifully into so many store windows. I looked at my reflection in the glass. I was pretty. I was, in fact, radiant. That was what this man did for me. He made me happy. I kept my mouth shut.

"You know, Stephanie, just after I met you I had a very important dream about you."

"Do you dream a lot?"

"Mmmmm."

"Tell me. I adore dreams. Was I in it?"

"No. No, you weren't. But in the dream I broke through to a new level."

"Really? Of what?"

"Oh, well, I'm not sure . . . you know, of consciousness, getting rid of the old hang-ups."

"You don't seem awfully hung-up, Richard." Here we go, Miriam. I'm taking notes, baby.

"The usual, you know, insecurity, afraid to feel . . . but I knew when I woke up that you were going to play a very important part in my life."

"Richard, don't overinterpret," I warned myself.

"Stephanie, I know I'm not overinterpreting because with you I'm not afraid to feel."

50

If ever there were a classic Richard remark that was a classic Richard remark. I was busy thinking about whether he felt anything about the other woman. What I should have been thinking about was whether he meant he *would* feel something about me or that he wasn't afraid because with me he wasn't worried about feeling. I always got trapped with Richard on the easy responses, as in the nots, while he was levels beyond me. I did know enough to note insecurity for Miriam, realizing that if I were to get involved, it would be useful information and I remembered thinking then that I wasn't hooked because I was able to consider critically and objectively the fact that when we walked into his apartment, WRVR was going off the air for the night and the last glorious rousing strains of a jazzed-up "Star-Spangled Banner" greeted us. Richard stopped, placed his hand over his breast and moved his lips silently. I think he was practicing for a conditioned response as in bandstand, podium, inauguration. Finally a distant voice chattered through the wavelength and Richard looked at me as if we'd just taken communion together.

"God, Richard." I took off my coat. "That's how I started to masturbate. Sixth grade, you know, with my hot little hand over my hot little breast. I couldn't wait for the pledge. I never passed a flag. . . ." Either I was offending the Governor or boring Richard because he took my coat to the closet and as I was about to tell him that I keep a flag over my bed just to turn me on which was an exaggeration but I thought amusing, he disappeared into the kitchen. I let my voice trail off and wandered into the living room. In a very few minutes, long enough for the blush to fade, Richard carried in a Plexiglas tray of brie, sardines, crackers, coffee in a MOMA glass pot and a clear bowl of fresh whipped sweet cream.

"Whipped cream? Are you somebody's pussycat?"

"Oh, people feed me," he answered vaguely, setting

the tray down on the coffee table before me and returning to slide closed the double doors to the rest of the apartment.

I stuck my finger in the bowl and licked it, hoping he would explain. But he did not.

"You know I think you can really understand my goal, Stephanie. Whoops, forgot something. Meet my family. I'll be back in a minute." He indicated either a continuous bank of gleaming fish tanks or, above them, a blown-up gallery of relatives, and then, opening the closed double doors quite softly, he left me alone to decide what he meant.

"Do you like them?" he will ask me. And he will touch my hand, tapping it as he taps me, and will say solemnly: "I want you to like them." And I really won't know if he is referring to his fish or his family because I had learned from Richard in these few days that his messages were two-pronged and either prong, although I was free to choose, could stick me good. I wished he would hurry back. I moved around his room, trespassing on the thick lawn of unbleached wool, feeling very large and very conspicuous. A toilet flushed twice. I heard water running. Was it in this apartment or the next? Perhaps he was washing or changing into something contrived and dreadful like silk pajamas and maroon mules, as terribly civilized as his apartment which included all the items New York eclectic decorating is expected to include. Except the awful fish tanks and the blown-up relatives. I liked neither.

The tanks themselves were filled with crystal objects as if someone had dumped an entire display shelf from Baccarat into each of them. I heard voices, a man and a woman close to me, muted, muffled. I strained my ears but the siphons and filters of the many tanks drowned the other noises. At last, the doors slid open. Whatever it was he had forgotten, he had apparently not remembered because he came back, unchanged, empty-handed, and again closed the doors softly.

"You'll have to meet them all, Stephanie. Except my father." He touched a jug-eared man under a beach umbrella and sighed. "Four years now and my mother has never been the same."

Recklessly, I looked up into the enlarged faces of his relatives, gray and white spotted specters who may somehow know my future but clearly not my past. Why are you doing this, Richard? I came at midnight to make love, to sleep with you. Why are you doing this?

"And my mother. Do you love your mother, Stephanie?"

"Mmm."

"I don't feel anything toward my parents. Maybe that's why I tend to compartmentalize my relationships."

His mother, young, was wide-hipped, sweet-faced, dark-haired on the beach in a pleat-skirted bathing suit with his father's thin arms encircling her waist from behind and his face, squint-eyed, jug-eared, over her plump shoulder. She didn't look crazy at all. "What do you mean compartmentalize?"

"I mean one person for one thing, one for another." We moved to the next picture. "This is just after his first heart attack."

"Oh, I'm sorry." The father, still squint-eyed and jug-eared, gray-haired now, on a wicker-chaired porch with pine boughs dipping in the corner. Richard, I am not interested in your father's coronary. Not yet. I'm not even interested in the future yet. I have to go to work tomorrow. His father frightened me. He looked like the kind of man who makes the women around him grow old and mad, while he grows healthier and meaner. I wondered how the mother outlasted him.

"And Richard as Dickie-boy. I didn't become Richard until my bar mitzvah and soon after that I was 'The Gov-

53

ernor.' " My heart turned over. Richard at three or four with masses of light curling hair, pouting lips, dancing eyes. The phone began to ring somewhere beyond the closed doors. It rang many times. He didn't seem to notice. If the call were from the woman he was involved with, he wasn't too involved. "And this is Blossom, my sister. She's older. She and her friends always teamed up to make me cry." Who calls Richard at one in the morning? Who does he ignore who might be crying her eyes out and going mad because he wasn't answering? Will it ever be me?

"I guess I better answer it. No one else is going to. I'm sorry, sweetheart. This is so special. I'll be right back." The doors closed again. It was simply a remark. Who else would answer it? He was being amusing. I looked back at his baby picture. I loved him. Blossom was beautiful. Her eyes were straight and honest. She didn't look crazy either. I found her pushing Richard in a pram on a boardwalk, his chin barely reaching the side of the pram, sweet and fat and drooly. He was a funny baby. Blossom was better looking, with an antique enamel face, like a doll, and rosebud lips. Farther down the wall, I found her standing on a pedestal, glowing with her own beauty and pride, a trumpet-hemmed wedding gown twisting around the pedestal, making her eight feet tall. Then Richard at six or seven, slump-chested, bandy-legged, hipless, jug-eared with a pail and shovel and knobby knees. Beach umbrella with wide stripes, soda bottles stuck in the sand around an old blanket, middle-class, earnest people on the beach. My life had been inland, PX's and Officer's Club pools, separate from relatives, army brats on concrete shores, always shifting. A life apart. But I was certain, somehow, different as I was, that when Richard with his knobby knees knelt to get a sandwich from the A&P bag leaning against the wooden pole of the beach umbrella, I was certain it was an egg-salad sandwich with a slice of tomato and when he bit down, he hit sand in the egg-salad. I was certain of that although I'd never known his life and I really wanted to ask him. Goddammit, who was he talking to out there beyond the doors? I could feel his life somehow, wonderfully, as I stood before the pictures. I wanted my own place up there on the wall. I didn't know then what it would cost to hang there, in a middle-class, East Coast, jug-eared Jewish family, closed to outsiders, but it had the same sense then to me, although far removed, as the Armengols' Gothic Chapel and the peace of their tombs and I wished to belong.

Which could have been a death wish. I tore papers, I knew, because I avoid tearing at myself. What kind of man has his ears flattened? Why would anyone go through all that pain and shame and bandages so he wouldn't look like his family and still hang all of them on his walls? I didn't know if I would be part of Richard's life or part of this joke before me. And he'd still come up with a little jug-eared, dancing-eyed baby anyway. I would knit lots of funny hats with pompons until he was old enough to have his ears flattened too if he wanted that.

"Forgive me, forgive me, forgive me." The doors opened; the doors closed. "My mother. She has a pain. She always has a pain when I haven't called her for three days. And who is dear Stephanie smiling at? Do you think we're all funny looking?"

I was smiling, thinking of his jug-eared baby and smiling because I had felt Richard's eyes as he came into the living room, shining, like warm fires, within me. I had a deep and sweet internal sense of him without looking at him. Just as I had known about the egg salad.

"Richard, was there sand in the egg-salad sandwiches?"

"Of course. I must have been out of college by the time I found out they don't necessarily come with sand."

And then, because of the sandwich and because he was standing just in front of me, his back to me, I slid my arms around his waist as his father had his arms around his mother's waist. "Richard, why didn't you tell me it was your mother?" Richard stiffened perceptibly as I asked my question. "I thought it was another woman at the Cloisters." He slipped away like a piece of dental floss, leaving me with a pair of extra arms which could find no place on my body to rest comfortably and humiliation burning my cheeks into ashes. Either my question or my touching him was a tactical error. Or both. I used my hands to smooth my hair. Richard adjusted a screw on a siphon tube running into the tank.

"My mother wanted to meet you after I told her you were in the top three."

"Top three what?"

"An expression. I told her you were fantastic and she found out from Terry—Terry's my sister's friend— where you worked. I didn't send her, Stephanie. I didn't tell her what to do. But she tried to meet you and you were rude."

"Rude?" My voice peeled into something belligerent which I couldn't cover. "How should I know who she was? I didn't even know your last name. I didn't even know why she had come."

Richard grinned and wagged his finger at me. "Hostile, hostile. You called my office so you must have known my last name."

Richard, what are you doing? I am here to hold you and kiss you and stay in your arms. What is happening? We'll be fighting in a minute and I don't know how to draw out of the morass you've led me into. "Is that an accusation?" I asked as softly as I was able.

"You *are* hostile, Stephanie."

"You *gave* me your phone number. I didn't know your last name." I spoke with my back to him. I examined the ugly black fish.

He continued calmly, ignoring my increasing anger and anguish. "My secretary said you were rude also. I told her you didn't strike me as rude. I think you are really sweet."

"Oh, Richard," I turned to him, almost pleading. "I'm not a rude person."

"I know you aren't. Here, come sit down and have our coffee." He patted the sofa and sat down, waiting for me. "Now, tell me what's bothering you."

"Is your mother crazy, Richard?"

"My mother's invested a great deal in my career, Stephanie." It wasn't the question I should have asked. The question I should have asked was "What do you want from me?"

Instead I continued, "I'm not rude, Richard. You have arranged situations for me which leave me no alternatives. I don't know how to act. I didn't mean to offend her. I don't know what to expect." I remained at the fish tanks. He waited at the sofa.

"Ah, when we begin to expect something of each other, the excitement is over . . . you see? I can't handle expectations. Don't expect anything and I won't expect anything from you and whatever I receive I'll be grateful for. You know, Stephanie, I think probably, Stephanie, that you are a romantic person, that you are not rude at all and if you do hurt people, it is unintentional."

The combination of "would you like to go to Atlanta?" with the expectation shtik told me he was willing to pull anything with me. And if he could do that, I could resort to anything to draw the attention back. "I really am a romantic, Richard. I really dreamed of princes in white uniforms with gold epaulets waltzing me across marble floors."

"Well," he said, "come over here now, finish your coffee and then we'll put on some romantic music for a romantic lady and we'll dance. I've left my epaulets at the palace. Will you forgive me?" He reached his hand out. As I came to him, he used it to spread brie on a cracker and offered it to me. "Would you like to dance, Stephanie?" He didn't stand.

"Very much." I sat next to him. The sofa exhaled as I sank into its plush and a cat, the same ochre as the sofa, leaped away. I hadn't seen it at all.

"Platypus."

"Funny name." I tried to mold my face into a dreamy, exalted mien, like a kid in a *Seventeen* ad for Keepsake Diamonds getting her engagement ring. It was difficult. Richard had brought in delicate rice paper napkins which I lusted to rip.

"It is a funny name. I never thought of that. I didn't name her."

"Oh." I asked no questions. The cat loped to the fish tank nearest us. She was wide-faced and scarred. Richard, it seemed, would have had a Siamese.

"Well, I'm really excited that you're here finally." The sweet twitch began at the corners of his mouth. He sought out my eyes, peering, searching for something I hoped would be there. The fish in the tank below the glass coffee table swam in circles around my cup. I looked back into Richard's eyes which seemed not to blink. If I had allowed myself to watch the circling fish and then look at the sardines on Richard's tray, I would have become very ill with little more effort. I wanted to go home. I tried to keep my face dreamy and exalted. His eyes were as I had remembered them, gray-flecked and sincere. He tapped my hand. "Stephanie, tell me honestly, what do you think about my fish tanks?"

"Mmm. That 'love is all there is, is all we know of love.' " I couldn't help myself. I understood the frustration of Emily Dickinson who also said she would wait forever for her love if he would only tell her how long forever would be. I thought I would soon be in a position for measuring forever. I would also thank her for the line. If I hadn't had it, I would have screamed.

"I knew it! The minute I saw you. A true romantic."

Below me a pack of feathery armed fish pressed near my saucer. They reminded me of Sissy. "Listen, Richard, I love your fish tanks. They're terrific." That was the second time he discovered I was a romantic.

I found a napkin to tear. I tore it at the side of my hip away from him with my two-fingered act and slipped the shreds under the pillow as he explained his collection. "My five-thousand-buck fish tanks. I'm not really a spender, but once people found out I had fish, they kept giving me more, some kinds that couldn't live with each other. I tried to keep everybody apart for a while but it got to be too much and now all those precious expensive fish, Blue Angels, all of them . . . you can't tell what they were."

I tried to keep my eyebrows up, alert and keen. Touch me, Richard; feel me, or I will cry or go home or scream. Whatever I will do will be utterly disturbing to both of us. I reached for the napkin on Richard's lap. He snapped his legs together.

"It's more of an indulgence," he added quickly. "Not really a collection. And it needs constant attention. Just keeping the glass clean and changing filters and feeding them."

"You have help then?" Was this what I had come here for? The important talk about the future? Who gives you the fish? Who gives you the cream? Who waters that gorgeous asparagus plant in the stainless steel pot out there in the hall? Who else is there? How will you keep all of us apart in our compartments? And will we all end up in faceless, mutated, ruined, quivering heaps? Goddammit, not me. I don't want to be aggressive with you, Richard, but I want to strangle everyone who shines your glass and feeds your fish and fills your refrigerator. Every other woman. "Do you have someone to help you, Richard?" I repeated.

Did I have to make a pass at him? I had, I supposed, a psychic need for this man to make love to me and yet he sat there grinning and being sincere and I sat there tearing up his rice paper napkins and talking about his damn guppies and I wanted to leave, to go home and dream about him rather than be with him. He put his arm over the back of his sofa. Although he wasn't touching me, it was a step forward. "I couldn't do it myself," he said cryptically.

"What?"

"The apartment."

"Oh, no, all that glass." Let's get started, Richard. I have to go to work in the morning.

"Listen," he sighed. "People would come in and I'd be rattling off the names of all the fish and I'd be an absolute prick. I'm not boring you, am I, Stephanie? Here, put your head on my shoulder. Let's just sit quietly for a moment."

I sat quietly. He didn't. He talked about bucking the system, how to remain a politician and keep your integrity intact. With geological timing, I moved closer to him. Finally, quite happily close, I whispered, "She's watching us. I'm uncomfortable."

The muscles along the right side of his thigh tightened like rubberbands. "What?"

"Platypus, she's watching us."

"Oh, I'll get rid of her. You know, you really are wonderful. God, you are nice!"

I would have to remember that because he took my hand. "Stephanie, for all the cool and all the style, you really are old-fashioned. You make me so damn happy. Do I make you happy, Stephanie?"

What had I done to bring about this delight? I had told him what to do. I had given him a command, not advice. I would remember because he leaped from the couch, allowing my head to bump against the sofa, pulled me up, threw his arms around me and hugged and whirled me around and around until I began to feel his joy. "Let's dance. Let's really dance, Stephanie. Records. Let me . . . now you don't move. Stand just as you are, right there, so I can remember this minute. Stand still. I'll get some music on."

He licked his lips and danced with his arms around an imaginary me to a complicated stereo with a noisy mechanism. "Music for a romantic girl. For an old-fashioned romantic girl who makes me happy. Next time you come here, I promise, no more cat. Promise. Show tunes. Ah hah!" He knelt at the stereo. I explored the lines of his back and buttocks and tried to recall desperately what exactly it was I had done that had so appealed to him. It couldn't just have been that I had told him what to do. I think what I had done was to have avoided relating to him in any way whatsoever all night long. And then told him to get rid of his cat. Jesus. Or a combination of both.

We danced finally. I don't recall what we danced to except for the last tune. I was warm all over and tingling, soft, weightless, dreamborne, at peace. I wanted to stay in his arms forever. He sang vague words into my hair, into my ears, into my forehead, his chin leaning on my nose. I followed his footsteps. I would follow him anywhere for this contentment. The noises of the apartments began to fade, the bubbling and pumping of the fish tanks was more and more faint. The cat was gone and we danced.

He pulled away slightly so I could look into his terribly solemn eyes. His lips twitched. I wanted to kiss them and still them. "I was a prick to make you come running down here in the middle of the night, wasn't I?" If his eyes hadn't been so soft and his arms so good around me, I don't think I would have answered as I did.

Someone else would have murmured. But I knew what he wanted to hear although it was not what I wanted to say and I said it. "What's a friend for?" I knew, later, it would cost.

In response, he held me closer. It had been the

answer he was waiting for, although it had been, to be accurate, a question. I had no idea, still, into what my role as friend would really translate. "You're the right girl, Steph. I really mean that."

"One night at a time, Richard," I reminded him.

Miriam, I would say tomorrow, he's making it too easy. And Miriam would reply, when it's meant to be, it's meant to be.

"Stephanie, do you know what my favorite meal is?"

"Tell me."

"Breakfast."

"I should have known."

"Strawberries and whipped cream and tossed salad with blue cheese and fresh ground coffee."

"Croutons in the salad?"

"You are so smart. Not with garlic."

"Of course not."

And we danced. A toilet flushed somewhere as the records lifted and dropped on the turntable. It sounded very close.

I whispered, trying not to break the moment, "What's that?"

"Sounds like a toilet flushing." He paused, holding me still, at arm's length. "Oh, here's the song I've been waiting for." And then, although there were no epaulets on his sweater and the floors weren't marble, he became my fantasy for he stretched out his arms to me as the music began and folded me to himself and we danced to "The Girl That I Marry." I smiled into his shoulder. I nuzzled into his turtleneck. He had planned this when we were walking on the sidewalk so long ago this evening. He didn't need a white uniform. Rather, I didn't need a white uniform; he had created my dream and it was happening. Sweet, magical, solemn.

" 'Stead of flittin' I'll be sittin'—Next to her and she'll purr like a kitten. A doll I can carry, the girl that I marry must be." Richard lifted me from the floor when the

62

song ended and carried me to the couch. I kissed his cheek
lightly as he put me down on the couch. It was then that
he said, "I have a lousy speech writer. I bet you could help
me with my speeches." And it was then, before I could
answer, that I heard the shower running and a girl singing. He settled down beside me and pulled my head back
onto his shoulder. I think if he had touched my nipple,
forget the shower, forget the speeches, I would have had
an orgasm with no further effort. But the shower was
forcing its way into my consciousness and the dreamy film
drifted and lifted away because I heard, I thought, and
then was certain I heard that same voice of the girl at the
party singing that same song Richard had just been
singing to me and singing it in Richard's bathroom or,
more accurately, in their bathroom somewhere beyond
the closed double doors of the living room and in the
direction of the beige plush bedspread I had so wanted
to be spread upon.

"My God!"

"What's wrong?"

I rammed open the doors. Her voice rang clear and
powerful in the hallway. I wrestled with hangers for my
coat and fled from his apartment. He was shouting after
me and she sang on, trumpeting triumphantly while my
walls came tumbling down. I looked back once at Richard's
astonished face. "Will you be all right? Call me as soon
as you get home. I'll take you home, Stephanie. Call me."

By the time the cab reached my building, little
pearly bits of hope were penetrating the black roach shell
of anger in which I had encased myself and by the time
I pressed the button in the elevator I was no longer certain that the voice I'd heard had even been in Richard's
apartment. A neighbor may have heard the song and sung
along. Walls are thin. I hear the couple next to my bedroom fighting late at night. Next time I would listen, perhaps even ask. Next time. I walked down the long hall
with all its doors locked and bolted, a long empty feeling

63

of no one to say hello to when I came home. Next time. And as I neared my own door I heard the phone ringing and ringing and ringing and I ran down the hall, the roach shell slipping away, the keys jingling in my fist, and my spirit lifting and stretching to the phone. My heart pounded. "Hello?"

"Thank God you're home. Stephanie, why are you so hostile to men? What is this hostility? Why did you leave like that?"

I couldn't begin to think. Am I hostile? I didn't even know why I'd left any more. "Richard?"

"Oh? Do you do this kind of thing twice a night? Are you some kind of castrator? Of course it's me."

The shell was gone and I had no skin to cover me up. Hope slid out like an oyster. "It doesn't sound like you. That isn't the way you talk." It was after three. Four crosses were arriving by ship tomorrow and I didn't know how I would wake up for work. Nor could I imagine how I would sleep. I had made a terrible mistake and I wanted to hang up before I made another one. "If I didn't care so much for you, Richard," I tried, "I wouldn't have left. I thought . . . I thought there was someone else in your apartment."

"Dumdum." His voice was gentle at last.

"I'm sorry I didn't stay with you, Richard."

"I'm sorry too, honey. I was so upset and worried about you running around the city in the middle of the night. I wish you would have let me take you home. Say, did you lock your door?"

"Oh, no. Hold on." I knew he could care less but I would be damned if I were to give him the satisfaction of hearing anger in my voice. But he must have heard some of it because when I came back to the phone and told him the door was locked, he made his next move.

"Honey, when can I see you? I must see you. Would you like to go away for the weekend? Are you free the weekend after next? I don't mean to beg. . . ."

Cold water splashed on my collarbone. Had he said beg or bed? What was wrong with *this* weekend? My mind began to click into place. "Do you know what I would like, Richard? I'd like to put my head in your lap and have you stroke my hair until I fall asleep."

"Poor baby. You must be so tired. I would sit next to you and hold your hand while you slept and if you woke up, I'd sing you back to sleep."

"That's what I'd like. And I'd like you to brush my hair."

"You have lovely hair. Next weekend. I promise. Now you lie down, close those beautiful eyes and think about me stroking your head and singing and holding your hand. And try to get a good night's sleep. I'll call you tomorrow and tell you where we'll go so you can plan your clothes. Could you meet me next Friday at my place at four-thirty? I'm in court and I'm not exactly sure when I'll be out but you can take a drink and I'll be there within the hour."

"Richard, I don't want to go back there."

"No one will be there, Stephanie. No one. I'll have the key sent up to your office. Do you want to go anyplace in particular? Sun, sand, surf?"

"Anyplace." I was drowsy already. I would sleep, charmed. Seek the stars.

"Stephanie, one last thing. Whatever the reason you left, whatever I did or you felt I did, I'm glad of one thing that I've learned about you tonight."

"Mmmm?" How is it that this stranger can detoxify me so? What magic has he that softens me and reassures me?

"I'm glad that a girl of your caliber, a girl like you, that you're just too wonderful a girl to be small-minded and jealous. I'm so glad of that. Now, put that head down and sleep. I'll call you tomorrow." He clicked the phone down. My fingers stiffened on it, clutched.

When I could release them, I took the Manhattan

classified to bed with me and tore every page under Ranges & Stoves—Dlrs. & Svce. in the yellow pages. Then methodically, I began with Appliances—Built-In and worked toward completion. I had to check every crack, scratch, chip, mark, quality of stone on those four crosses tomorrow before I accepted shipment. God, it's the only situation in my entire life in which I am actually able to judge authenticity. Maybe there was a girl. Maybe there was no girl. There must have been. Why else would he mention jealousy? But he was so surprised. Was he surprised that I would leave or was he surprised that someone else being in the apartment would bother me? Am I really that square? I shared bedrooms once with another couple and a date in a beach house. I didn't adore it but I didn't drown myself either. Why was I intellectualizing this man? Why couldn't I just accept the magic he offered? If he made sure I was home safely and my door was locked and brushed my hair and sang me to sleep and held my hand, he might even pin that note on my chest when I die: She's gone to seek the stars. It was small to be jealous. To nag and ask questions.

My pillow became his lap and I could feel his hands on my hair and his voice soft and mellow. "She'll wear satins and laces and smell of cologne. . . ." I'll have to buy some pretty gowns, diaphanous, and we'll sail away for a year and a day to the land where the bong tree grows and there in a wood . . . God, I wish my breasts were fuller. And they danced in the light of the moon, the moon. And I would buy some underwear like Anne Bancroft wore in *The Graduate*, serious grown-up sexy stuff and when he begins to really trust me and be sure of me, he'll be less ambiguous. I know it. I woke up the next day with a drumming headache, very late, in a bed of yellow confetti with the lower half of Women's Apparel—Retail intact, the page clutched in my hand next to my cheek. And I'd have to get a new phone book.

During the next week I learned a number of things. I learned that Miriam in the name of love was going off the wall. I learned that Sissy in the name of love was going off the wall and that Richard in the name of love was pushing whoever it was who loved him off the wall. I learned that Richard and the Unicorn more or less equaled each other, which meant that the more I knew about either of them the less I knew them at all. I had an inkling that the fiery script on the wall would spell Stephanie and that sooner or later I would have to choose between in the name of love and the wall. By the end of the week I had reduced all of my equations and theorems to the lowest common denominator—which is a fairly reasonable vantage point from which to view romantic love—a simple maxim: love and truth do not a marriage make.

I had hoped that the week as it progressed was simply the kind of week in which everyone in New York goes to his astrologer. Then the universe moves forward a notch and once again morning's at seven. It wasn't that kind of week. Sissy for instance was going to the hospital.

She called sobbing Friday night. Could she have

Monday off? I allowed her Monday off. For only one day I didn't feel obligated to ask what was wrong.

"Aren't you going to ask what's wrong?"

"No."

"Why?"

"Because I trust you. If you need the day off, it's your business. I wish you well. I don't want to know. I'll pray for you."

"Pray for the baby." She hung up, cursing me to a third party before the phone reached its cradle. I didn't hear from her until Tuesday. Nor did I call her. I rationalized my not calling her but I knew the reason was that I couldn't stand hearing whatever gothic tale she had to tell me.

Richard, who was obviously into phone calls at erratic hours, called me again early Saturday morning, offering to bring steaks over that night and, because it was a forsythia–sky-blue day and I was happy and part of me really did want to be the right girl, I borrowed pieces of furniture, sheets, and dishes from everyone in the building, lugged home four flowering azaleas and a ficus tree that probably would impair my spine for a lifetime, licked the apartment clean and prepared strawberries Romanoff, readied a Caesar salad, whipped up more cream just in case and, among other things, sang Richard's song about the girl he would marry all the day long until he called at three to say he had to leave at ten but would be over at six, had his alarm clock set for six and would take a nap. The free spirit asked no questions. The free spirit was learning. But he hadn't come at six and I was wildly angry and called him. Error. I woke him, he said, as his alarm went off and he'd been dreaming about the owl and the pussycat. I was no longer wildly angry. The synchronicity, like Merlin's sand of enchantment, flung me into my darkest mythic levels. Instead of asking practical questions like where are you and when will you be here, I wanted to know what level our reality was on. What did our meeting really *mean*?

"I have a friend," he told me, dreamy and groggy, "who insists that the owl is a girl. I say boy. Who would you identify with, Stephanie, girl that you are?"

If he hadn't said friend, I might have said pussycat. I have a friend who rolled over on a hot August night and said, dreamy and groggy, to his wife, "Honey, I gotta go home." Who do you talk to in your sleep, Richard? Who are you dreaming with? The veil of enchantment was lifting rapidly. I said, "The owl, definitely."

"Really, I could have sworn you'd say pussycat. She says the owl," he told someone else. "Well, I told my friend we'd have to accept your decision because you are a born romantic. But why the owl?"

And there's one born every minute. Who does your friend think you're talking to? "The owl because every time you mention another goddamn friend I want to ask who."

There was a sharp intake of breath on the other end and then silence and then, quietly, pleasantly, "Hold on a minute, honey, while I splash some cold water on my face and answer nature's call, okay?"

Nature who? But I held on and when he came back many minutes later, perhaps seven, perhaps ten, he said, "Jesus, it's really late. Would you forgive me if I freeze the steaks and take a raincheck? By the time I shower and shave and dress and get over there, I'll have to leave and that would be unfair to you."

What was I to do? Ask him if he were constipated? I murdered petal by petal our centerpiece until the petals were red pulp in my hand but I held because he told me in melodious lilting words about poetry and silly things like owls and pussycats and how talking with me on those levels really turned him on because he loved to hear me dreaming and someday he would catch me asleep and when my eyes were doing those REM things to show I was in a dream state he would touch me on my lovely ivory shoulder and ask if I would let him into my dream before it went away. And he told me how lucky we were to find each other, that it was part of a cosmic design and he extracted a promise from me that if I ever thought he was full of shit—his words, not mine—I should tell him so because it makes him feel secure that someone can be totally honest and care enough to help him. Even if it hurts. I would have saved myself a lot of time if I'd picked up on the "even if it hurts." At that point though, I couldn't imagine hurting him, tempted as I was to love him and I was still slightly enchanted while I listened to his promise that he would think only of me until we were together again and signed off with his "Catch you later." The catch you later lifted the final veil. It wasn't until I looked around at the very real ficus tree and the four azaleas and the red pulp in my palm that the white anger rose in my volcanic neck.

I am such a sucker for myth, magic and cosmic promise. Again I had allowed myself to be charmed. I had allowed him to break the date without a murmur, without a question. Why would fifteen minutes, I tried not to think, make any difference? If he had to be at my place at six, why had he set his alarm for six? And why did he have to leave at ten? And why, if all he did was sleep on Saturday, couldn't we have gone away this weekend instead of waiting for the next? I had a strong feeling he was manipulating me.

But I couldn't really expect to understand him that quickly, I thought, and I decided not to think about him or the weekend or the owl. Maybe he had diarrhea. At any rate, I had a new ficus tree and my apartment was gleaming. I gorged myself sick on the whipped cream and stopped thinking about Richard.

Until Sissy arrived on Tuesday, slung her knapsack

on my desk, and burst into large tears. I handed her Kleenex, the knapsack and bills of lading to retype. "How's Monica," I mumbled as she left my office, heaving.

"Don't ask."

I didn't ask.

Forty-five minutes later, she stormed into my office. "I really appreciate your concern. Thanks a lot."

"How's Monica, Sissy?" I offered more audibly.

Her mouth turned down into tears. Through the tears she looked at me with proud and defiant animal eyes. "She kept the baby."

"What baby?"

"Monica is pregnant."

I had been right. I couldn't stand hearing whatever it was she needed Monday off for. "What do you mean pregnant? What do you mean pregnant?"

Sardonic now, superior. "I mean she is going to have a baby. We Lesbians aren't barren, you know."

"Oh." I looked at Sissy and I felt her pain thundering into my own center. I recommended what I saw as a logical and sane solution. "There are agencies, Sissy. Miriam can help."

Sissy gagged on hot fresh tears. "Only a man would say that. You better not try anything!"

"Look," I tried again. "Tell me how it happened."

That too was the wrong approach. I could feel the walls closing in on me. Sissy sat down on my desk, pushing papers into piles. Her shoulders shook. All I could separate from the strangling noises was Baskin-Robbins. It didn't help much.

"Sissy, dear . . . get a grip on yourself." How I wanted to run from that office and scrape all of the plaster of her insanity from me. "Here, try to tell me how it happened."

She looked up at me with her sudden killer clarity. "How the hell do you *think* it happened?" And rooted

71

around in her knapsack and handed me a Muriel. I tried to hold on. "It was important for our marriage and so we found a father."

"Oh my God."

"It isn't easy. Don't think it's easy, Stephanie. We're not programmed the way you are. We live on a frontier."

I swung around to my window, hoping the bases of her choice were at least worse than my own. Hers seemed more rational.

"We're going to write about it someday and we're going to emerge better people for it."

"Forget the philosophy. How did you choose the guy?"

Sissy was very at ease now. The Muriel was in shreds in my lap. "Straight leg, flare leg. Elimination. We got stuck on Oshkosh painters but dropped that. Lees or Levis, that took days but we ended with straight Levis. Then all the guys in straight Levis who bought ice cream cones. See?"

"Of course."

"And then Rocky Road or S'Mores."

"Rocky Road?" I didn't know where the responses were coming from, a hole in my head, floating out to the hole in Sissy's head.

"You *do* understand. I knew you'd understand. Then three scoops, two scoops or one. Two was moderate. Then chocolate sprinkles or plain. Then who licks and who chews."

"God help me."

"Lickers cling and are too sentimental. So she went home with the one we liked. It was a very troubling time for both of us, you know. If it's a girl we're going to name it after you because we love you." She found another Muriel and passed it to me. "Try to smoke it this time."

"No way. No way. Don't get me involved. I lick. I hate chocolate. I don't want any part of your insanity. No way, Sissy."

72

"It isn't insane, Stephanie. It's just because you're programmed. Straight people are programmed on straight lines."

"The hell I'm programmed."

"She almost lost the baby, you know. I feel so guilty."

"The hell I'm programmed."

"Once you realize you're programmed, you'll be free. But you are programmed, believe me."

"Why didn't *you* have the baby . . . you're programmed too then . . . she's the woman, you're the man."

"Shit, I just didn't like ice cream. That's all."

I asked Sissy to take the rest of the week off and stay home with Monica, but she refused because she couldn't do it to me, she said. She knew how important a week it was. She would stay by my side. "Look," her last remark of the day was, "you're lucky you're programmed. Don't feel bad."

It was after that remark that I began to think about Richard. I began to think about Richard a great deal that week. The museum had closed my chapel. The Armengols were shrouded in spattered drop cloths and a pockmarked painter in Oshkosh paint pants replaced the windows with sixteenth-century stained glass. I became so assiduously aware of his pocks and his pants, even though he was quiet and pleasant, I could find neither solace nor solitude in my chapel. Miriam was finally so annoyed that I'd called her as often as I had to ask why Richard hadn't called me that she, explaining she had a heavy case load (one of which was herself), locked me out. "Stay off the phone, honey, and give him a chance to call you." And so I spent my lunch hours that long week, except for one, with my Bison Brand in my briefcase and the Unicorn in the Hall of the Unicorn Tapestries.

I thought of myself as a rational well-centered woman who could think as well as feel. And so I sat before the Unicorn each day and forced myself to think. Mostly I felt. The Unicorn always did that to me, which was why

I avoided the Hall, the romance and the charm. The gentle magic beast in its millefleur fields and the happily married Anne and Louis, Queen and King of France, were, as I had known they would be, simply too much for my rational nature and I was soon lost in the immensity of the tapestries, the tiny beasts, the delicate flowers and the utter charm of my friend, the Unicorn, while I sat and considered Richard. I considered what Richard had said, what Richard had done, what Richard would say, what Richard would do—a dozen conversations I held before the Unicorn, and then I considered what I had said, what I should have said, what I had done, what I had not done, and then I seriously considered Richard's acts and words and how my acts and words would change his acts and words, how my moves would change his events. Sweet, heady, androgynous, lucid tête-à-têtes before the Unicorn and each one ended with the smug decision that my legs were plenty good enough and ended with me in a pastoral scene—something between horny Cretans and langorous Tahitians with Richard humming and rocking his head to a mythic melody as we undressed under the thatching. And when I had come dead end in my consideration of Richard, I would then consider the Unicorn. Eventually during that long week, I began to think of both Richard and the Unicorn together, and my romantic daydreams were becoming Skinnerian—I was trying to control the behavior of another human being.

I wanted to tell Miriam where I was with the Unicorn but when she finally called late Tuesday night, whispering into the phone, I knew she wasn't ready for the Unicorn. "This one you'll never believe. Guess which late-maturing adolescent spent the weekend in the hospital?"

"Are you all right?"

"I was an early maturer, but our friend has a broken foot and a broken arm. I have to stay home and baby him because he thinks I tried to kill him."

"Did you?"

"I didn't try, but I almost did." She began to laugh, that absurd, wild laugh she releases after her Il Duce stories. I couldn't stand it. "I can't help laughing. I have stomach cramps every time I walk into the bedroom and see him there. But I have to stay home: he won't have a nurse. Comic books, chocolate chip ice cream and we're playing pishy pashy like it's a Russian chess meet."

"So?"

"My late-maturing adolescent decided to paint the eaves Saturday morning, which aren't aluminum? And he's a little shaky all the way up there on the ladder, so he ties a rope around his waist, okay? Throws it over the roof and ties, oh God, the other end to the bumper of my car." She started to laugh again. "It worked fine until I ran out of cigarettes."

"Miriam, how far did you go?"

"Just . . ." the giggles, ". . . just until I heard him bouncing across the roof. Every time he told the story in the hospital he had the nurses in stitches because he was so serious. And soon he figured out they thought he was funny and then he was Jack Benny and they rolled him around the place in his wheelchair. He had a ball. He's almost grateful."

"But is he okay?"

"Oh, yeah. He's too mean to die." I heard him calling her in the background. "Got to go."

Part of me thought it was a great story. The other part wondered if she really had intended to kill him. Miriam wasn't into objectivity. For myself, I returned to contemplating the Unicorn. The next day I called her and she answered thoroughly annoyed. "Miriam, I think Richard and the Unicorn have a lot in common."

"Sure" she clipped. "They're both horny. Listen he doesn't like me on the phone." And hung up.

I knew more about the Unicorn than I knew about Richard. But some information did ring true about both my friends. The Bestiary described the splendid horn of the Unicorn as anfractuous and chocleary. Chocleary wasn't even in the dictionary but anfractuous certainly applied: winding, roundabout, devious and tortuous. That resonated. Actually I really knew nothing about Richard and nobody really knew anything about the Unicorn. All was conjecture. The only conclusion I reached after those lunch hours was that both Richard and the Unicorn were absolutely charming and completely elusive and regularly unknowable.

Finally I stopped thinking about the meaning and I began, slightly nonconsummated as I was, without even being aware that I had begun, to consider how I could capture my Unicorn. How I could get Richard to lay his head in my lap. For I also knew from the Bestiary that not a single Unicorn had ever come into the hands of man alive and although it was possible to kill them, it was impossible to capture them. Except, another strange archaic source offered, "if a virgin be led to the woods where the Unicorn lurks and he will see her and lay his head in her lap and allow himself to be caught." That was interesting. But if the Unicorn—all spirit, all knowledge, enlightenment—allowed himself to be captured, he must have known his program. That's when I began to reconsider Sissy's remarks about programming. If I were programmed, then Richard too was programmed and maybe he was programmed for a girl like me. Maybe that's what the right girl meant.

And he had reacted to my owl remark, unkind as it was, because he was already committed to the programming. I *was* the right girl. He wasn't angry because I had said something a right girl shouldn't say and thereby showed myself as the wrong girl. What he'd found was that the right girl, the one he might not be able to avoid, had bitch in her. That's what bothered him. He was fighting his programming. And I mine? Actually, it might have meant I could do no wrong. Once the right girl, always the right girl. The worse I became, the more he would realize I was the right girl, because if you are programmed in the ways we are, then the right girl is your nagging mother or your castrating big sister. The wrong girl is the one who is loving and kind and open. There was a great deal to say for the Queen capturing the Unicorn by wounding him instead of laying *her* head in *his* lap. At any rate, the concept was far more appealing than a two-scooper straight-legged chocolate-sprinkled Rocky Road chewer.

I had no idea where my line of thinking was leading me but day by day I drove closer to my low conclusions. I was beginning to put together patterns and I needed to tell them to Miriam. But poor Miriam, it seemed, already had the plaster under her fingernails and was clearly out of control. I realized that when she called me at home Wednesday night. There was no laughter behind her voice this time.

"Vus machsta?"

"Oh, Miriam, I'm so glad you called."

"You packed for your weekend?"

"I don't know where we're going. Listen, I have to tell you. . . ." Miriam wasn't listening any longer.

"Pink, blue, soft lushy things, don't forget. Listen, I gotta tell you this story. . . ."

Why did she have to tell me? The hostility between Miriam and Il Duce was beginning to horrify me. I wasn't amused. I didn't want to hear. I couldn't afford to hear. And anyway, I didn't want to tie the phone up in case Richard were to call. "Sure, Miriam."

"Remember I told you how the nurses pushed him all over the hospital and he went avisiting? Remember? It seems that he went into one room where a kid is drawing illustrations for a medical text. Okay? She's taking her pictures from a slide projected on a wall, a huge slide. And it's a diseased vagina or some goddamn thing. He can't stop talking for days in between the pishy pashy about the picture and how young and innocent she is. And

77

how honest she is. And how honest she is. And he's in love."

"With the kid?" Below the wisecracks, somewhere, Miriam had to feel something, some pain.

"Says so. Says she's honest. He respects her for her honesty, and he wants some time off when he gets better because she promised to see him 'socially.' But, he wants to be honest too and not sneak around so he wants my permission. Is that cute? How do I compete with a young kid? Innocent, I'm not. Diseased, I'm not. But I thought I was honest at least. He got boxes of candy from her already and little cuddly cards. The whole kindergarten shit, bunny rabbits, mice with fucking bonnets. And he shows me everything because he thinks . . ."

"Because he thinks he should be honest. That's really stretching the intent of honesty, isn't it? Rubbing your face in it?"

"Listen to this one. 'Heal those gorgeous limbs, from Francine.' Okay? I really thought I was honest. He said he's never met anyone so honest. I was the most honest woman in the world, he told me. Before we were married. But you can't be honest if you want to stay married. It doesn't work. But I *was*—honest and open. I could do with a little less of his goddamn honesty. And a little less of his pishy pashy."

"Do you care, Miriam?"

"Nope. But I'm plenty pissed because I get to stay home and bake and he keeps screaming about how she cares because she sends him a card. Mice with hats. Are you lucky you're the other woman. Are you lucky!"

"I am?"

"Sweety, the whole thing is a damned Mexican stand-off. You get hung up with the morality of who shoots first, what is fair, what is just, what is honest, you die. Okay. Don't get hung-up like I did on being honest. Honesty isn't exactly the coin of the realm when it comes to marriage."

Miriam didn't pause, couldn't listen. She didn't even need somebody on the other end of the phone.

"Listen, she'll do him a lot of good. She'll drop him for a sexy intern and he'll come running home. No problem. I'll let you go. I just had to tell you. Is that a scream? If I let him do this maybe he'll stop thinking I tried to kill him."

"And you must know just the intern."

"Of course." She laughed, but it was a different laugh. "I found one who looks most like Richard Chamberlain and told him that the girl in the audio-visual room was troubled because she liked to give blow jobs and her dates felt threatened."

And wore straight-legged Levis. Christ, another one. "Miriam, I love you. I have to get to sleep. I'll talk to you." There was pain. When had she begun to love him?

I didn't sleep. I lay in the dark wide-eyed with my cynical uncertainties. At that point I only thought Miriam and Sissy were crazy. Love seemed to be the problem. And if I were to love, I too might go off the wall. It took a phone call from Richard and lunch with Jack to complete the picture and turn my night thoughts into cynical certainties.

Sissy told me I was lucky I was programmed. Miriam told me I was lucky I was the other woman. Richard told me I was lucky I wasn't in Atlanta. Had I had a choice? It was muggy in Atlanta. His voice was faint and distant as it had been when I woke him on Saturday. "Steph, darling? Can you talk? I'm so down. It's so muggy in Atlanta." It was four A.M.

There were certain responses to this immeasurable man which drew no blood and I had begun to rely on them. "What's a friend for?" Come lay your head in my lap. I won't hurt you.

"I'm so alone tonight, Stephanie. I feel so abandoned."

"Oh, Richard," was another of those responses. I added, "Darling."

"I wish you were here."

"Oh, Richard." So far, so good. Why hadn't he asked me before he left? Did he want me to think he'd asked me?

"I need to be with someone who's my equal. That's what I need."

"Poor dear man, what's the matter?"

"You don't mind listening. It's pretty personal, honey, but I have to talk to someone. Look, I'm in Atlanta, okay?"

"That's nice." I was noncommittal. Was that hostility I heard?

"And I took my friend with me, okay?" He *was* challenging me.

"I understand. I can't help wishing I were with you."

"I wish that too." He was very quick. "But I took my friend because she was really looking forward to it and she's been working her ass off."

"I'm sure." My God, he wanted my approval. Then he really was programmed? "Richard, we're not committed to each other. Don't worry."

No response to that. The only person who had responded to me all week had been Sissy. He was going on. "Well, I had a conference and I was two steps ahead of the sheriff all week and busy as hell and she just sat in the hotel room and didn't do anything but wait for me to finish with the conference. You know how conferences are."

"Why didn't you take her to the conference?"

"I didn't feel like it. She would've been bored. Anyway there's plenty to do in Atlanta."

"I know, I've heard the Eastern ads."

"Haven't you ever been here? I'll have to take you sometime. Anyway she sat in the hotel room all day waiting for me to call. And when I finally came in . . . it was after two in the morning . . . I even took my shoes off so I wouldn't wake her up . . . she screamed at me. Is that fair? I think everyone in the hotel must have heard her. Is that fair?"

I was becoming increasingly aware that even though I was jealous I hadn't gone to Atlanta, I was exulting in the trouble brewing down south. "Richard, did you call her to tell her you were going to be that late?"

"No, I guess I should have but by the time I realized it was so late I didn't want to wake her up. I wasn't with another woman or anything. I was just goddamned busy."

"Didn't you realize she'd be worried?"

He hesitated. "Funny, that's just what she said. But that isn't what she meant. She expected me to come back and take her places. But she had no reason to have expectations."

He took her to Atlanta and he left her in the hotel. He dragged her a thousand miles and spent good money on her just to show her she shouldn't have expectations? Richard was a sweetheart. "That's true," I said, echoing something he had once said, "when you have expectations the excitement is over."

"And she left hopping mad. But not until everyone on the floor heard her. Colleagues, Stephanie, colleagues."

"Oh, Richard." I knew then I should be defending her, but he had pushed her out and called me. Richard simply wasn't up to confrontation with her but he was looking for a way to break up—and she took the worm. Or I took the worm.

"She said some awful things to me, Stephanie. I'm very upset about some of the things she said. Can I talk to you?"

"Of course."

"You're a wonderful girl. I'm a lucky guy."

And you must be a shit, Richard, to set her up like that. To take such pains. I would have torn you limb from limb if you tiptoed into my bedroom at two in the morning, skyline panorama, revolving restaurant, glass shaft elevator, Underground Atlanta or not. Carrying your shoes?

"She kept telling me I didn't belong in politics. Now that hurts. And that I only like middle-class women anyway. And that when she first met me I was almost a Marxist, a Maoist, and then within weeks I had shifted to a *Village Voice* liberal and now I'm a conservative; whatever way the wind blows, she said, because I have no center. But I have a center. I have integrity. She thinks my priorities are false and that because I treated her the way I did I could never deal honestly with human concepts."

"Oh, Richard."

"I'm very upset about this, Stephanie. She said that I'd never be governor, that if I got to be a mildly corrupt senator I'd be damned lucky."

What was I supposed to say? I found myself nodding in agreement with the other woman.

"She must be very hurt, Richard. I'm sure she doesn't mean all of that."

"Hurt? I didn't have to take her to Atlanta. Do you know how much a double at the Regency Hyatt costs? I don't need to hear those things. I had to speak this morning and it was almost impossible I was so depressed."

I think that may have been my authentic moment of clear certainty when the goal became more important than the truth. "Oh, she knows you have it, Richard. She's just neurotic about you."

"Do I, Stephanie? Do I really?"

It was so easy. "Of course." Everything that woman said was true but I wasn't going to be dumb enough to tell him the truth. Men don't marry women who tell them the truth. That much I had already learned from Miriam. How that girl must love Richard to be so painfully honest. Or she didn't care. But she cared. I had seen their apartment. She left him though—at least for the time they were in Atlanta. So now if I wanted an opportunity to get him, it was mine.

"God," he was saying, "I'm so glad to know you believe in me. You don't know what it means to me. I'm so tired of angry women." Richard continued talking in that thumb-in-the-mouth voice about all the women who had hurt him. All the questions they'd asked him: Is everything all right? Can I get you anything? What's the matter? Why didn't you call? Where were you? I was worried. These were the patterns Miriam meant. Too much love. All those women hunting him with love like the troops of huntsmen in the tapestry tracking down the magic beast. Giving, giving, giving. The girl wasn't harmful. None of the women he mentioned seemed hostile. He really was searching for someone to blame his hostility on. Me? I'd always wondered how my Connecticut friends could pull off their dears and their darlings and now I knew. They didn't feel. They had no illusions about their husbands. They had very little invested. I was ready to lie. I *had* lied. I *was* lying. And it was so easy. Why? Because I wanted the romance, the man, the big bed in the Regency Hyatt? No, I wanted the win. Well, maybe it was more than just the win. I really was scared of growing old alone. Even after I suspected the dream wasn't quite as dreamy as I had hoped, even after that, I still wanted the dream. There is always that blinding egotism in us that says . . . with the love of a good woman. . . . Richard's girl hurt him very badly and he loved her more than ever. He was dreadfully depressed. Obviously they had much invested in each other. My advantage was that I didn't have very much invested, just a little illusion, just a little hope.

"I'll be back in the city tomorrow, darling. And then Friday we'll be together. I feel so much better now. You don't know what it means to have someone who believes in you. What I'll do is call you first thing Friday morning. I'll send a messenger up to your office with my key and then you can wait at my place until I get there. But I'll call and let you know exactly where we're going after I make some phone calls Friday morning. Now, get a good night's sleep and I'll talk to you Friday for sure and see you about four-thirty, five? Okay? Hey, I love you." He waited. "Aren't you going to say anything? I said I love you."

How could he think I believed in him? When had I begun to believe in him? Did I? "What, dear?" Christ, I wasn't even from Connecticut. What was my next line?

"Don't you love *me*?"

"Oh, Richard, of course. Yes, darling. Yes, I love you."

My head was working like the electrical connections in a pinball machine. There was no way to call Miriam but the next day, fortunately, I thought at the time, I would have lunch with Jack who understood me so well that being with him was like thinking. He would help. I ran my head along all the tracks, all the buttons, switches, go-backs, tilts and free games, a maze with Unicorn at the end. Well, this was the game.

"You don't have it in you to play that kind of game, Steph." Jack kept looking at his fingernails on one hand and stirring his Senegalese soup with the other, endlessly. I had told him about the phone calls. Jack is still a little in love with me and lunch always becomes pathos, bathos and tragedy because he orders great amounts of food, sets up conversations in which I am bound to reject him and then is too upset to eat, but keeps ordering food and trying to order food for me in quantities. "You're not that kind of girl. You don't have it in you. You'll never catch him if that's what he needs."

"What do you mean, I don't have it in me? Am I too stupid? Do you mean I'm not capable of playing the game?"

"I mean you shouldn't sell out, Stephanie. You're not that kind of girl."

"You are so goddamn vague."

"The soup is fine. Why don't you order some."

"I don't want soup. I want to know what you're talking about. Specifically."

"Specifically you aren't the kind of girl to tell anyone

he's full of shit. Not that you're weak. You're a nice, decent, kind girl. You aren't a calculating female."

"How do you know?"

"I know."

"Considering the assholes you end up with, I don't see how you're such an authority on what I am and what I'm not, Jack."

"*Me*? Oh. Good try. I'm not impressed. Has to be a direct attack."

"Be honest with yourself. All the times you've come crying to me, how could I have picked a loser like that? Remember the girl you took to Turkey? I always thought you set it up so you could get a loser and then run off. Remember you used to say you'd pick the biggest ripest blackcap in the raspberry patch so when you reached in for it, you'd get trapped in the nettles? Every time? That's you."

"Okay, Stephanie, then learn from my mistakes. We know each other very very well. Is this man so terrific that you would change your behavior? Is he some kind of hotshot? What's so special about him?"

"I don't *know*, Jack."

"Well, he's got to have something." Jack was asking to be hurt again and I would have to play Richard down, but then Richard really wasn't terrific or a hotshot or handsome, or, beyond fantasy, any good in bed. Jack shifted his hands and examined his other set of fingernails. "So?"

"So. Ever see a Madison Avenue lawyer in a three-button-roll button-down, Brooks Brothers, stuck on a traffic island, holding his attaché case in one hand, his stainless steel tennis racket in the other and tapping his blue suede Adidas impatiently until the traffic lets him through to his tennis lesson at lunchtime?"

"They're not buying Adidas anymore. They're buying those high-rise brown ones from France."

"Well, one of them is him. I mean, you wouldn't notice him."

"Corporation? Securities? Is he good in tennis, at least?"

"He had a book on municipal bonds in his place, with margin notes."

"I don't know anything about municipal bonds. I don't *care* about municipal bonds and you don't either. What firm is he with?"

"Don't know. I don't ever ask him questions."

"Crazy. Sounds boring as hell." Jack was a staffer for *Time* and everybody's job was boring as hell.

"I know it's crazy, Jack. I don't understand it. I've been trying to figure it out all week. He's got this magic. Like the stuff with the owl and the pussycat. He sort of steps into my fantasies. He's got a little magic and he's very elusive and he connects up with my dreams and he is very, very charming, sort of wild, shy, charming."

"You know how long that lasts, the mystery? Until he farts." Jack's job wasn't boring. Jack was boring. He knew it.

I saw him blink rapidly. "I'm sorry, Jack, this isn't the most supportive subject for us." He examined his fingernails and cut through a chicken breast laced with wine, cheese and ham.

It was a hot day, too early for summer heat. The food I had eaten was massing, heavily, in my stomach. Jack asked nonchalantly if I wouldn't consider forgetting a bad risk and going to the Hamptons with him for the summer; at least I knew, he said, what I would be getting into.

"I don't know what I'll be doing this summer." Again, he had set up the rejection. "You know, Jack, I'm just playing . . . I'm not committed or anything. Sure it has possibility, but I'm not making any decisions."

"I say you're out of control."

"Oh, you know me, I like to edge. But I always pull back in time."

"Yes and no. Yes and no, Stephanie. This guy, what does he talk about? Say you're at lunch, what does he talk about?"

"Adolf Berle."

"Are you interested in Berle?"

I shrugged. "You know, I'm interested in things . . . mostly how his mind works, so I listen."

"You're not interested . . ."

"It's fascinating. It's . . . oh, you know, Rexford Tugwell, that era."

"You know what your problem is, baby? All you museum types. You want to get saved. The guy's gotta be into politics."

"I'm not a museum type." I didn't respond to the politics.

"You're leading to it—unmarried. Your clothes are getting blacker and blacker. Soon you'll be into all black with one piece of heavy jewelry, locked in a room, labeling death, skin drying up, pale, pale, dandruff from your old flaky hair on your black sweater which is getting greener year after year, all the time waiting for someone to discover you, whisk you away to Hollywood, Washington, anyplace but the archives."

"You're really a bastard."

"Also my dear girl, you haven't mentioned sex at all. Something is really rotten."

I shrugged. "I haven't mentioned sex because we haven't gone to bed yet. He doesn't want to make any mistakes."

Jack laughed and waved his fork. Bits of chicken flew from the sides of his mouth, he laughed so hard. He finally managed to ask, "How far wrong can you go? You screw, you screw. I'll bet he's Jewish."

"Jesus, Jack! You are so goddamn *twisted*."

"Makes sense, you used to love me too. He is, isn't he?

Don't you know the myth that Jewish men are womanly? That they grow up thinking if they screw another woman, they're betraying their mother and the only way to really break loose, to really betray your mother is to marry a . . ." He pointed his fork at me. "A shiksa. And then he never forgives her because she's not like his mother. It's wonderful as a racial failure, like sickle cell."

"You are so jealous. You are so bigoted. You are so small."

"Ho, ho. Compared to whom? Listen, if he were screwing you, I might really be jealous. Right now it's just a professional courtesy, okay? Stephanie," Jack's voice lowered. I supposed he had had his revenge on my summer refusal. "Stephanie, really, think about it."

"I don't see why you and I should discuss it."

"I know you so well, Stephanie. Listen, there are two kinds of power. Political power and sexual power. Men have political power. Women have sexual power. Don't you get it? You've lost control. He isn't going to allow you to have sexual power. You're out of control, Stephanie." Jack shoved his platter of chicken at me. "You should eat something."

"I don't want the chicken. I didn't want the soup. I wish to hell you'd stop asking me what I want and giving me things and taking care of me. I wish to hell you'd leave me alone. I know what I want and I know when I want it."

"Boy, there's *gotta* be something else you aren't telling me."

I decided to control myself. I needed to talk to Jack.

"It doesn't exactly amuse *me* to talk about a man you love, Stephanie," he was saying. "If you recall, I still harbor some feelings about you. And that's the only reason I'm willing to listen."

I looked away from his eyes. "Okay. Richard reminds me of the Unicorn. I mean I adore the Unicorn. I want the Unicorn. I love the Unicorn. He fascinates me the way the Unicorn fascinates me. Okay?"

"Hah." His hah had no exclamation point. It was a depressed hah.

"Hah, what?" I knew I shouldn't have brought it up.

"Hah, do you know what an asshole image that is? Do you have any idea what the Unicorn means? The Unicorn, dear lady who shouldn't forget that Hitler played the Second World War by myth which he understood a lot better than you, means eunuch. Medievals played word games. It's a homophone relationship. Unicorn is the Gnostic, mystery stuff, the self-realized man, kundalini, tantric, the lowest chakra exploding into the head, the semen bursting up the spinal column into the brain center of ultimate God-consciousness. The horn's the penis. That, my love, is why you catch a Unicorn by letting him lay his head, which is his now intellectualized conscious-risen penis, into the lap of a virgin. Mind-fucking. But, darling girl, the Unicorn is the heretical castrated eunuch trapped in the sacramental fence of a Catholic Church which was just finishing up inquisitions, et al. The little drops of blood are the sacrifice of his sensual nature . . . of his poor balls. Yeah, your Richard and your beast *really* do have a lot in common. If you're going to live by myth, girlie, you better understand myth. The enlightened gentleman will be enlightened because you're going to cut off some of his best meat. Boy, do you deserve what you get!"

"Okay, bastard, how do you know all that? Read it in the *Nazi White Paper*, did you?"

"I just made it up. But it fits. It really fits."

"I really hate you, Jack. Deeply."

"Goodness, it's been years since I made you cry."

"Shut up."

"You're making a big mistake. A little magic, a little charm and you are absolutely blind. No brakes, out of control, downhill. You're really being stupid and you're going to get stuck."

"I'm in control."

90

"You're still going to get stuck. At least I've never been stuck."

"That's because you purposely choose dumb shits so you won't get stuck."

"Purposefully." Our conversation always ended when he corrected my English. I didn't make another date for lunch. I'd never been that depressed in my life.

"He's a masochist, darling," Jack told me as he kissed me good-bye on each cheek. "He's a masochist in search of a sadist and he turns sadistic when he can't find a sadist. The guy wants to be hurt."

"You just defined yourself," I yelled at him.

"Yeah? Well, maybe it's all of us. I'm sorry, Stephanie."

Even though I could still feel the poison of that lunch trapped inside me, I promised myself that Friday would be calm and wonderful. I would forget Jack and his clever, twisted envy. I wouldn't eat. I wouldn't scream. I wouldn't respond to Sissy. My crosses were coming in at eleven. It was the second shipment and I had still not recovered from the thrill of watching the first shipment and touching their rough sides as they emerged from their crates. Our exhibit was only a few months away and so far Sissy had been thoroughly spontaneous and supportive with not a touch of jealousy. She took an uneven sort of pride in me. Knowing how hysterical her plans with Monica had made me, she had known enough to keep the ensuing details to herself. She hadn't even watched me as I sat before the Unicorn all those lunch hours. I hoped somehow she and Monica had done the right thing . . . at least Sissy seemed more centered than she ever had before. And by nightfall, and by nightfall, I would be sleeping with Richard. Then the world might look sweeter to me. And perhaps not. It had been a long week and what I had learned by the end of it was the rules of the game. I didn't know if I could play it, but at least I knew the rules. And so when I arrived at the office Friday morning I was not un-happy myself, knowing I would be driving off into the sun-set with a very attractive man who wanted to spend the weekend with me, who wanted apparently to marry me and it wasn't a bad way to begin the day except that Sissy was grinning like a Cheshire cat which meant I was once again the canary.

Not today, Sissy, please. Today is calm and wonder-ful and I'm not going to fight. She was delaying for some reason, opening and slamming drawers, rummaging for a pencil, sharpening one pencil, another pencil, another. Somehow she would ruin my day. My perfect, perfect weather, my crosses in the morning, Richard in the after-noon, and somehow Sissy would ruin it. I knew it. I could feel it. I waited for her at the arched window of our tower and looked down at the pigeons on the red-tile roof of the Froville Arcade below and the flower beds along the wind-ing upper driveway. Blue hydrangeas were in bloom. Rich winey irises opened to the sky. I forced myself to my desk. If I began, perhaps Sissy would begin. I didn't want to fight, with Sissy or anybody.

A key strung with mottled African trading beads and tied with a faded orange shoelace had been placed signifi-cantly dead center of my desk. "What's this key, Sissy? Sissy, I must have the camera with film in it by eleven. I go to the docks at eleven."

"It's Richard's key," she called, still at her desk.

"Oh." I slipped the key into my pocket and patted it for its promise. "Are we about ready to begin?"

Sissy finally came into my office. "Wouldn't you like to know who brought it?"

"Not particularly. I would like to know how much film is in the camera and if there is not enough, order some fast. And I need the bill of lading and some author-ization forms and . . . take some notes now and then do the camera."

There was a message on her face I couldn't decipher

and since I had no time to play her games and had promised peace, I turned to my office. "Bring in your pad."

Sissy continued to grin but didn't move.

"Swallow something, Sissy?"

She shook her head.

"When you feel you're ready to stop playing games, Sissy," I told her calmly and a little officiously, "you'll find me in my office lacerating my breasts with impatience."

"Don't ever say I'm not a good friend to you because no one would have done what I just did."

I said nothing.

"His fiancée brought it."

I covered my eyes with my hands. I would open them soon and everything around me, the sun on the Palisades, the pigeons cooing on the roof tiles, the happy spots on the Rhenish virgin's cheeks, everything would be the same. My hands trembled against my eyelids. "I don't think I can handle this, Sissy. I don't think I want to hear about her."

"I let her think I was you. Isn't that good?" Sissy waited for me to commend her. I was unable to speak. The phone rang. "Was it bad? I was just trying. At least I tried." My head throbbed in response to her whining. The phone continued to ring. "Do you want me to call Miriam? Do you want some tea? I really tried, Stephanie. I made believe I was you."

"Whatever you did was wonderful," I murmured and indicated the phone with my chin. "Please."

"Miss Boxwell's office." Sissy touched my shoulder gently. "Do you want to talk to him?" she whispered. "You can just listen. You needn't say anything."

How does she know so much about me already? I took one hand from one eye and held the receiver at arm's length before plunging once again into his sea. Someone is lying. Someone is clearly lying. Are they using me to work out their own problems? She didn't leave him. She just went home to wait for him. His fiancée.

"Richard! Welcome home." An exemplary Connecticut greeting.

"Hi, sweetheart. I thought you were a secretary. I didn't know you have a secretary. Are you packed?"

"Yes." I had indeed told him what I did, about the crosses, and he had indeed told me to decide where we would go. He's really marvelous, like a battleship zigzagging across the Atlantic to dodge torpedoes.

"Great. Did you get the key?"

"Yes, as a matter of fact," I said matter-of-factly. "Your fiancée brought it up this morning."

"Great." There wasn't even a pause. His voice was impersonal and clipped. How could he have said nothing? "We're going to see my Uncle Myron in New Jersey. I'll pick you up at my place at four-thirty give or take."

"Where? We're going *where*?"

"Leisure Village West." Richard dropped his voice. "It's really important, honey. Everyone in the family listens to Uncle Mike. He's the executor."

"I don't understand, Richard."

"Just a minute, Nancy. Of my father's estate, Steph."

"Oh, Richard, I thought we'd be alone."

"Jesus Christ, Stephanie, you always make me feel inadequate when you criticize me. We'll be alone but right now it's important that you meet my family."

"When have I had the chance to make you feel inadequate by criticizing you?"

"Oh, Christ, it must have been someone else. I *am* sorry. Listen, I know I've been a real chauv not letting you make any of the decisions and not letting you know until the last moment. I'm really sorry. It's just very important this time. I know you'll understand." He spoke to someone in his office.

Score one for Stephanie. I had made him feel inadequate. But it wasn't what I wanted. I wanted to wear my jeans and the old shirt and bikini I'd stuffed into my duffle and lie in the sun and sleep naked and make love and make plans to spend the summer together. I didn't want to meet his family. God, if I'm meeting your family, Richard, who the hell is your fiancée? How many rings do *you* carry in your nose? One for each of us? Over the phone I heard pages turning. "There better be a bong tree in Leisure Village West." What I really wanted was a little assurance he could make me happy.

"Excuse me. The brief was a mess. We'll find a bong tree. From there we go up to my sister's in Westport. You'll love her place. She's so excited. She said to tell you she started the cooking yesterday. State occasion: Beef Wellington and she's taking out her Bing and Grøndahl china."

"Richard, I'm not going to wait for you in your apartment and you know very well why."

"Stephanie. I have to be in court in fifteen minutes and I'll be there all day. Look, I'll pick you up at work. Let me put you on hold and you give Nancy your address. Shit, I'm going to be really late. I love you. Sit tight. Look nice. Here's Nancy."

"It's the Cloisters," I told Nancy acidly.

"Sweetie, you're lucky he remembers your name. Don't take a burn. He means well."

He won. My hands shook on the teacup Sissy offered me. Richard is incredibly brilliant, accurately sadistic, thick, insensitive, all of the above, none of the above. Or simply on another wavelength, one I'll never pick up on. What is he *doing*? "Sissy, don't I look nice? I mean right now, do I look nice?"

"You always look nice." Sissy poured sugar in my tea. She frowned. "Don't go, Stephanie. He's engaged to someone else, for God's sake. How do you know he isn't going to take you to Leisure Village West and hack you to pieces and bury you in the sand and steal the Cornish crosses? How do you know? I think you should call the FBI."

There is a point at which Sissy becomes completely useless. We had reached it. She watches too much tv.

I dismissed Sissy from my space. "Don't say I didn't warn you," she said over her shoulder. I stood and watched the sun slowly burning the fog from the river. Sissy walked between our offices, round and round, chanting.

"Don't get upset. Don't get upset."

I caught her finally by an arm and stopped her. "Sissy, I would like you to tell me what that girl looked like."

"You won't get upset?"

"I may."

"You've already torn up my shorthand pad."

"Dammit, Sissy, mind your own business."

She pulled away from me and I pulled her back. "I'm getting very upset," she advised me, rather rigidly.

"Just talk. Objectively." I held her arms tightly. As she studied my face, I managed a comforting smile.

"Well, I would say, she's . . . well, she's nice." Sissy watched my face change and edged from me. "I'm sorry. I didn't . . ."

"No problem," I assured her carefully through my teeth, nodding like a piano teacher at the Spring Recital. "Please begin again. What she said. What she looked like."

"Well, she comes in, says hi, hands me the key. Sort of hip, a little far out on the clothes but attractive. Not beautiful. Uh, striking. Nice teeth."

"I don't care about the teeth. Was she sexy?"

"Ooozing." She shot me a fleeting glance of triumph.

"Sissy, for Christ's sake."

"Just my opinion. Everything is relative."

"So she wasn't really what a man would see as sexy?"

"No. She said I looked familiar. I said she does too and then she asks if I . . . well, we probably belonged to the same group and it seemed like maybe there was a consciousness-raising group years ago before I came out that maybe we were in together. She says to leave the key in the kitchen. Then she asks if I have a minute and I said sure and she sits on the edge of my desk and lays on how Richard fucks like crazy." Sissy giggled.

"She *said* that?" Braggart, it's hardly a solitary act.

"Not exactly. Do you really want to hear what she said?"

"Don't play with me, Sissy."

"The semen is always flying—absolutely flying."

"I can't believe that."

Sissy shrugged. "She says Richard is kind of lousy the way he runs women around, gets all of them crazy and then sort of steps back and says how come everybody's crazy?" Sissy was pleased with herself. She had me going. The girl sounded so honest and friendly. Why? My intestines lurched with every new bit of information.

"He needs lots of rope, she said, and it's tough for her to talk like this but she thinks women should stick together and if he ever starts playing one of us against the other, well, we should keep in touch."

"God!" I sat at my desk, my fingers stuck through my hair. What does that girl want from me? She wants to keep tabs on me. But why would she tell me so much? Flying semen. Flying semen?

"Oh, she said to have a nice weekend and I said don't you mind and she said she does but she's got something going anyway. And then says put the key in the first drawer on the left of the sink."

"She's really smart. Bitch."

Sissy crossed her arms before me and shook her head, smugly. "I'd say she's really into sisterhood and that you are wrong this time."

"When it comes to men, no one's into sisterhood." Her shadow was cast.

Sissy walked behind me as I trod the floor. She swept up scraps of her shorthand pad, sprinkling ostentatious handfuls into my wastebasket when she passed it. "I think she's nice and I don't think she's up to anything at all

98

except sisterhood even though that man Richard is her whole life. She said that."

"Years ago, Sissy, you would have been a great fanatical Catholic. Now everything you know, sense, smell, taste, has to be interpreted as Movement. Did she really say he was her whole life?"

"Yes. And 'when he swings, he sings and when he comes, he hums.' "

"Just make that up?"

"No, Stephanie, I had forgotten it." Sissy really didn't approve of me. She had approved of Richard's girl. "You have to be at the docks at eleven, you know. It's getting late."

I sat rubbing my forehead. I wish I had seen the girl. "Her name? Did she tell you her name?"

"No."

"Sissy, this is important. You know a lot of women. Did this one look crazy? Did she seem out of control? Desperate, dangerous, anything like that?"

"No. No. She was friendly and easygoing, sort of together, you know. A together girl."

I would have preferred her to be mad so I could hope that my love, the love of a good woman, would put Richard together again. But *she* sounded like a good woman. She had made her peace with Richard. Somehow she had as much from him as she needed. He really was in love with her. I had been correct. I didn't think I could love him as much as she did, certainly not more. Oh. Oh. Loving him less was the answer. And hurting him more. Wow. The unethical imperative. Men don't get hostile from their mothers. They are naturally hostile and they spend their lives looking for a woman to blame it on: she hurt me. And usually it's a woman who loves too much. Maintain your manhood through hostility; most of the other battlefields are closed. Richard wanted all the trappings of love, the dears and the darlings and the homemade pies, but not the love. Jack was absolutely correct about Richard controlling sexually and politically, but I still had an area of control: I could control his behavior. It was immoral. I was dealing with the devil for the illusion, buying into fantasy. I didn't want to. I didn't want to hurt Richard or anyone. I could see the soft deer eyes of the Unicorn looking up at me: "Stephanie, did you have to hurt me? Why did you hurt me?"

If that lousy bastard Jack was right and Richard was the eunuch/unicorn waiting to be castrated, why would my Unicorn who had all the wisdom let me hurt him? "Because," I told myself in Jack's voice, "because he's programmed for the wrong destiny. Wrong set of cultural values. He's off the path, lady, and so are you. False principles. Wants to be Governor. And that's the way he sees you—as the Governor's Wife. It's an ego trip for both of you and that's not self-realization. But I don't care about him," Jack would say, "I care about you. Quit messing around with myths you don't understand. They're more dangerous than love."

I informed Jack in my head that I still hated him. I had once been in love with him. Then I could never get attention from him. But ever since I turned off he's been waiting for a chance to give me another go-around. I was out of control with him then. Not now. Because now I don't love him. Everyone I know is off the wall with love. Not loving, you stay in control. Loving . . . aah, when you love, you are out of control. I didn't know then if I really wanted Richard or not; it was more an intellectual challenge. Armed with the rules, I wanted to play the game. And it was such a lucid, simple decision to play. The game could be warm and sexy and entertaining as long as I didn't fall in love. After I caught him, then I could decide what to do with him as long as I remembered not to fall in love—and that would be the easiest part, I knew, because he was such a shit. Anyway, I decided, folding up my doodles and shutting the drawers of my desk hard and decisively, if I'm going to do it, I may as well do it right.

I'd rather go to Bendel's any day than off the wall. The right girl has to look like the right girl.

"Sissy! Sissy! Get ready. You're going to the dock and accept the crosses for me."

"Me?" Her face lit up. "How about you? What's wrong with you?"

"Something's come up."

"Oh, Stephanie. I can't let you do this to yourself. Don't let a lousy man do this to you." Her face had changed and her eyes were like the Unicorn's. "It's the highlight of your career."

"Christ, I don't have time for emotions. Listen, I've been thinking of switching careers anyway," I teased. "He's doing *nothing* to me. I'm doing to him. And watch my steam. Look, seriously, you're going down to the docks, authenticate the crosses, take the pictures and accept them for the museum. I'll show the crosses to you in my book. These are the Cornish ones, not the Irish. You can take the book with you if you want. Okay? Be sure to say 'I daresay' a lot. I did last time. It works."

"What if they're forgeries?"

"No one's going to forge tons of stone, for God's sake."

"What if they find out I'm not you? I'll lose my job." Her face fell. I chucked her under the chin.

"Tell them I forced you into impersonating me and then you can have my job. Come on, Sissy, it's very simple."

Sissy blushed and seeing her blush made me feel warm toward her. She had always wanted my job, but I was also someone she admired terribly. Then I blushed. I understood why she didn't want to go to the docks for me but I needed her to. "C'mon, Sissy, there won't be any problem. You don't have to say much. Take a clip board, write down a lot, work slowly. Just act mature. No one will ever know."

Fat tears rolled down her cheeks.

"Please, Sissy."

"I can't do it, not even for you. I'd do anything for you, Stephanie, but you shouldn't be doing this. It's immoral and it can ruin your reputation in your career."

"Don't judge me, Sissy. I don't judge you."

"No man's worth it."

"Look, Sissy, I appreciate your concern but forget it; we'll be old ladies together and I'll rock and you'll rock and I'll say 'Sissy, remember when I almost got married just to see if I could pull it off?' "

"I'm going to spend my life with Monica and our child, not you."

"Dammit, I was just being metaphorical."

"Well, I'm not. This is very real. You're selling out and you're too wonderful a person to sell out for a man."

I can remember that conversation so well. Sissy, as she spoke to me, as she refused to go, was taking notes on the areas of the crosses I would need photographed. She found the camera, loaded it, studied its manual, studied the crosses in my book and pinned up the hem of my dress with paper clips—I'd pulled the hem while Richard was talking to his secretary. I turned as Sissy patted my leg. It was very disconcerting to have her look up at me, kneeling as she was and yet towering above me. I had never before measured her interior.

"You are going to do it, aren't you, Sissy?"

"Yes. I have to."

"Sissy, when you and Monica . . . I can't even imagine what you do in bed. . . ."

"For beginners, it's sort of like trying to braid your hair in a mirror. After a while you get used to it."

"Well, I try to accept it. I have tried. To me, it's wrong. Please don't judge me. What am I supposed to do? What alternatives do I honestly have if not marriage? Loneliness? Lesbianism? But I'm a heterosexual. I want a man. There's no other way. I don't have the courage to be alone and honest. And I'm afraid to wait too long—I'm not getting any younger or any prettier. So I've got your act or a house in Scarsdale. I want to get married. You can respond to loneliness, can't you?"

She nodded and then looked up at me, locking eyes. "I guess we all have to do what we have to do. I guess."

On the way out of the Cloisters, Sissy walked beside me as if she were a casket bearer. She was clearly bereaved for my soul. I was calculating the shortest way to get to Bendel's. She hadn't even asked me what I was going to do. Somehow it was better she didn't know I was going shopping for clothes to impress Richard's family. I kissed her cheek at the bus stand and gave her a ten-dollar bill for cabs. Astonished with the kiss, she began again to cry and I matched her this time tear for tear. We both fumbled for scraps of tissue and sniffed into our sleeves. She was crying for me. And I suppose I was also.

"Get pink," she sobbed. "Pink is the color."

I knew she'd ruin my day. She made me feel like a kamikaze pilot all the way to Bendel's where I wrapped myself in silks. I looked, when I went back to the Cloisters, very much like my Connecticut friends. So what if he doesn't make governor? I could do worse than a mildly corrupt senator. Truth is a lonely mountain. I'd rather have a man. Jesus, I hope he's good in bed.

I didn't think about Richard's driving that weekend. I should have because Richard didn't respond to traffic signals. As a matter of fact, Richard didn't respond to traffic. But I took his nonresponse for blitheness and spirit although I don't know why I didn't then become just such a combination myself. Because my consciousness was fast slipping into my lowest chakra, I related Richard's relentless detachment directly to Genghis Khan stealing me across the steppes, dragging me into a lonely tent while all China waited, pulling me toward him by my long and flowing hairs, taking me, his eyes slanted, his mouth open, and his topknot loosening as he jammed me in the white tiger skin tent, horses and prime ministers braying uneasily without and cold winds whistling across the steppes. I've always preferred claim and conquer. Once an Irishman drove me from an airport to a distant motel with his hand between my legs all the way all the way. I didn't move. His hand dark in my white slacks simply remained there like a territorial flag. He had said to me, "Do ye want to?" And I'd said yes. With Richard I felt as if I'd signed a nonaggression pact gagged and blindfolded.

Richard was whistling also. A lot. Whistling he drove through to New Jersey whistling and whistling he left behind a chain of severely adrenalized drivers as his yellow Mercedes made its singularly swift approach to the condo in Leisure Village West. But windows up, air-conditioning purring, majestic music on the FM, both hands on the wheel at ten past ten as in Drivers' Ed.—I didn't think about the driving. I thought about sleeping with him and I thought about wrapping my legs and arms around him and sinking away to Dvořák's *New World* into Richard's soft/hard magic. I squirmed in my bucket seat and thought about all of that while between whistles he talked about his sister Blossom's big mouth.

"I could never marry a woman with a big mouth. Blossom used to make me cry. She'd always have a friend over and the two of them would plot ways to make me cry."

"Really? Does anyone make you cry now?"

"Not unless I want them to."

"Oh."

"You understand that." It was a statement, not a question.

"Of course." Not.

I mulled that conundrum and listened attentively to the swelling variations on the theme of mother/sister/father/uncle/women who had victimized Richard. Even when we passed a tractor-trailer whose trailer wasn't quite tracking as we swung in tandem down a steep grade and the Mercedes had to thin itself out to pass on the downward hurtle, even then I listened attentively while Richard warned me to look out for his uncle. He said nothing about the tractor-trailer.

"Watch him. I was involved once. My uncle met her, took one look, said 'not a penny' and turned his back on her." As the left tire bumped up and off a concrete meridian he told me that he needed someone to help him cry.

"When I get off airplanes, I'm sick with fear and I can't cry. You're the kind of woman who can help me cry. To face my fear realistically. I know that instinctively."

Richard would understand later that he had the correct instincts but the wrong interpretations. "Richard, why don't you tell me about your mother. Should I feel threatened?"

"My mother? My mother is a sick woman. She drains me. She gives me diarrhea. She gives me backaches, biological relapses, boils. If she informs you of my bowel habits by the grams, don't be surprised. And she will begin every conversation with, 'So what's new in your court, Governor?' No matter what I tell her, which is less and less each time, she says: 'There is one law, Richard. A man marries and has children.' 'And has sons,' my uncle will say, 'so someone says Kaddish for him.'"

Richard continued to talk about relating and not relating and whistled show tunes against the Stockhausen on the FM. I allowed myself to think about Richard as a large, glorious hickory tree and I wrapped my arms around him for strength and heard his heart beat and he moaned softly and moved under my whispers while I nibbled at his pith. Later I lay in his shadow and his leaves touched my forehead and our sons danced around us, straight and strong.

"And watch my mother. She manipulates. Do you know how many nice girls whose mothers live in Leisure Village West or ride the bus or play in the Monday canasta game or shop at the same butcher call me at the office because my mother told her mother we'd have a lot in common and she was just passing through the city? Maybe two a week. A lot in common means she's Jewish, she lives in one of the boroughs and has done anacrostics occasionally . . . sometimes I screw them to get even."

He turned and smiled at me to see my reaction. "To get even with my mother," he said.

"That's not very Christian of you."

"Of course you won't make references like *that* around the folks."

"Of course not." That's not what I should have said. What I should have said was: Funny, Richard, you make yourself sound like such a victim but you sure come on like Attila the Hung. But I kept my mouth shut.

I should never have kept my mouth shut. You miss a line, it messes up the rhythm. I was deep into silent metrical lines about honesty, openness and moral purity, when an old black Chevy, its trunk filled with tires and tied down precariously with thin ropes, roared ahead of us from an access road, went over a bump on a level stretch and threw up a tire. I squinted at it, wishing it away, as it bounced into the traffic, up and down, high and happy, like Genghis's topknot, unwinding itself inexorably in my path. Other cars swerved, brakes screamed, but Richard advanced steadily on the tire. The tire couldn't get his attention. Mine, notwithstanding a certain detached fascination, was no problem. I clawed upholstery and braked all the way. Richard, lobotomized, easy on the wheel, face serene, the governor's governor set at 65 mph, still— although I had the impression he murmured moron at one point—ignored the oncoming tire.

"All she really wants is photos. She sits at the pool and all the grandmas have letters from camp and those long plastic fold-ups that flap down. . . ." The tire hit the undercarriage of the Mercedes lifting my half quite in the air. "Blossom's kids fill some of the spaces. . . ." On two wheels we continued down the now empty highway. "The ladies at the pool think I'm gay because I'm thirty-three and not married."

"Christ died at thirty-three," I managed to whisper through my teeth.

"Non sequitur," Richard accused happily. "Do cool the references, Steph."

A few inches more and the Mercedes would have been on its back but Richard was obviously oblivious to the

107

ramming and ripping of fenders and bumpers, to the cars throwing dust and gravel up as they retreated to the shoulders away from the still energetic tire. Other drivers we passed in what must have been only three or four minutes watched us with open mouths. It occurred quite irrationally to me that men who are shocked look very much like men who are coming. I wondered how Richard looked and if I would live to see such a moment. Hanging men have erections—where the semen lands beneath their swinging feet, the mandrake grows. I vacillated between visions of myself on my back, of the Mercedes on its back and prayer. And then the Mercedes came down perfectly in a four-point landing on the highway in the very lane in which we had begun our ascent.

"Used to be if a son didn't marry it was testament to the fact that no other woman could make him as happy as his mother could. Now, we're suspect. 'It's not normal, Richard. They don't elect men like that, Richard.' 'Like what?' 'You know.'"

Nothing moved behind us. Soon the next pack of cars would catch up to the disaster area. A blue Subaru was turned facing up the highway and steam vaulted from the folded hood of a silvery T-Bird. Richard reached over and squeezed my knee. We passed the Chevy on the shoulder of the highway, its four doors flung open and its four young men examining the ropes and remaining tires. "You're a good woman." Good woman moved closer on her bucket seat but the knee action was non sequitur also. "They're all nuts but they're all decent. Once they accept you, they'll turn the world upside down for you."

I didn't know if Richard was doing Genghis Khan or Evel Knievel. At one level, he was unaware of the tire. My knees, both of them, were shaking in what I wanted to think was desire but I knew wasn't. Little wonder the wrecks and near wrecks piled up behind Richard. The rest of us, I would find out, his traffic, would sit inarticulate with rage, giving him the finger from our shattered windows, stalled and steaming at the shoulders, while he, ignoring us all, arrived at his chosen destination, sighed mightily over a gin and tonic and remarked: "Christ, the traffic was a bitch."

It was Sanka, Slender, and Sucaryl. "Christ, the traffic was a bitch. Folks, this is Stephanie."

The sigh was as I had imagined, as was his mother and his uncle and the plastic, urethane, Syroco-cast indoor-outdoor condo at Leisure Village West. On the last leg of the trip Richard had recited chapter and verse from the "Book of the Dead for Brides-to-Be" and each place of judgment and weighing of my heart that he had fore-warned me of, I passed. The uncle said nothing about pennies. His first remarks were: "Good teeth. Hasn't she got good teeth? Good teeth, a fur coat and big ears to hold her down with, that's all you need in a woman." Then laughed at his own joke and asked me what my father did for a living.

I pretended not to hear him.

"And this is my mother. Mother. Stephanie."

"I'm so happy to meet you. Richard's shown me your pictures."

"Likewise, I'm sure." Except Richard had no pictures. Not of *me*.

"Say, you look like a girl whose father is a banker."

I continued to ignore Uncle Myron. Richard winked at me and I ignored the wink. His mother looked nothing like the blown-up photos. The full doll's face had dropped to bitter fat cheeks and the splendid hips into thick legs swelling painfully at the ankles to fold over the sharp leather edges of black Enna Jetticks. Unblinkingly, turn-ing me into a photograph, she continued to stare at me with sea-shell eyes, rather deadly I felt, and served up more Sanka, Alba, rolls from egg whites according to Weight-Watchers and Cool Whip with something I would have thought, except under those circumstances, should have been real cottage cheese. Richard continued to wink. He was no different here than at the Four Seasons. His mother, who shuffled rather than bend the ankles into the tops of her shoes, simply became all nine waiters and he responded to her in the same way he had to them. I was touched by her loneliness and wondered what her name was. They were not bad people but simply desperately anxious to have Richard married. They were on my side. Later, his mother asked me quite covertly while the men were discussing no-fault, if I liked old things. Her tone suggested porny pictures but she meant, and pulled out for me from a box stuffed with newspapers, a lovely collection of Baleek, then majolica, then Imari.

The men ignored us. We were behaving quite properly as women should until I mentioned my work in the museum.

"That must be so *exciting*." Her eyes came alive.

"It is. Right now . . ." and I only brought up the subject because I had a strong feeling no one had spoken to her in a decade except to ask for the Cremora and find out what suit she was coming in, ". . . right now, I'm bringing together a collection of stone crosses, ancient Christian crosses. One of them has a man with a tail on it. Can you imagine?"

No-fault stopped. Apparently I had—at least one. His uncle's eyes and his mother's eyes, four little sharp shells, crackled at each other. Richard opened a plastic box of plastic cards with Boy in Blue and Girl in Pink and suggested a little canister (his word, not mine) if his mother would clear the table. She flushed. "You'll have to excuse me. I'm not what you call liberated." I didn't know if it was the tail or the Christian and felt awful that I had embarrassed her. Later she told me quietly that she had boxes of old things in storage and that her daughter Blossom only wanted new things that matched and if I didn't mind she'd like to give me some. "Delft? Maybe Wedgwood?"

She was the trader with the beads and bracelets. I was the Indian. If I gave her pictures, she'd fill my china closet. All I had to do was keep Richard happy. Which meant, of course—though only I understood—making him cry. I looked forward to meeting Blossom.

"A piece, Myron?"

"A piece thin."

We had more Sanka and piece thins of Baskin-Robbins ice cream pie and continued to play canasta. I thought about Richard through seventeen hands, through a vague steady heckling about what fathers do for livings, and I was still thinking about sleeping with Richard when I laid down three jokers and a deuce to announce my need for fresh air. He was not, as he demonstrated so succinctly on the sidewalk, of like mind. He had not been thinking at all of sleeping with me. I put my arms around him and drew my body into his under streetlights and trash cans, just like the first night, and he backed away quite nimbly, begging me, then and there, not to turn him on.

"I think we'd better define terms, Richard."

"Aah," he responded mellifluously. "Defining terms is a form of legislation. Every man becomes his own legislator. You can't legislate a thing like this. It's cosmic, darling, a higher law."

The girl that he marries shut her mouth rather than offer up her own logic about the inviolability of cosmic spaces and the insufficiency of his argument. Making love would of course be following a greater natural law. "Richard," I said clearly and simply, "I want to sleep with you. I really want to sleep with you." It was not unacceptable for a free spirit to speak that way.

"Oh, God, I know, Stephanie. But the way I feel about you, if I were to take you to bed without knowing you, it would be jumping into the void." He spoke so quickly I decided he had had the response ready in a brief somewhere in his pocket. Prepared by his secretary.

"Richard, I need to sleep with you."

"Oh, honey, I want *you* terribly. I am very attracted to you. But you are a gift from God, Stephanie. I can't misuse you. Look at the couples. Look at the divorce rate. God has given you to me, crossed our paths, and we can't . . . we must try to do this right."

"Couldn't we just go someplace and be alone?"

"How would they feel if we left them, those poor old people?"

"Richard!"

I adored the way he looked under the streetlight. I had felt the strong full body he would offer me and I really hoped he was kidding. I tried again. "Richard, I don't care about your mother terribly. I want to sleep with you. I want to make love with you. I want to go to bed with you."

"You don't care about my mother?"

"She's a nice person, Richard, and your Uncle Myron is okay too. I care about you."

"So, that is precisely why we are going to do this right. We're not going to clutch wildly at each other in a dirty bed. You understood, Stephanie, that there were rules."

Richard wasn't kidding.

"I never knew the rules," I said with a great emptiness. And anger began to flow quickly into the emptiness. "Okay, Richard. Okay. I have to ask you some questions. Just what do you mean by doing it right?"

"Don't ask questions, Stephanie. It isn't becoming."

"I have every right to ask questions. Every right."

"Why of course you do. Of course you do. But you see it annoys me." Richard held my shoulders. Maybe he was kidding. "We're not a couple of teenyboppers. I'm in love with you and I'm going to marry you. What more do you really need to know?"

I have to make a phone call, I thought. "I have to make a phone call." Electrical charges and synapses and nerve sheathes were tightening and shuddering toward hysteria. "Can we go in there to make a phone call?"

I ran up the steps of the Harbor Village Spa. Faces, like ghosts, all fed on chemicals and pills, with open mouths, watched me from the bar. All layered like Richard's mother, all polyestered and knit pantsuited and newly toothed, all long-nailed and polished and painted, like the lobsters in the case next to the phone booth, twitches and pulses and pacemakers, all waiting to catch somebody, something, long since gone, all afraid of dying alone, and I remembered the Armengols with the peace on their carved faces. Who would I call? My mother in Munich? And tell her I am in love with a man who wants to marry me but he doesn't want to sleep with me until we're married? "That's lovely, darling, thank you for the good news. But we have guests right now. You'll have to forgive me." Jack? God, no. Dial-A-Prayer was busy. I called Miriam.

"Miriam, he really isn't going to sleep with me! Can you believe it?" My voice was too loud. The painted people at the bar swiveled en masse and studied me.

"Christ, he really wants to marry a virgin."

"It's not so easy to become a virgin overnight, Miriam. Even a week or two."

"It's not so easy to get married either. Look, it's a good sign. Just keep reminding yourself. It's a good sign. He's going to marry you. That's why he isn't sleeping with you. Okay?"

"Call Terry, Miriam," I whispered. "Find out what the girl is like."

"Terry?"

"From the party."

"Oh, Terry."

"Please, Miriam."

"Okay, but that's not what's important. What's important is that you're meeting his family. He wants to marry you. I have to hit you over the head with that.

Don't get into rejection. You're the right girl. He's going to marry you. Anyone can sleep together."

"Miriam, don't say that. That's what he said."

"So he's right. Now, look. I'll call your Terry. You come here Monday night for supper. It's our anniversary."

I hesitated. I had learned to hate Il Duce.

"He's very different now. Come after work."

"I'm a wreck, Miriam. Why doesn't he want to sleep with me?" I didn't mean to yell at her. "You sound like my mother. My mother told me if I was going to be an actress I shouldn't believe men who told me that swallowing improves your voice."

"And your mother also probably told you to walk straight, smell good, answer politely. And wear a gardenia in your hair. I'll dance at your wedding. See you Monday night. Be good."

Richard was whistling on the steps. I managed to look as if I'd twisted my ankle as I ran to him and he leaped to steady me as I came reeling down. He held me in his arms. It was what my mother taught me: deceit.

"Sweetheart!" He carried me to the lowest step and sat down next to me. "Is it awful?" The gold chain around his neck danced in the mercury lights of the Harbor Spa. I didn't like him.

I rubbed my ankle and wished it to swell. He rubbed it. I laid my head on his shoulder. He stroked my hair. It wasn't bad. As a game play, it had limited life, but it wasn't bad. Except when you run out of limbs, the next moves have to become more degenerative. Four steps to herpes.

"Let me try to carry you home. Can you put any pressure on it?"

"I don't think it's broken or anything, Richard. Oh, Richard, how foolish of me."

"Foolish, silly girl, wonderful girl. Here." He hoisted me into his arms and carried me for a while. I wondered why it was he preferred me broken. I'm not that small.

Richard began to breathe badly. "We're going to have to do something else. You're getting heavy."

"I could take my clothes off. I'll weigh less."

He carried me back, struggling bravely, to the steps of the Harbor Spa and promised to return for me with the car. He kissed the top of my head. He broke into a run. What if he didn't come back? But I knew he would. Some of the painted people from inside walked by me down the steps. I considered breaking into a run in another direction away from the entire scene, finding a train and going home to my ficus tree. The ankle didn't even look swollen. Pinching it murderously, I considered bending it back and forth to stretch a ligament or something believable. He was back, three steps at a time, carrying a single rose.

"I prefer gardenias, Richard."

"God, I'm sorry. I stole this from someone's garden." And he carried me to the car. I tried to remember how I should act if I were in pain. Laying my head on his shoulder and sniffing the rose seemed appropriate. Commonplace, but comfortable.

"Gardenias are really exotic. Roses are so Mother's Day, you know."

"I know. I'm sorry."

I received an Ace bandage, a cup of cocoa, a croissant with fake marmalade and my very own pillowcase embroidered "Hers" when we came back to the condo. Richard tucked me into bed. Then he tucked his mother into bed.

Lying next to his mother that night on the Castro Convertible—she breathing fitfully but smelling nice— I thought seriously about the girl at the piano. It was so easy for Richard not to sleep with me. Bind my loins with an Ace bandage and tuck me in next to your mother, safe and sound. Damn. He's perfectly satisfied. They fuck like crazy and I'm going to end up like this old snoring woman next to me on the Castro. Her career: shopping. Her goal: someday, someday her men would need her for something more than chambermaid. Waiting, preparing herself to be needed, one of each in the cupboard, two of each in the medicine cabinet. We both lie here bound against the sins of the dark. The temptations are for other women. The wives get loyalty, life insurance, birthday cards, a new outfit each season, the paycheck every week and wait forever for an emotional commitment. Anything but that. No matter what it costs in Gucci's and Pucci's, anything but that. That's on reserve. The girl at the piano has it right now.

We didn't go to Westport. We had a late breakfast on Sunday. Uncle Myron brought his flyswatter to the table. Almost, and probably exactly, on signal, Uncle Myron and Richard's mother left the table and retired to the corners of the room, like the trainers at a prizefight, and Richard took my hand. "Just tell me what your father does, Stephanie. They really want to know and it's pretty rude the way you've been avoiding it all weekend."

"He works in Munich." I shrugged. I'd told him once. But he hadn't believed me. Or, more likely, hadn't listened.

"Stephanie, their coffee is going to get cold. Just tell me."

"I didn't tell them to leave the table." I wasn't being the girl that he marries at all. As I defended myself from my corner, I remembered Mrs. Slentz's scene with the crocus plants at the Cloisters and I was inspired with a wonderful thought. If I had only blushed, my work would have been without flaw. As it was, it wasn't bad. I waved the mother and the uncle back and then hung my head in shame while Uncle Myron tapped the table with the dangerous end of the flyswatter and I told them so softly and so parenthetically that because my grandmother had been a Hebrew—the flyswatter hung in the air—my grandfather's gun factory in New Haven and my father joining the army as a career officer had nearly driven her berserk and I thought, that is, I stuttered and stammered, wishing for a blush or a provocative tear, that they would be offended if they knew we had become rich from war and that my father was a general. Of course no one heard a word beyond "my grandmother had been a Hebrew."

"It is all right, isn't it?" I ended with a fine quaver. The antique euphemism, in its Episcopalian inversion, was super. The word "Hebrew" plus the flyswatter hung over my lowered eyelids.

And all the while I had woven my tale, I had delicately, infinitesimally tipped my coffee cup in order that the cloth in front of Richard overflowed finally into his lap. He hadn't moved.

The three of them were afraid to look at each other, incendiary as a shared glance could be at that moment. Over the fake marmalade buzzed a fly which ought also to have been fake. The fly and the steady drip of coffee from Richard's lap to the floor were the only sounds until his mother broke the silence. "It's okay. They should only look like you, sweetheart. See, Richard, her teeth. That's what I mean by Connecticut teeth."

"And the ears," added Uncle Myron. "If the kids have her ears, we'll save a fortune."

I raised my eyes demurely to Richard whose temples were pulsing visibly. "Liar," he mouthed at me.

"Richard! Shah!" His mother slapped his hand lightly. Either she lip-read or she intuitively understood. I couldn't tell then.

"It's the Eighth Army," I added lightly. "I'll show you pictures."

"About your grandmother," he braved, "I find it particularly difficult to believe. Whatsoever."

I began to pat politely at his pants, delaying my napkin over his inner thigh and not responding to his challenge. The muscles twitched along his leg.

As if it were Richard, Uncle Myron picked off the fly. The marmalade slid to the floor under the impact and

I, in my still small voice, as I joined the family unit as a compatriot, spoke: "Surely, Richard, it isn't important to you one way or the other, is it?"

Uncle Myron laughed very loud. His mother covered her mouth. I allowed a smirk at the corners. Richard left the table.

The only thing Richard said to me about my grandmother scene was on the way back to the city. Since he didn't have to be home until seven, we were going to the Cloisters. I didn't ask who was at home. I knew. "I have a friend," he mused, almost quizzically, as if somehow I could convince him he didn't. "This friend would die before she made a fool of me in front of my family. I know she would."

"Is she the one Uncle Myron wouldn't give any money to?"

"It's not important. Just that she's a very nice person." His voice was dreamy. I didn't want to see his face.

"Richard, do you think your family liked me?"

But when I looked at his face, it was changing from the look of love that was for her to the bright charm and false smile that were for me. "Dear girl, of course; they adored you. You are everything any of us wanted."

While I sat on a bench resting my ankle before the Unicorn, Richard wandered through the Cloisters whistling, rocking on his feet before exhibits, hands folded behind his back. I could hear his heels clicking on the stone floors. A very handsome, magnificently dressed woman sat next to me in something gray and soft. She had the same face as the Armengol woman in the tomb, great carved peaceful planes. She looked at my Ace bandage.

"How did you do it?"

"I'm faking it."

"Oh." She waved to a man passing by who said he would be back in a minute.

"Are you happy?" I asked her, astonished at my involuntary question. But she began to answer in an astonishing way.

"Yes. Now. Once I had a husband. We used to go places together. On Saturday afternoons. But that wasn't enough. So I got rid of my husband and took a lover. But then I never went any places on Saturday afternoons and I spent Saturday and Sunday waiting for him to call and take me someplace. We always slept together on Saturday night."

"Why didn't you stay with your husband and keep the lover?"

"My husband understood that he wasn't capable of being both. But I didn't understand no man was. Now, I don't sleep with the men I go places with and I don't go places with the men I sleep with and it isn't bad. My date is going to call the girl he sleeps with for tonight. I'm not unhappy. I'm not happy. I just don't have to stay home on Saturday afternoons and wait for somebody to take me someplace. I go a lot of places now. I'm very busy on weekends. Men just aren't capable of handling both kinds of relationships with the same woman."

"I thought it was because they're bastards."

"Oh, not at all, poor babies. They *can't* do both. It's not their fault." She put her hand on my knee. I kicked my bad ankle, again involuntarily. "Women can."

I really wanted to take her hand off my knee. There are too many battle-scarred bisexuals already. And I was still in there fighting.

"Except you'll die alone," I told her. "That's the problem."

"Yes," she answered thoughtfully. "Yes, it is." She took her hand away.

Richard turned to me and smiled. Then he came over and offered me his arm and helped me limp out. "Who was that?"

"I don't know."

"Why did she have her hand on your knee? I don't like that at all."

"I didn't ask."

"Sorry," he answered nastily.

"Oh, Richard, I'm edgy with this pain. I'm sorry." Actually I wanted to think about the woman's words and remember them. I didn't want to talk or listen to Richard. I had never recognized the duality. Richard is unable to do both things with the same woman. That's what Miriam has been trying to say. That's what Richard had been trying to say. "Anyone can make love. I want you to be my friend." That's precisely what he said and precisely what he meant. He needed me to be his friend. And I would be. With a vengeance.

And as I discovered when we parked in front of my building, friends do indeed go many places, most of which are rated by *New York* magazine and transferred verbatim into Richard's little Gucci notebook. Some dates in Richard's notebook were already circled in pink marker. He did not use pink marker for my dates. "On Tuesday, can you meet me at Madrigal? And let's go to the Saint Regis on Wednesday and Thursday or Friday—which is better for you?—La Toque Blanche. Then can you meet me next Monday after work at Bosphorus East? Do you like Armenian food?" I calculated how many hours a week I would lose going downtown for lunch. I told him I loved Armenian food. "And how about next Tuesday for lunch at La Grenouille? You'll really like that. Thursday . . . why don't you suggest something? Unless you want to go back to Madrigal. Maxwell's Plum is always good on Thursdays. And that weekend, let's see, it's the first weekend in June, isn't it? That weekend we ought to hit Westport. And after that . . . I don't know what the schedule will be. We're pretty open until August when . . ." he flipped through pages. His hands were shaking. "August fifteenth I go to the Hamptons and then I get back after Labor Day."

"Oh." Speaking in the singular. It wasn't with me. I bit my lip. I wanted very much to be the girl he loved.

It was all right, I kept telling myself as I took my overnight bag and my kiss on the cheek and my wilted rose. And it was all all right, I continued to tell myself as I kicked the vacuum cleaner and cried into the shower and tossed one of my mother's three Rose China plates against the wall. "These are for you when you get married, Stephanie . . . take care of them." I had refused his offer of aid in the elevator. "I'll be all right, Richard. Really, don't bother." The sound of one plate hitting the wall sounded wonderful and, as if I had made it happen by tossing the plate, the phone rang. It was himself.

Himself was terribly sorry. Was I busy? I'm throwing rare plates against the wall, I didn't tell him. He had to change a date. He had just glanced at the calendar at home and there was a grossly boring banquet he had promised a friend he'd go to and would I mind if we left for Westport on Saturday morning instead of Friday night. I didn't mind because I still had two plates to go. He sent a kiss over the phone. I sent the plates against the wall and left their precious shards on the parquet until the next morning when I scooped them up, wrapped them in newspaper and shipped them from the museum to my mother in Munich and then sat for many unproductive hours while Sissy directed a score of workmen casting platforms for the crosses and I bit my lips, wrote my dinner and lunch dates neatly into my calendar and tried hard to keep my head from exploding until I could take my agony to Miriam's where I would be going for her anniversary dinner. I really wanted to be loved. I really didn't want to die alone. I really wanted to get married. I really didn't feel like eating at the same table as Il Duce and I really wanted to talk to Miriam.

I couldn't really talk to Miriam. There was another element at the table, a pretty one, the medical illustrator and she didn't like peas. Miriam avoided my eyes and filled the dinner table with superb food while everyone else avoided the eyes of everyone else over the lace tablecloth. There was a fine and terrible line of sweat beads on Miriam's upper lip as she refused offers of help and carried steaming bowls to and from. "You should try your peas," Il Duce advised me. I nodded with a mouth full of peas. "You should try the peas," he said to the medical illustrator. "Miriam grew them from seed."

The medical illustrator, demure, embarrassed, mumbled that she had never liked peas and Il Duce, with a look of knives and no words, directed Miriam to the kitchen to get the girl something else and we waited for Miriam to come back while the girl talked about what a fantastic cook Miriam was and Il Duce talked about what a fantastic cook Miriam was and I talked about what a fantastic cook Miriam was and when Miriam came back I told her what fantastic peas she had grown as she served the girl corn on the cob which the girl ate dutifully in large desperate noisy bites. After mousse, after espresso, I caught Miriam in the kitchen.

Steam rose from a pan of dishes to cloud her face. "Don't ask."

"I don't have to ask."

"Look, your friend Richard's friend is a nurse. Poor family. First generation. The patients all love her. Speaks Italian to the old ones even though she's maternity. She's lived with your friend for a couple of years now." Miriam laughed that edging laugh. "So we both have little nurses."

"And Richard Chamberlain?"

"Two weeks more and he's off maternity. Then it'll be okay. Meantime," she jerked her thumb toward the dining room. Soap bubbles ran along her wrist. "That's his present. A temporary sacrifice."

"There's sacrifice and there's crucifixion, Miriam."

The girl came into the kitchen and stood at the sink with us. She was very embarrassed. "Are you sure I can't help with anything?"

"No, no, you go out and entertain him. That's *your* job." And the girl left smoothing her hair, not that embarrassed. "He's improving, isn't he? It's working. Just time, time. You see, it proves my point. Richard isn't sleeping with you because he's going for the Big M. Il Duce wouldn't dream of marrying that kid. I'm his wife. You don't get rid of husbands. They don't really leave."

"I prefer the Big O."

"Listen, dewy eyes out there is getting the Big O. But she's never gonna get the Big Shit because the Big

Shit is married to me and there's no way to budge him. That is why you must have patience with your friend Richard. He is ready to get married. Don't mess it up."

"I think it's abnormal. Don't you think he *wants* me?"

"Darling, worry about want and love and all that after the ceremony. Just don't iron his shirts."

"I also think he really loves that girl, Miriam. He said she's nice, that she'd never make a fool out of him. I mean she's an honorable woman. That's what bothers me. I've sold out . . . right down the river. I've sold out to the devil. I used to be nice."

"Devil, shmevil," she spat as she tossed silverware into the sink. "I have to beat you over the head. You want to be moral? You want to be nice? Go over there and put your head in my oven and turn it to self-clean. You gotta be very rich or very young or very thin before you can afford to be moral. You see the ad? What's a nice girl like you doing in an oven like this? You've seen that? You can't stand the heat, Harry, get out of the kitchen."

Miriam was hysterical, offering one strange homily after the other. I dried the dishes she passed me. The water she used was burning hot as if she were punishing herself. "Let me tell you about a moral act. Let me tell you my scenario for this evening. This evening I am flushing a bottle of Darvon down the toilet, pulling a suicide, and when he tells me I have to throw up, I'm going to make him throw up first. The whole anniversary dinner, the peas from seed, the mousse, the works, he's going to throw up. Choke and gag and vomit and I'm gonna do it after you leave but while she's still here and listening. So I'm on *her* conscience. Now, Miss Purity, Miss Honor Before Marriage, is *that* a moral act?"

I couldn't answer.

"Here, allow me. I don't take yoga for nothing." Miriam stretched out on the kitchen floor, hand draped as in Ophelia, the scrub pad on her breast, eyelids fluttering, slurring. "I-can't-live-anymore-like-this. I-can't-wait-

124

for-it-to-end. Watch-my-breathing-Steph." She breathed
very faintly. "Heart-slows-down-all-the-way-to-nowhere. I-
hardly-breathe," she said slowly and convincingly. "I-can-
hold-it-eleven-minutes." Then she popped up. "Want me
to teach you? Isn't it good? I've really been working on it."

"Are you crazy, Miriam?" I knelt beside her. "Do you
want help?"

"Crazy? Like a fox. I'm just not nice." She stood up
and smoothed her apron. "And I'm running out of
weapons."

When the dishes were finished, she and I went upstairs. The record player was on in the den, the door
closed, "The Shadow of Her Smile." Miriam had a great
idea, she told me, a wedding present. Her bedroom was
romantic, frilly and female, with perfume bottles of
extraordinary shapes and cloisonné music boxes lining a
French provincial dressing table. "I've got it figured out."

The record player stopped on a bar. It continued to
play the bar. Miriam and I looked at each other. "They're
not dancing, Miriam."

"Funny about record players, isn't it?" She started
rummaging through drawers. A cigarette dangled from
her lips. As she bent I saw that her eyebrows were gone,
totally removed, from under her bangs. "You know someone's gonna stop it soon but you just don't know if you
can stand it until someone does. It's that space in between
that's so tough."

"I'll go down."

"I believe that is already occurring without you. Let
them be. Listen, I'll become the second Mother Cabrini,
crucified on my KLH. That's funny, isn't it?" She plowed
through dresser drawers, shoving clothes away in closets
and dumping old suitcases on to the bed. "God, where
in hell did I put them?" The record player was growing
louder even after Miriam kicked the bedroom door shut
with one foot. "Clothes closet. Aah, linen closet. It can
wait. What we really have to do is find out about your

nurse and just how serious *that* deal is, which means we have to do a number on her."

There is a certain kind of woman in New York who can use the telephone the way other women use their hips. Miriam was expert at psychological harassment through Ma Bell. We'd worked together before.

"What's the number?"

"Let's not. What if he's there?"

"Would you prefer a house call?"

"Miriam, what if she's the right girl? What if she's really the right girl?"

"No such animal."

"But what if . . ." She was poised, one finger above the first digit.

"One in a million . . . okay, then we would have to get rid of her before he finds out she's really the right girl. But she's not. Nobody is."

"I think she is."

She dialed the number. My heart stopped. "Just breathe in and out, Steph. Say 'Hawng' to yourself as you breathe in, 'Saw' as you breathe out . . . relax. Just sit, don't be scared of her. You're the girl he's going to marry. She's in troub—Good evening. My name is Carol Good from the Bye Dee Diaper Service and your name has been submitted to us by a friend who told us your very happy news which means we have a free gift for you and your husband a beautiful layette for the baby with a market value of thirty dollars plus a six weeks supply of Ivory Snow and a certificate for a studio portrait of the baby dear good for a year. Oh?" Miriam laughed, high and mad. "Someone is being *funny*. Isn't that *wonderful*? Maybe your husband, maybe he *wants* you to have a baby. Do you have any plans . . . so I can file your card? After September. I see." She nodded to me wisely. I tore pages from her phone book. "Let me write that down. Very good. You should know then. We'll have our representative call on you with your gift and explain our service to you then. Very good. And that's S L E N T Z?"

Miriam took away my phone book. "Oh! *That* after September. So I should file this for sometime the next year. Well, we'll be sure to call you. The very best of luck."

"I can't stand it. I can't stand it."

"Hawng, Saw. Hawng, Saw."

"I want to throw things out the window. She's going . . . is she . . . going to marry him? Is she? Something is going on there."

"She's making a decision. She isn't certain. Obviously she is in for a major disappointment."

"Or I am."

"Oh no you're not. Oh no you're not. Let's just get to work. Come on, I'll go through the closet again. I know the stuff is in there."

"What stuff?"

"Weapons."

Miriam talked as she worked in the closet but I couldn't hear her muffled words. I sat on the bed. If I were home I would have shredded my own coverlet. But I didn't shred blankets; I didn't throw perfume bottles. I had until September. It was almost June. July, and then two weeks in August before he went away. And I had to face it, went away with her. I could forget the two weeks as a matter of fact because she'd be packing with him then. I had June and the month of July. "Miriam, she wants to have his baby. She's a nice person. This is really lousy. Anyway, don't people have throw-away diapers now?" I leafed through the phone book. There were still some diaper supply companies. "You have to admit there are very few women left in the country who genuinely want to have a baby," I told Miriam. "That really says something for her."

Then she burst from the closet. "Here! Are they gorgeous?" Triumphantly she tossed me an old white T-shirt and a grimy shoulder bag. "Is this terrific?" Across the breast of the T-shirt, running from shoulder to waist, was written in red, "Daniel Hechter." "Would you believe that's a fifty-buck Munsingwear T-shirt? And this . . . see this ratty thing . . . plastic piece of junk. That's my Louis Vuitton bag. The shoulder strap is leather. In the sixties, my number two, the shrink, in exchange for fifteen minutes of me acting out for him a patient's fantasy, gave me this bag which then cost him one hundred and eighty-five bucks and the older it is, the longer it looks like you've been rich." She kissed me on both cheeks. "Welcome to ze regiment, mon petite. Maybe someday you'll earn your own."

"Did your bedroom look like this with your second husband . . . all the toile?"

"No, with him it was arty. With number one it was intelligentsia/bohème . . . posters and blue lights. Now this home, hearth stuff. Don't you like my gifts?"

"I don't really like status symbols, Miriam. It's really out of my . . . uh, experience."

"Oh, sure, that's because you are a status symbol yourself. Listen, the act is no longer being a Jewish mother. What you lack attitudinally is life-experience at being a Jewish princess. It's easy enough to be a mother. Now, you have your princess uniform. It's a far more subtle act. The secret motto of the legion is: attack. But subtly. Never the jugular. Always the capillaries. See? Do their possessions, not them. Mothers attack *them*. Princesses have a more delicate touch. If he brings you rye bread with seeds, sigh and say you've been lusting for rye bread without seeds and if he brings you without seeds, sigh and say, et cetera. Always an A minus. Keep him coming back for the A. Never give it. Never! If you want to marry him, you have to keep him in line."

On Tuesday at Madrigal I told Richard his tie was outrageous and he ought to try Tripler's. On Thursday at the Saint Regis I suggested Dunhill's because Tripler's had obviously lost their buyer. Although I let down for La Toque Blanche, by the next Monday at Bosphorus East I advanced my position with the suggestion that he try Brooks because my father had always been able to depend on Brooks to be appropriate and by the next Thursday when I arrived at La Grenouille carrying my worn and filthy bag and wearing my yellowed T-shirt with women examining me hood-eyed and more men who looked more like Richard looking at me more than usual and Richard standing and waving, obviously pleased and proud as I joined him at a rose-laden table and I intentionally ignoring all through lunch his rather lovely tie of British silk, muted paisleys in ambers and beiges, Richard finally broke down and said: "You were right on about Brooks, Steph."

"Oh." My smile was wide and lovely. "Is *that* from Brooks?"

He returned my smile above the table. He grabbed

my forearm under the table. "Stephanie, what the hell is wrong with *this* tie?"

"Richard, please. Really, this is so inappropriate of you. This is all so unimportant. It's just a tie."

His teeth were slightly clenched. I thought it was sexy. There was a delicious space between them large enough for the point of my tongue.

"I want you to tell me. *You* started this, Stephanie, so you'll finish it."

"I? Look, it isn't written that I have to like your ties. I don't care about your ties. I don't give a hoot about your ties. Hoot hoot." I thought he might recall our discussion of the owl and the pussycat but he was rather rigidly centered in on his tie. "I care, Richard, about your body and your heart. I am your friend." I rolled my tongue across my lips. I found his agony very satisfying, a certain violence brewing which could well be translated to Body English in bed. "It isn't cosmic enough." He wasn't amused. At all.

"Every day, Stephanie, I have to present myself to hundreds of people. The slightest off thing can shift a jury. I need to know precisely what you're thinking about this tie." He lifted its point to my face.

"It's a jungle out there, isn't it, Richard?"

"And war is hell." Richard ordered a third cup of espresso for each of us. This would go on.

"Richard, you are a sexy man and I know, I just know that you've really got your orgasm together. Waving that tie before me is indeed a phallic suggestion. I'm beginning to like that tie more and more. But I am not thinking about it. I'm feeling it."

"Either you start thinking about my tie or I'll walk out of this place." Richard was hissing.

"I'll be delighted to think about it. Okay." I closed my eyes. "I'm now thinking about your tie. I actually have it in view. I'm thinking." I waited and he waited. I began to squirm visibly on the chair. I could keep him here all afternoon. "I'm ready."

"Well?"

"I keep getting phallic images, darling, and I lose the tie." I pursed my lips. "Rub the end of your tie across my cheek, Richard. And then I'll tell you."

"Not here, for Christ's sake. Stephanie, please concentrate. I don't ask much of you."

I sat up straight as an arrow. "I've got it." I put my hand on his arm. "Now, look, don't get angry." It was delicious to watch him hanging on my words. Surgeon, turn on the oxygen, more pressure, vital signs reducing quickly. I was becoming an elemental necessity to Richard's vision of himself. Drown in your narcissistic pool, baby. "Look, Richard," I took a deep breath, then gulped loudly and started bravely. "It's a little . . . uh, a little J."

"What?" He squinted in disbelief.

"J. Yes, I think, yes, that is clearly what I responded to."

"Jesus Christ, you are the most bigoted woman I have ever met." It was said, that line, with a hushed reverence.

"Oh, Richard," I kissed his cheek. "I'm sorry. I mean it's all so stupidly unimportant."

"There is no such thing as a Jewish tie or a gentile tie. Completely and totally irrational categories." He took my hand. "Is there?"

"Bigotry is irrational. Anyway," I continued lightly, loving the soft warmth of his hand around mine, "I don't recall saying there was a difference. It's just the way particular ties look on particular people. Try it this way, Richard. From the top? When the salesman shows you ties, does he pick out four or five and tell you they'd look good on you or does he just let you go through all the stock yourself?"

His anger was gone. His hurt was gone. He seemed passionately, alertly, curiously involved.

"In the better stores?"

"Yes, go on, darling."

"He picks them out."

"Well, there's your answer."

"Do you mean . . . ? Then it doesn't matter what kind of tie I wear, it will always look like a Jewish tie? Is that what you're trying to say? . . . Or do you mean they pick out 'J.' ties for me because I look Jewish?"

"Dammit, Richard," now I hissed. "This is the stupidest conversation. Why are you so hysterical about being Jewish? Such terrible self-hatred. I mean you're the only one who cares. I think it's very nice that you are a Hebrew because we know you make good fathers and wonderful husbands and excellent providers. We have absolutely no objection to whatever it is you believe in or what ties you wear and so on and so on." I had really lost my train of thought.

He turned toward me with that certain violence I found appealing. "We who?"

"Darling, this discussion is simply not worthy of us, is it?"

"Aah, Stephanie." He took my hand. He actually took my hand and kissed the center of it and then all my little fingers. B&D? S&M? He had found his sadist. "Come with me and help me buy ties. I'll take the afternoon off."

"Oh, no, Richard. I'm setting up the first section of my crosses. I have to supervise the construction of the platforms and . . . well, I could *never* do that to a man. Perhaps after . . . well, it's something a wife does, you know, and I'm just not ready to commit myself to playing that role yet." I sighed prettily. "You know." He sucked on my palm and I was about to slide off the chair.

"Of course. I understand, sweetheart." He continued working the center of my hand which seemed, like acupuncture, directly connected to other vital centers of my system. "Someday."

We sat still for a while, touching knees, heat climbing through my body and I knew through his. This man was a very possible man. Afterward, long after the check arrived, the restaurant almost empty, he asked, breathing hotly into my ear, "Stephanie, when I wear a tie like this do you mean people like yourself look at it and say that man must be Jewish?"

"Of course not."

"You did."

I shrugged. "You forced me to that conclusion."

"All right, what *would* they think?"

"Do you mean these people here for instance who know you? The various ones you spoke to as they came in?"

"Yes, and others, juries, judges, clients."

"Probably, and this is only a probe because I can't speak beyond my own experience, of course, probably they'd think, if they stopped to think, there goes a Jewish tie."

I might have overdone it. On the way out into the sunny afternoon, Richard buttoned his raincoat up to his neck.

He called me that night. He said nothing about ties. Instead he asked me to hold as he turned up a record, blasting music into my ears. I held and listened. It was "The Emperor." I never liked it.

"Is that gorgeous?" He at last removed the music. "Isn't that the most moving, most brilliant? That passage is the finest."

"It's a fine performance. Who's doing it?"

"Do you know what it reminds me of? Listen to this. It reminds me of . . . the way I see it? Two primeval creatures like Prometheus with new worlds rising volcanically above them, fighting the last fight. Water, fire, streams of lava, red sky and the last fight is meaningless, because it's all coming to an end. But . . . but . . . no one is sure if the world is really coming to an end and the fighting is useless or if the last fight is in reality producing the new world. Don't you see it that way?" He was very excited.

"Not bad." It really wasn't. I thought I would listen to it myself someday and then discuss it with him. I felt a recognition. If one could talk about new worlds, one might talk about God and the perfectability of man. I was very happy and was about to bring up that very subject when he perforated the faint connection we had made.

"God, it's late. As FDR used to say, gotta run. Catch you later."

Click. But I had really expected no more this time.

Those two weeks of dating were grim. The calendar hung like a lodestone around my neck. I had just a little more than two months before he took the girl at the piano to the Hamptons, before he discovered that she was really the right girl. On another level, though, I enjoyed the two weeks, enjoyed being with Richard for all those lunches and early dinners. I liked being seen with him. I liked the way other men looked at me. He liked the way other men looked at me. I often caught him searching for an authentic face, trying to find someone he might someday look like, someone he might become, someone who seemed content. I would see him from moment to moment, pensive, staring through windows, distracted by a distant troubling thought and then he would turn and smile his utterly charming smile for me. He was playing games also but not as well as I was. There were other factors operating during those weeks. His shirts were wrinkled, buttons occasionally crushed and hanging awry. I had seen a fluff of Platypus's orange hair on Richard's well-styled locks and knew he'd slept at least one night on the couch. And, as if he weren't eating fresh strawberries and whipped cream any longer, his face was touched, just touched, with a gray cast. I knew he was in conflict. I knew my public presence helped him. He constantly measured other people's reactions to us as a couple. And as lightly and as pleasantly as I greeted him for our dates and conversed entertainingly, looking like a girl, acting like a lady, thinking like Machiavelli, I worked like a dog to find his openings, to find some soft painful spot where I could dig in and dislodge the virgin before my time was up. Privately, my presence ate him up alive. I knew, because he began to seek advice from me quite desperately. Advice for her. As the problems worsened, he made less and less attempt to cover himself and finally began talking directly about her. And I got mean.

At odd hours from odd places, Richard began to call me. Bars, drugstores, street corners. I always asked where he was and he always told me at his place. Buses and trucks ran through his place, cash registers rang often and short order cooks called out in Chinese from his kitchen. Nevertheless he called me and I couldn't complain. We discussed moral issues. We discussed the problems of "my friend" or "an acquaintance of mine" or "someone I know."

"I want to try something out on you, Steph," he would begin. I was becoming an authority on Richard's someones, which boiled down to, I was certain, that one girl at the piano. And as I grew to know Richard more or less—I was never sure which—the someone seemed to have greater and deeper problems each time Richard called me. The most rewarding call came after a lunch date at which he had yawned a great deal and eaten ravenously. I had suggested that perhaps he had had a fight with his friend and that he'd had a bad supper/night/breakfast. He reminded me that we had promised each other not to ask questions. I told him it was a statement. He told me not to expect a response, be it question or statement.

And late that night he called. Very late.

"Where are you, darling?"

"At my place."

A cash register rang behind him. "Steph, you're a mature woman. Let me try this one out on you. Do you think if a woman loves passionately and deeply, that she has to give up the possibility of reaching a higher level of truth? I was just talking to a friend and the question came up. I said I knew exactly who'd have an answer."

"It's after two in the morning, Richard."

"Just off the top of your head, huh, honey?"

Sure I know the answer, Richard. I know my *Antigone*. But I'm not supposed to be bright. "Not for me was the marriage hymn, nor will anyone start the song at a wedding of mine." Prefer honor. What was happening over there? He was downstairs in a phone booth. She was upstairs crying over her honor, trying to choose between motherhood and morality? And he came downstairs for some pastoral counseling from the other woman so he could run back upstairs and climb into her bed against her body and relieve himself into her and think of me fleetingly or perhaps even imagine she was me just to bring a little extra joy into the bed. Jesus, I'll never really get her out of his head. He is so worried tonight. What is this? Marriage versus career?

"Dearest Richard, you are so philosophical and I'm feeling so horny and I just want to think happy horny thoughts."

"Try, Stephanie."

"Is it awfully important?"

"Awfully. Yes. Well, she thinks it is."

Terrific. Just terrific, Richard. "Offhand, she sounds like my gay secretary. Guilty about screwing. Hasn't got her man/woman thing worked out yet. Is your friend a little latent?"

"I never thought about it."

I knew those lines too, from Sissy: she fucks like crazy and the semen flies all over the apartment. "Tell your friend when you see her that a woman who already is mature doesn't have to make those choices. She is better able to integrate passionate love and morality, truth, honor. She doesn't have to worry about growing up. Will that help?"

"Well, would you say another way to say it is it just takes time?"

"Yes." June, July, August, September, October. "Yes,

that's very good. Lots of time. Months and years before a woman is really mature enough, knows enough, for marriage. Tell her to be very patient."

"Thank you, Stephanie."

He couldn't wait to hang up, to dash upstairs and hold her in his arms and stick my knife into her. And he wouldn't even realize how he had hurt her. How deeply. Just keep whistling, Richard, and drive right through. I felt sorry for the girl. Sort of. I felt sorrier for myself. I felt very little for him at that moment and that, considering how shattered I would have felt if I loved him as deeply as she did, was a relief. Thank God I don't love him too much. I have to remember that I can't. The answer to that question he'd asked me weeks ago . . . I have the answer. Yes, Richard, there has to be pain and suffering. For you. For her. Not me. He needed to get married. I just wanted to.

And, like a wound, he couldn't stop examining his conflict. He called very late that night. He talked softly. He called me darling. "Darling, do you ever feel that I strangle you? That I suffocate you? Do you feel that with me?"

"Not at all, Richard. Not one teensy little bit." God, what a way for a grown woman to talk.

"I've been accused of that. That's not me, is it? Don't you feel I have the ability to commit myself? Haven't I committed myself with you?"

"That argument, Richard, dear, is not going to impress her."

"Who?"

"Whomever it is you're talking about."

"I'm talking about us."

"Oh, well, I've never accused you of that."

"I know. But you remember, before, there were women who have accused me of not committing and I just thought . . . I hope this isn't what my dear Stephanie sees in me."

"I don't. You are kind, wonderful, sweet, charming, committed. My heart is full. I love you."

"You don't like the way I drive."

"I never said that."

"I can tell. But that's incidental. Listen, do *you* think I'm hostile?"

"You? How?" This would be an endless conversation. I couldn't recall if he'd had an analyst or not. He had now. Me.

"I've been accused of limiting someone's chances at a higher level of truth because I loved her."

"That's not hostility, Richard."

"Oh, no, but just out of curiosity, do I strike you as hostile?"

"I really don't like the way you drive."

"Say hello to Platypus."

"Hello, Platypus."

"You're the first one ever to mention my driving. Nobody has ever accused me of hostile driving before."

"Because I care. I'm the first one who has cared enough to risk hurting you in order to help you. And I'm probably the first one who cared enough to tell you that your earlobes didn't come out evenly. And if any woman says she loves you and then isn't honest with you, then you are both indulging in the luxury of an emotion raised by a false belief." I had no idea where my phrases came from. But they were very sound and wonderful. He hung on them.

"Maybe she never noticed my ears."

I didn't answer immediately. I sighed as if another awful truth were forcing itself to emerge to the surface. "If only I could be with you and hold you while I tell you these things. We need to grow together, Richard. You were put in my path and I in yours and I must help you as you must help me to become what it is we must become."

"Yes?"

"Richard, what are you eating?"

"Hershey kisses."

Richard deserved everything he got. "What God wants us to become. Richard, I realize you are the victim of your own myth. I understand that. I know what it means to feel you must be hostile, you must be aggressive, you must be a man and . . . and . . . forgive me, darling . . . and strut."

"I don't strut."

I continued without acknowledging his response. "Your personality is warped because you are corrupted by your unearned victories and ascendancies. You are your own victim, darling, but you can relax with me. You can trust me. I understand you."

"What do you understand? I don't understand what you understand."

Oh, God. I didn't understand either. "That you are a man and as a man your primary purpose of manhood is defending and maintaining your manhood."

"How do *you* know what *my* primary purpose in life is?"

"Isn't it to be happy?"

"Yes. Yes, that's really all I want."

"And that is all you ask of life."

"Yes."

I sighed. "Progressive education. It is the fault of progressive education. Everyone loves you and you do what you want. An entire generation brought up on stimulation and motivation. Spoiled. And you are simply adrift, still looking for pleasure. New stimulation, new motivation. And that's why so many men like you . . . do you know, last year I asked all my girl friends what their lovers most wanted from them and they said anal sex. Anal sex is the living end. And then I asked all their lovers what they thought about anal sex and they couldn't even *admit* they *thought* about it. That's this generation of men. Torn between decency and funk. The typical New York man,

Richard, is an expert in natural foods and unnatural acts. Do you think about anal sex, Richard?"

"Christ, Stephanie, I don't even care if I eat processed *cheese*." So she was into the strawberries and cream.

"You ought to care about the sugar in those kisses . . . too toxic. But that's what I mean, leaping from one funky motivation to one kinky stimulation when life should be based on value and tradition and continuance. And you are *sadly* adrift, aren't you? That is what I understand. But at one point you will have to nail yourself into history, into commitment, values, marriage. At one point, you will have to give up your dalliance and become a grown man."

"Stephanie, I didn't call you to hear *that*!"

"Hang up, Richard, if you need to. If it's part of your myth. I'll know if you're a man or not in other ways. So if you need to hang up because I am telling you the truth, I'll understand. If you need to hang up because you have to show me your manhood, I'll understand. I'll really understand because I care."

"You've been very understanding, Stephanie. And I appreciate that. Only an intelligent woman like you could be so understanding."

"I try, Richard. I try." And I am so very good.

"I love you, Stephanie. Love you because you are enormously generous and good-natured and you are really my friend. I know you'll be a very important influence in my life. A real help. Stephanie, you're kidding about the earlobes, aren't you?"

"She never told you?"

"She once told me my nostrils were crooked. Look, let me try *this* one out on you. I finally convince her that it'll feel better if she gets on top of me and she gets on top of me and she looks up and says, 'Gee whiz, Richard, I never knew your nostrils were crooked.' "

"Good night, Richard."

"I . . . I'm sorry. I just . . . you're so understanding. I'll call you tomorrow. I'll call you at eight sharp in the morning. Before you go to work."

"Good night, Richard."

"Eight sharp. And I'm really sorry, darling."

"It's all right, Richard, I understand. It's just that you are sometimes so inappropriate." And I hate you a lot.

He called at 7:45 the next morning. It had helped to tell him he was inappropriate. The nastier I became on the phone, the more often he called me.

And then, it was June and I knew he and the girl were having trouble, and we were off to Westport under a promising sun and blue skies and I was satisfyingly optimistic about Richard and myself as we wove our fateful skein through the traffic to Connecticut, disregarding all the signals, certain that if we were to sleep together, the agony, the self-searching, the grimness would fall away and release the old shining Unicorn magic. All of this heaviness was simply pre-pubic agony. We'd both be getting pimples soon. I knew he had to feel about my body as I felt about his. And I wanted him. I was certain he wanted me. I'd seen him looking at me.

Those hopeful thoughts may have been why I did that awful thing at Westport. Sissy, in a way, although I can't blame her, had suggested it. Late Friday afternoon, Sissy came into the office. She walked very straight and had improved her whole being. She had grown since I'd become so dysfunctionally in love or whatever it was I was in. I went so easily from optimism to grim determinism, I wasn't certain any longer.

"Stephanie, do you have a few minutes to spare?"

Part of my dysfunction was not to trust, but the other part was not to care, so I didn't respond with the usual sharpness. Besides, she had worked her job and mine all these weeks while I doodled, daydreamed and vaguely planned activities for her. Also I had ignored her. At any rate, she hid a flashy gold and magenta gift box behind her back.

"Oh, poor Sissy. You've really been working, haven't you. Sit down."

"Well, Stephanie, you see . . ." she started, quite uncomfortable, the package stabbing her in the lower back. "My mother and father . . . they were married."

"I never questioned that, Sissy."

"What I mean is, I see that you and this Richard character are really going to get married, at least it sure looks like you're on the winning team and I want you to know I'm rooting for you. Not that I believe in marriage . . . in your sense . . . but if that's what you want, I sure want you to win, Stephanie. I sure do."

"Thank you."

"Well, it's not just that. I think, well, look, my mother, she was pretty *overt*. You know. She'd insist on a kiss and a hug from my father and I think she nearly attacked him in bed. And he was passive. She'd always grab his tush when he walked by her and I never saw it but I'm sure she grabbed him all over, you know? She always teased him and turned him on and attacked him. But he loved it. He loved getting attacked."

Sissy was helping me. She was decent. "Did you ever notice if she insulted him?"

"More like challenging him. She would say at supper with a smile, a look, just for him, 'I guess you're too tired to go to bed early, huh, Frank?' I never figured that remark out till much later. Until now, really, when I was trying to think of what you . . . well, if you, if I could help you somehow. So, look, I brought you this." She swung the box to me. She was very embarrassed and very real. God knows what was in the box. I hoped I could say the right thing. The box was from Blackton—Fifth Avenue. No way would it work with the Louis Vuitton and the Daniel Hechter.

"That's the kind of thing my mother always used," Sissy said as I opened the papers to a G-string triangle of hot green and yellow felt with gold and fuchsia spangles spelling SUPERWOMAN across the crotch and two cones spiraling with the same colors in bangles, no more than an inch in diameter, lovingly wrought, striptease items. I didn't even know the name for them. They were so cheap and in such bad taste and yet I knew how hard it was for her to do. It was beyond my imagination to imagine Sissy shopping in Blackton's. But she had. For me.

"Oh, Sissy, they're . . . they're so sexist. I love you."

"I hope they work."

"I'm so touched, Sissy. I am very touched."

"Christ," she dropped her voice. "Men are so stupid. You must have to draw them pictures. Somebody's gotta work around here. I gotta go. I suppose they'll fit," she added with a lecherous grin. "I'd love to see them on you."

"Sissy . . ." I began to scream at her. And then I spread my arms out, quite empty. "Sissy . . . it's just the way it is. That's all. Thank you."

"Come down and look over the blueprints later, will you?"

"Sure."

It was the closest we had ever been. She buzzed me on the intercom before she left for the day with a small sociological commentary. "Listen, another thing, my mother told me that Jewish guys don't marry girls who swallow."

"That's wonderful of you, Sissy. That is extraordinarily important data. And how is Monica?"

"Yeah. See, I care about your problems. That's the first time you've asked in almost a month."

"I'm sorry." I walked out to her desk. "How's it going?"

"It's okay. See, we are making new rules so no one knows what to expect. You at least know the rules."

"Don't like them. Know them."

"Well." She wanted me to talk to her and I did owe her something. Primarily, I owed her some attention. She had been carrying the responsibility of the cross exhibit entirely by herslf, covering for my three-hour lunch dis appearances, and caring for me. I sat on a corner of her desk. "Sissy, I always wondered how you know when you meet a girl whether or not. I can usually tell with men."

"Oh, Monica was simple. She walked up to me at the movies and said 'Let's take a walk.'"

"Just like that?"

"Just like that."

"Just like that. Listen, I hope this all works out." After she left, I slipped the blazing gift into my bag. Just like that. It wasn't quite just like that at Westport. It was pretty awful in fact. And I couldn't blame it on Sissy altogether.

The closer we came to Westport, the more constricted Richard became. He tried to whistle and then stopped trying. He tried to hum. He tried to find something on the radio. Station after station, nothing pleased him. And then we arrived at the barn which had been a barn but was no longer a barn. It was now an exquisite home set behind boxwood and mulberry with only the shell of the original New England indicating its humble beginnings. The folks inside spoke with a strange combination of Port Jervis and Boston accents with "fuck" sprinkled like sea salt throughout. The mother and daughter must have been at one time very short. Now they wore six-inch platforms that stilted them far above the father and son, the sort of shoes cripples wear one at a time to even up a stunted leg. But the mother and daughter, Blossom and Pamela, wore the shoes two at a time and towered over everyone. Both children, although they had perfect complexions and shining rows of braces, blinked constantly and uncompromisingly. And Pussycat, the father of them all, was wonderfully, neurotically overweight; expansive and generous and perspiring with no apologies, a good man. Mark, the son, was neurotically underweight and much shorter than everybody else and kept saying he was getting nervous. And because everyone was so ill-bred, a pair of perfect Borzois licked their feet. Good breeding, I decided, was to be free to buy your dogs at the ASPCA.

Blossom, still as lovely as her wedding picture, thin, stunning, her nails—toes and fingers—polished in deep red, showed me the barn. The stone walls of the kitchen and family room were certainly barn and the high beams and rough woods of the next three floors were certainly barn. But the bookcases—all book-club editions—and the French windows and the Chinese carpets and stainless stairwells and rosewood lofts in the bedrooms were not barn.

"Hey, Little Mother," Pussycat bellowed upward and the stainless steel spirals shivered. "Get down here and feed everybody." I would, he explained, see the rest of the house later.

The evening wasn't bad. The family wasn't bad. They all cared and touched each other. Blossom was still angry with Richard about the Beef Wellington and the Bing and Grøndahl china that first weekend when I lied about my ankle and we didn't continue on to Westport. So she (her words) ordered out and we had (her words) chinx. I didn't mind. I was thinking more and more about that G-string over a flat belly as I picked delicately over the chow mein and assorted exotics. We ate and watched *Mothra*, a Japanese sci-fi movie about an enormous moth who wipes out airports. Mark could do an excellent Mothra death scene and did it often throughout the movie. Blossom wanted to know how old my Louis Vuitton was. I told her I couldn't remember. Pussycat stretched out monstrously as he asked what made me choose a little guy like Richard. Mark repeated Mothra's death howl with no variations while all of us ate from the cardboard canisters and cuddled near each other on the family room sofas. Pamela wanted to know what kind of perfume I wore, what kind of lipstick, what kind of eye underliner, where I bought my shoes, did I douche or use the pill or wear a device and all the other normal questions of the contemporary fifteen-year-old woman. She wore a device and most of her friends did. A couple were still on the pill. Fifteen, I thought, moving closer to Richard, who became stiffer, fifteen and probably starting at thirteen. And I was almost thirty and not allowed. I cuddled next to Richard, rubbing my forehead against his shoulder. Mark had him nailed on the other side and, between us, Richard couldn't move.

I cuddled harder and began to think with greater clarity of intention about my superwoman G-string. Richard was very withdrawn although he tried to be avuncular and tender equally to Mark and myself. That night Richard would be sleeping in the family room. I was to be in Pamela's room on the second floor. The master bedroom, well out of earshot, was on the third level. I never found out where it was Mark slept but he looked as if he never slept. Actually, as it happened, that night he was around quite a bit. But then, so was I.

Before intermission ended Pussycat was out and back with hot fudge sundaes in more canisters. Mothra gave her death scream. Mark his, surpassing hers. Happy ending. Pussycat stretched toward me again, a huge round lion, belched, smiled at his belch, and measured me for a take-out treat in a cardboard canister. He wasn't lecherous. He was just a hungry man. Blossom took me aside as the kids punched off the tv set.

"Listen, Steph, after everyone's settled down, it's okay with us if you want to come down here with Richard. Just don't let him come up to Pammy's room. And listen, can I borrow that T-shirt for lunch next week? I'll mail it back. The girls will drop dead."

Pamela, lacking the finesse of her mother's generation, whispered with equal generosity, "If you two are gonna ball, don't get any come on my sheets."

And Pussycat led me upward to Pamela's bedroom

*148*

while Blossom did the dishes, an interpretation of an act manifested as burning the cardboard in the incinerator. Pussycat brushed me as we walked up the stainless stairs. I climbed faster and faster because every time I slowed down I could feel his chest, stomach, something, against my backside. If there had been more stairs, I am certain he would have had a heart attack. I didn't wish it on him but then I didn't wish him on me.

He opened the door to Pamela's room.

"Good God!," I hadn't meant to say. Now I understood Blossom's and Pamela's anxiety about the sheets. The bedroom out-Bloomingdaled Bloomingdale's. The walls were patchwork, the sheets were patchwork. The spread, the dust ruffle, the padded rocker were patchwork. The towels were patchwork. The ceiling was patchwork and the floor was stenciled in patchwork and covered with forty thousand coats of shellac.

"It's something else, isn't it?" Pussycat, exhausted, laid my suitcase at my feet. "And you know that fucking kid of mine. She comes in after the decorator and four carpenters finish and says, 'But where's the straw rope on the bed? I wanted a rope bed. How can you have a patchwork room without a straw rope bed!' Can you imagine that?"

Pamela was a natural. She'd never need a Daniel Hechter or a Vuitton.

"Listen," Pussycat was still breathing hard. "Should I look in on you so you don't get in trouble? Maybe I should lock you in. Hey, let me know if you get in trouble. I mean, if you need help. These young guys. You gotta draw them fucking pictures, for Christ's sake."

I watched him blush. "I'm sorry, Pussycat, I didn't hear you. Could you say that again?"

He repeated himself unevenly, the great blush rising and fanning out across his great face. It was the third time I had been advised that Richard needed a picture drawn for him. Didn't they know about the other woman?

As I closed my door on Pussycat and climbed into my four-poster and lay knee-deep in Jewish Appalachia, I began to fantasize about green and gold and fuchsia–spangled peak moments in the family room.

The house was very still. Freezers buzzed, pumps sumped or sumps pumped, the incinerator hissed away. Richard slept below me, troubled, I knew, and withdrawn. It wasn't easy for him to be with his family and he felt shame and pressure. He was only a half flight down the spiral staircase on softly carpeted steps and I thought about him and about my blazing superwoman G-string and drawing pictures and Sissy's father and mother and finally, applying my spirals and triangle that glowed quite wickedly in the dark, I slipped into my robe and out to the hallway, patting my way along the wall, intrigued by my own luminosity. Once I thudded against a velvet Borzoi who groaned. When I found Richard in the family room, I slipped off my robe, laid it at the bottom of the sofa and touched Richard's forehead.

"Richard?" I whispered softly. No answer. I patted my way down to his chest. I put my hands on his face quite gently. Awake or not, he allowed me to lift his blankets although first I had to break his fingers because he clutched the satin hems so tightly. He allowed me to slip one leg in beside him. He breathed steadily. I didn't trust him. I knew he was awake.

"Richard?"

And then he screamed. A karate scream, a Mothra death scream, a lion wounded, and I had time only to leap backward.

"What are those lights? Help! *Help!*"

I was about to accuse him of faking, of sounding too much like Tevye's wife but Blossom and Pussycat and the two Borzois and Mark and Pamela were with me in my luminous shame and the lights went on like a surprise party. Nobody sang happy birthday. The two Borzois had been in the den. I had tripped on Mark.

"S-U-P-E-R . . . superwoman, it says. It says super-woman. Boy, am I getting nervous. I'm getting really nervous, Mama."

I glazed my eyes over and stood very still.

"Blossom," Richard said sanely and appropriately. "Take your children away. I'll take care of this. She's obviously sleepwalking."

"Why don't you keep her down here, then, so she doesn't get loose again?"

"Shh, don't wake her up. She gets very upset if you wake her up and she'll know what she did."

There I stood with Richard defending me, my eyes glazed, my blazing shameful triangle and tits glowing obscenely in the family room. Richard was wise. I must offer him that. "Just let her out. Just open the doors and let her go. Stand out of her way."

I simply turned, keeping my eyes wide and frozen, and passed beyond the family with my outstretched arms, up the spiral stairs and into the room of the princess. I heard the door lock from the outside. When I climbed into bed, I wanted to die. When I woke up in the morning, I wanted to murder Richard. Choke him with the G-string. There was no need for him to scream.

But the scream that came shivering up into my sleep wasn't Richard's. It was Mark's froggy deep voice bursting frantically up the spiral staircase, covering quite well my own crisis with his own crisis. "There isn't one fucking package of Froot Loops in this whole fucking house and I'm getting very nervous."

"Mark!" Blossom yelled from the third floor, "is that you?"

And Pamela from nearby: "Who the hell else do you think that *could* be?" Bitchy lady.

And Pussycat. "Isn't your Uncle Richard down there? Ask him to find you something to eat."

Blossom began a strange liturgy I would hear repeated many times on our visits to come. "There's Cap'n

Crunch and Grape-Nuts and Grape-Nuts Flakes and Chocula and Heartland with nuts or plain and instant oatmeal, with the cinnamon and apples like you like, and frozen waffles. . . ." She continued while something heavy and large and loving stumbled down the staircases, slammed a screen door, tore out of the white chip driveway with a screech of Lincoln brakes, and, some few minutes later, brought back the Froot Loops. The crisis was over. I buried my head in the patchwork. No wonder Richard was scared of marriage and commitment. This is what he had seen and poor Mark is whom he might have been. And he wanted to lose himself anyplace but back in that scene again. Mark's anger was of course unmitigated ultimate terror, and it was why Pussycat, who understood the terror as only a man can, kind and fumbling, nearly fell down the stainless stairs to get those Froot Loops. Mark's life as a man would start only soon enough. My Richard, for whom I felt pain that morning, was also in terror. Of me, of marriage, of the whole thing. Richard didn't have to be governor or wear the right ties or drive the right car. God, I so wanted that morning to hold Richard and tell him he didn't have to, that I knew his pain and his fear and I'd always have the Froot Loops for him. But I couldn't. The girl at the piano was the Froot Loop distribution center. I gave out the terror. I wanted to get married and I couldn't give out Froot Loops. I had to keep him frightened.

Draping the superwoman G-string on one post of Pamela's bed and sticking the pasties on the tops of two other posts, I packed to leave with Richard. The family was so embarrassed for Mark I was able to be gracious and forgiving over a standup breakfast of chocolate-laden coffee cake and real coffee. When I left, Blossom kissed me and whispered: "I'll be around if you have problems. I know him like a glove."

Glove and I did not communicate on the way home.

Glove said things like: "An hour more." "Did you see that Lotus?" "Do you want to stop at a powder room?"

I said things like "How far is it now?" "No, I didn't." "No, I don't."

And when we reached my apartment and pulled up to the curb and he reached into his overnight case and gave me my Very Well Folded Robe which I had last seen the night before through glazed eyes at the bottom of the family room sofa, I said, "You didn't have to scream."

"I was scared. You honestly scared me, Stephanie. You get into my right hemisphere too fast." His eyes were the same solemn gray-flecked sincere eyes I had first loved. He touched the sides of my mouth. His lips twitched ever so slightly. "Listen, let's write in the little book again. I can plan ahead the next three weeks but after that the schedule changes. No weekends, though. They're tied up. Then in July we can plan on some weekends together." He drew little circles on my hand thoughtfully. "Isn't it strange how we're still planning dates when I feel as if I'm already married to you?"

I was back to my old responses. "Oh, Richard." What the hell was wrong with weekends? When he had tucked the datebook away and pulled my luggage from the trunk and waved good-bye and roared off into the traffic toward her, I didn't like him at all. I didn't like his eyes or his lips or his hands or his twitch or his datebook. I didn't like him leaving me on the street corner. Of course he felt married to me. I was acting like a wife, reminding him to wash his hands when he went to the men's room, talking about Piatigorsky when he whistled Bacharach, pointing out to him that his shoelaces were fraying, his knees were stretching, his eyelids had a trace of dandruff. Not because he was comfortable with me did he think of me as wife. But because he was uncomfortable with me. What a thankless victory the weekend had been.

As soon as I was in my apartment, depression coming on like a Class D fog, I called Jack, who was, as I had hoped, easy, gentle, comfortable on the phone.

"Jack . . ."

"It's been months."

"You better believe it. . . ."

"What's up?"

"How would you like to take me someplace absolutely sordid and make very dirty love to me?"

"How about your place?"

"Very funny. Anyway, I've cleaned it since I've become a serious prospective bride."

"Still?"

I didn't answer.

"The Biltmore is pretty repulsive. What do you want first, advice or love?"

"Guess."

He laughed. "Under the clock in forty-five minutes."

It would be like old times. Crazy and hilarious and ruined with Jack's torment over whether I truly loved him or not, but good, always good. Honest, that's what it was. Vile rooms, blue-movie scenes, pseudo-embarrassments in front of dumb desk clerks, like Jack pouring handfuls of ghastly dime-store jewelry out of his pockets into my purse as he signed the register. And fun. I had had no fun with Richard—and no honesty.

The Biltmore was everything we wanted it to be. If Van Johnson had walked in with June Allyson they would not have been noticed. It was still the forties. Our room wasn't altogether sordid but it did approach a special degeneracy in the coarse, iron-on taped sheets, the blankets thin, soiled and frayed and the pillows relentless as shredded wheat. Even though the bedspread was uncommonly repugnant and I very much the tarnished woman, it was no longer amusing. I bit my lip for the times I had been in places like this and thought I was in love with Jack. And when he said, "You've been on my mind a lot. I remember how you feel when you come," I remembered why I didn't want to marry Jack. But as soon as I hit the all too solid pillows, loosed my favorite little "oh," and let Jack become Richard while I lay six inches behind my own eyes, I was with Richard, nimble, quick and charming magical Richard and I responded overwhelmingly to my expectations of Richard as lover while the real Jack labored somewhere outside my reality. Whether Jack was aware of it I didn't know, nor did it seem to matter. Much later, much much later, he commented discreetly on my increased responsiveness to him. "Well, the bastard isn't screwing you yet, is he?"

"Go to hell."

"Later I want to tell you my Mick Jagger story." And then he fell into a deep sleep while I tossed and at last left the bed, paced the room, bathed and finally crawled upon a wide window ledge, wrapped myself in a blanket and Jack's sweater and watched the city skies turning from black to cream.

In the old days Jack and I would have been wandering the streets of the sleeping city searching for pastrami sandwiches and cheesecake to quiet his torment. The milk trucks were already banging over the Con Ed metal plates on the streets when Jack punctured my vigil. "Hi, lady. What's doing over there that's better than over here?"

"Do you remember me when I was a nice girl, Jack?" I think I might have meant when he loved me.

"Who is that over there whimpering? Come over here. You're still a nice girl, Stephanie."

I kept my place on the window ledge. "Remember Playland, on the beach, when you told me no one could see us because the roller coaster went too fast . . . you made up the figures . . . they'd be gone before they knew what we were doing."

"Under the boardwalk. And the cars got stuck. Hadn't calculated on the cars getting stuck."

"Why can't it be like that again?"

"First times . . . you can't go back. Not like that with your friend?"

I said nothing. He knew. I slid in beside him and he welcomed me. I knew it was immoral to cry into his shoulder over Richard, but I was crying too over Stephanie and what was happening to her.

"If I want him, I have to hurt him. I can't love him. That is, if I want to get married."

"Considering marriage a moral act, which I doubt, all morality contains the seeds of its opposites. On the basis that two human beings have to hurt each other to capture each other, marriage is immoral."

"There's self-preservation, you know."

"You love him?"

"Don't get personal."

"There's another woman?"

"Don't get personal."

"Come on, baby. There's another woman."

"You better believe it. But she's pretty Italian and he's into politics."

Jack laughed. I hated him when he laughed. "You mean he thinks you're a good political bet? A country club Christian with a Long Island jaw. Shit, Stephanie, a couple of hundred dollars, someone buys her clothes and teaches her to speak . . . anyway, if he's such a good politician he should understand that an Italian wife is much more negotiable than a Pound Ridge prize like you these days. Christ, Stephanie, I hope for your sake he's good in bed."

"I hate you a lot."

"You hate truth, sweetheart. Truth as I see it is you don't love the guy at all. He's not even sexually attracted to you and you're grimly goddamned determined to marry the poor shmuck. And you know what I think? I think it smells."

I pounded his chest. I smashed my fists against his ribs and he laughed, grabbing my wrists after a while. "Channel the energy, loved one. Don't deny your anger. It's a form of passion."

When I stopped hitting him, he held me and rubbed my head silently until sunup. And then I brought him my hairbrush and we sat cross-legged while he brushed my hair gently, braiding and unbraiding, twisting and smoothing, and told me his Mick Jagger story. I tried to listen. It was about a woman who wanted to sleep with Mick Jagger.

"Who left her husband and her kids and started balling rock stars and each time, each guy, she'd say, 'He was good but he wasn't as good as Mick Jagger.' In a few months she actually met the Rolling Stones. She slept with the equipment men first and said after each of them, 'He was good but he wasn't as good as Mick Jagger.' And then she slept with the audio men and she said . . ."

"Please don't drag it out so . . . and do the sides. Too much on the back."

"Well, she finally balls Mick and she says . . ."

"I don't want to hear it."

"I didn't think you would. But you should. She says, 'He was good but he wasn't as good as Mick Jagger.'"

The point being, I understood, take me, Steph. There is no Mick Jagger. I went into the shower and knew there was more than that to the story and that Richard, no man, was ever as good as romantic girls dream them to be and there was nothing ahead of me except disappointment. And I screamed. As long and furiously and maniacally as I have ever screamed. When I was hoarse and dry and out of the shower, Jack was gone. He'd never done that before. I'd really become a different person. Even Jack didn't like me any longer. That night with Jack, I think, was the last loving act, the last softness, I can remember. My last dance with truth.

June was not my cruelest month. I was willing to do anything to get Richard into bed but nothing seemed to work. I nagged Richard a great deal and although that didn't bring him to bed, it did keep him coming back for more nagging. Even though he was already talking about marriage plans for Christmas, I could tell from the way he looked at me that he was into the duality again. His someone seemed to be in pain—I could tell she was spending time away, running, threatening, returning to whip more cream. Richard wasn't ill but there was still something gray about him, which indicated that no one was caring for him the way in which he needed to be cared for. I knew from sentences he left unfinished, from a sad look on his face when he mentioned picking up bread before he left me one afternoon, from the pain he felt when I was cruel, that she was a good person who did not give him pain. I could imagine then that I would even like her. He told me once, unguardedly, before he could slip back into the neurotic act he usually had pretty much together, that her CR group was pushing her to be more independent. He was worried that she didn't have enough of her own life and he was encouraging her to find it. I hoped she might also. We had one long convoluted inane conversation about raising children. We used bottom lines in more paragraphs than the Sunday *Times* held, ending in ideas about identity. His. Hers. Mine. Richard didn't talk to me the way you talk to a person you sleep with. They were serious, our conversations, and real, but thoroughly objective. And then, at one point that month, he told me he had seen his girl's analyst. Not only was Richard's girl in trouble, but Richard was also.

He didn't know if it was time for him to marry, he told me. But he had narrowed his choice down to two people. "Guess who?" I didn't respond. She was in such distress, he said, and I seemed so together. I didn't think she was in such distress at all. I was certain she thought she would win by giving him everything he said he wanted: independence, freedom, sexual fulfillment, understanding, sympathy, whipped cream. But she didn't know Richard. He said he wanted all of the above but I knew at gut level the only thing that Richard would keep coming back to was a nagging woman. He wanted to be nagged and he wanted to take me places. She was waiting like a good wife for him to come to his senses, secure in the belief that honesty, truth, and all those items always win out. So she was giving him enough emotional rope. But I was making the knots.

I nagged him. He took me places.

She owned the weekends. I, the business days. There were all those long lunches and short dinners during the week—so little space in which to flaunt the archetypal nightmare I was supposed to be. I did work on the capillary action however. His table manners needed cleaning up. He ought to be more careful about how he put his adverbs before his verbs because it was indicative of second-generation American. I refused to talk about his ties when he asked but did remind him often that his suit needed pressing, cleaning, anything, that his shirts were not looking as good as they once had and that when he met my family, although *I* knew how wonderful and bright he was, he ought to be careful because, although I knew it was only sincerity and a desire to please, he had a way of running off at the mouth, which, I added, was fairly typical of bright self-made men, especially in law and it would irritate my parents a lot. I mentioned often that sooner or later I'd like him to meet my friends. He was very agreeable to that but I never brought him any friends.

We did meet Jack once. Jack pushed past us both in P. J. Clarke's and then swung back when he recognized me. He was very drunk and wobbly. It was only lunchtime. "For God's sake. Stephanie. Baby!" Then he looked at Richard, lifted the bottom of Richard's tie and said loudly, after examining it cross-eyed, "Jesus, Baby, where'd you pick that up, the Yeshiva?" I didn't know if he was referring to Richard or the tie. I should never have told Jack about the ties.

Richard bravely attempted a rejoinder—"I've got a buddy in Tie City"—but Jack had already stumbled away toward the men's room. I so wanted to run after Jack and laugh with him because I knew he was holding his sides over the sink, laughing or vomiting. I could have done both also. I wanted to be with Jack.

After lunch, Richard and I wandered along the streets, each trying to fill the other's emptiness. There was no radiance in my face this time, not like the first walk we took together. We looked at diamond rings in velvet windows and talked about the shape I'd prefer. Richard, because he knew his own pain, didn't ask about Jack. And all I could think of as we looked at pear shapes and emerald cuts was how easy it would be for the girl at the piano if she did indeed have a baby or simply announced a pregnancy or tried a suicide. But I knew she was too decent and in her decency she was losing. I was winning and I couldn't afford to deal with sentiments and sympathies. I couldn't afford to waste an afternoon and so as

I walked out of one jewelry store, I said softly to Richard, "I understand you and your girl fuck like crazy and semen flies all over the apartment."

Richard leaned against the door frame. He closed his eyes. When he finally opened them, he said, "Be my friend, Stephanie. I beg of you."

And I said, "Of course, darling. I understand. I just am fascinated by the expression. Is it true?"

"No, no. It's not true. Nothing is true."

"But she said so. That you hum when you come and sing when you swing. Or is it the other way around?"

"God, Stephanie, this is so personal. Please. Can't you see what you're doing to me?"

"You're going to have to face life, Richard. You are going to have to do something about her."

Of course I could see what I was doing. The horrible thing, the really shocking and disappointing thing, was that it worked. It worked too well. There were times I wished he would free me of what he was making me become. Fold me in his arms and whisper, "It isn't necessary, darling. Stop. I love you. You *can* love me. I want you to love me. God wants us to love each other."

But he never did take me in his arms. I always wondered if it would have changed our direction. One afternoon he called me at work to tell me he had faced the duality. He had told *her* analyst that he was in love with me. My modus operandi was operating only too well and on a Saturday morning in July, which *was* my cruelest month, we were driving, just driving around without direction, no place for Richard to go, and he faltered. He asked me for a Saturday night date.

"You mean a real date on a real Saturday night?"

"Would you like that?"

"I would. If there's a good movie. I hate to spend time watching a bad movie just to go to the movies."

He suggested three. I made up bad reviews.

"Well, we'll do something. Let me make a call."

When he came back from the phone booth, looking now sickly and sad, he told me it was off. "Something's wrong. I don't know. She's upset. She's really upset about something. God almighty. God almighty. I have to get home quick."

In the car, windows closed, heat turned up high, although the day was in the eighties—I had claimed a chill—I asked him one of the few questions I allowed myself in those times. "Richard, do you love her?"

He salivated and swallowed very hard. It took him a long time to answer. "I feel I owe her something."

"That's what I mean. You are so evasive. Why can't you be honest with me? I'm honest with you. Why can't you be honest with yourself. Why can't you face LIFE?" I didn't lie back. He was so unutterably vulnerable I continued my offensive until a very serious squad car took over for me and, howling at Richard, signaled him unceremoniously to the side of the road.

My harangue continued, counterpointing the trooper's. "You give him a ticket, Officer. Give him a big ticket. Make him pay, Officer. Make him know there's a price. *He* doesn't care what happens to anybody else. He just goes *his* way. *He* doesn't care what the speed limits are. I've told him a hundred times 'You're going too fast. You are going too fast!' You have to think about other people, Richard. You have to think about the *lives* of other people and do you think he does?"

"Ma'am?"

"Do you think he thinks about other people?"

"You have anything to say, Mister?"

"Stephanie, I can handle this."

"What can you handle? You can't even handle me. You expect to handle an officer of the law? You who think the laws are for everyone else? I hope you get put in jail." I folded my arms across my chest. "Tell him about the little kid you almost hit when you drove off. Tell him that, I dare you. And he wants to be governor. Can you imagine?"

"Okay, buddy, you just drive on. Just drive on. Try to watch the lights and the signs, huh?" The trooper patted Richard on the shoulder and walked away shaking his head.

"Jee-sus!" I said to no one out the window. "I'm going to trust my whole sexual being to this man who can't even handle a policeman. Jee-sus!"

"Take it easy, Stephanie, please."

I apologized and reassured him that when we slept together, I would be easier. I wouldn't be so uptight anxious, so angry. He said he hoped so. That was all he said. It wasn't much to go on.

Then it was the last weekend in July. Although I'd seen a lot of Richard and been promised a lot more of Richard, his Virgin still had the keys to the kingdom and I had yet to dislodge her. I spent my times without Richard devising new and wonderful final solutions for the Virgin. I had never consciously wished for someone's quick demise before and I was shocked at myself for finding those thoughts so close to the surface. And then we were going to Westport for Richard's mother's birthday party and I did not know what I would do because my month was almost up, nor could I gauge what I had already done. But somehow, Richard and I would have a showdown and it would have to be that weekend because after that weekend Richard was going to the Hamptons for his vacation and not, I had no reason to think otherwise, alone.

Richard's mother's birthday party in the den in Blossom's Westport barn was my finest moment. Mrs. Slentz was sixty. Richard gave her a three-month trip to the Greek Islands, Rome, and Israel. She tore up the envelope from the travel agency without opening it. I watched the back muscles of Richard's neck tighten and vibrate like catgut. "*You* know what I want for my present, Richard. *You* know."

"Mother, not here, please."

"And it shouldn't be short and squat."

Mark giggled and whispered wonderfully loud to Pamela, who was wrapped in pink angora, hair in curlers, curled in Pussycat's lap. Smug. "Innocent Marie." Pamela nodded knowingly.

"See, even the kids know. All I want, Richard, is that I don't get an Innocent Marie."

I started then to laugh. I laughed very hard and very well. I faked most of it, but I was good, holding my stomach in agony and wiping my eyes. "God," I managed through my desperate gulps for air, "is that a person's *name*? I never heard . . . can you imagine . . . naming an innocent kid like that? She must have been born with flamingos in her belly button. A pair. Did you ever . . . did you ever hear about the Ital . . . no, about the flamingos who got married? Oh God, and they bought a pair of Italians for their front lawn?"

And then, because it was time to notice that I laughed alone and that Richard's family sat alternately watching my alabaster face and Richard's reddening face, like a team of demolition experts between two nitroglycerin caps, the nitro is ready to blow, when will it go, how will it go, will we get any birthday cake if there's a fight? Then, I stopped laughing. No one breathed. If a moment were to be pregnant, this was the moment.

I released my tiniest, poorest, littlest little-matchgirl-selling-matchsticks-on-a-bitter-winter-night-to-support-her-dying-mother "oh" into the vacuum around me. "Oh."

I inquired of everyone's frozen face. "Is . . . is Innocent Marie a *real person?*"

Mark exploded. "His girl friend. Uncle Richard's girl friend."

"Yes," Pamela, cool and wicked, president of the sorority. "His Italian girl friend, short, squat, and bangs."

"Nasty child, Pamela. That's enough," Blossom managed unconvincingly. Blossom's children were, after all, holy. Also Blossom had just joined my team. Ho ho.

Menacingly, Richard rose from his Hans Wegner Bear Chair. "Stephanie, I really want to talk to you."

Where was the magic? It had been such a lovely line. Nevertheless, for old time's sake, I followed him into the next room just like the night we had met when he really wanted to talk to me except this time I turned to my attentive audience, mimed the long, angry eye-popping face of Richard, crossed myself in abject piety and exited left. A burst of laughter followed me. Richard closed the door on it. "Now, Stephanie . . ." Richard began but there was nothing for him to say. There was no now for him. It was *my* now. He had stepped out of time into dark limitless chaos and he knew it. I'd show him cosmic spaces. What he wanted to say to me was "Don't make a scene. Don't embarrass me," but, hydra-headed as I was, I had no intention of saving Richard's two-faced neck. I was through the maze and into the forest and I had the Unicorn at bay, almost in my virginal lap. Loose the hounds, sound the call. This may be it.

It wasn't it. But it was fun. As soon as Richard abandoned the closed door to take a position suitable for flogging, facing the bookcase, I opened the door, winked at my spellbound audience and filled my lungs because I was about to project as I had never projected before, the Yma Sumac of Westport, Connecticut, raising the Inca gods at Machu Picchu, a range unequaled in the long history of Woman Betrayed. Tragically, of course. And very loud.

I chose a middle octave, round, firm, accusative tones. "You, Richard, you to whom I am promised are living in sin." I moved to upper octaves. "And I hate SIN!"

"Please, Stephanie."

"I hate sin. I *hate* it. *Oooh*, I hate it."

"Please, Stephanie, let's discuss this sanely. Keep your voice down."

There was no way for him to close the door to his family as I stood before it, defending the fort, guarding the Nibelungen treasure, maintaining my indignity, and if he were, either gently or violently, to move me from the door—whatever—his flesh and blood, his mother and his executor, all of them out there would see his naked face. At that moment, only a shiny collection of Martin Buber, Winston Churchill, and Philip Roth could appreciate his naked revealed face, which I think must have been terrific, a noble prize. And I think, also, that Churchill and Buber would have been on my team.

I leveled into low octaves. "I am ashamed." Dirge speed. "I am ashamed. I thought the Jewish people were decent. Was I so wrong? I thought the Jewish people were ethical. Was I so wrong? I thought the Jewish people were moral. But this—*this*!" Although I was addressing Richard's back, I wasn't addressing Richard. I was addressing the nation of Israel, ancient and modern. If Solomon slept with the dark foreign Sheba and brought down Israel and the wrath of Jehovah, so could my Richard. I let it be known to all assembled that the judgment of the entire Christian world, of which I was a major representative and not an unheard voice, that the entire world's judgment of the Jewish tradition would pivot on Richard's behavior with the woman of sin. Actually, until that moment, I had never thought one way or another about which religion had higher morals. Men were men. Miriam had taught me that. Any other distinctions were after the fact. But it was gorgeous. Richard's shoulders shrank into his camel cashmere jacket. He managed a few weak Stephanie pleases.

I turned to my audience in the den. Low, vibrating, stage whisper. Ring out, sing out, fling out your empty arms. "Richard and I, that man, have never slept together. Richard told me we shouldn't sleep together and I believed him. Do you hear that? Richard and I have never gone to bed because he's going to do it right. And do you know what doing it right means for Richard? It means living in sin. With a woman. In *sin*. It means, Mark and Pamela, that while your grandmother and your grandfather made love and your mother and your father make love, your Uncle Richard fucks. That is the difference. That is sin. *And I hate sin*!"

"Stephanie," Richard said softly, still facing Buber, Churchill, and Roth, "you knew I was living with someone." He turned to me. His eyes were pathetic.

"How should *I* know?" I pointed to his family. "*They* all know. I'm the last to know. The woman is *always* the last to know."

"She brought you the key, Stephanie."

*"That?"* I resisted holding my forehead or clutching a breast. "That is Innocent Marie? Oh, no! Oh my God, don't let *that* be the other woman. Oh, Richard, why couldn't she at least be pretty? I wouldn't have to suffer this shame if she were at least pretty. Or honest, or decent, or famous, or nice or even had good teeth. Or smart. Some redeeming feature I need. Well-dressed. Would that have been too much to have asked of you, Richard? That if you had to sleep with someone, that she be well-dressed?"

"They sleep naked, Aunt Stephanie." Someone clapped a hand over Mark's mouth.

I clasped my shoulders, holding myself, and strode back and forth before the door. "I hate sin. Oooh, I *hate* sin. I hate sin so much." Richard somehow moved through my defense and closed the door.

"Now just hold on, Stephanie." Richard faced me and spoke to me between his orthodontic teeth in a pained whisper. There is something decidedly sexy about violence. I could see where folks could get off on it. Maybe that was why I was doing so well. Richard felt he had to hold back here too. Anything but an emotional commitment. "Now just hold on."

"Let me guess. I think it's Gary Cooper but I can't get the title."

"She *is* decent and she *is* pretty and she's smart and nice and honest and I won't have you talking about her."

I walked nearer the door. "I hate sin, Richard. Oooh, how I hate sin. Ooooh, I can feel it I hate it so much." And I opened the door. "Don't you hate sin too?" I asked his family raptly assembled. They all nodded at me affirmatively. "And her name is shitty, Richard. I never heard a shittier name in all my life. If you could only tell me one thing about this hippie women's lib ragpicker kook, one thing so I could hold my head up in public. I beg of you."

"She's an honest woman. She has integrity."

"Does anyone who lives in sin have integrity?" I

asked rhetorically of my audience. They shook negatively this time. Mark asked what integrity was and Pamela told him to shut up.

"One thing, Richard. I'm waiting." I crossed my arms over my chest.

Richard offered his defense to his family. "She's a nurse. She helps people." He really meant it. I would never have that kind of love from him.

I threw my head back and laughed. "You mean a Natalie Nurse?" Then dropped to my lowest octaves, quivering, deep, agonized. "You come to me from her, from the bedpans, from the staph infections, from the cancer, from the lymph nodes, from the bedsores . . ."

"White with foam," Pussycat sang out bravely.

"Shah!" Richard's mother commanded behind her birthday cake. "Shah, Pussycat! I don't want to miss anything. What did she say? Did I miss something? Isn't she wonderful?"

"I said she is death. I said that Richard comes to touch me and he comes to me from death. Richard touches his mother and these clean children and that birthday cake and he contaminates the people who love him."

"See here, Stephanie, she's maternity. You've got her all wrong. That's life, maternity."

I continued undeterred. "From the festering fetuses, from the bleeding wombs, from death. She is death."

"Go on, Richard, let her have it."

"Daddy!" I heard Pamela, as calm a little castrator as there ever was, "I can't believe that you would defend Uncle Richard's *sinning*."

"Pussycat doesn't mean anything, Pamela, honey. He's just sorry for Uncle Richard. We are all sorry for Uncle Richard."

Richard's voice cracked and rose on what he interpreted as sympathy. "She's a nice girl. She doesn't even scream like Stephanie. She's not a fishwife like Stephanie."

"You better believe it like a fishwife. You want to hear screaming? You just continue with your immorality, with your deceit, with your dishonesty, with your hypocrisy. God, to think you are allowed in a court of law. To think." I addressed now the heavens. "Oh, but they'll find out. The world will find out about you, Richard Slentz. The world will find out what you've concealed under that curly head. And if they don't, I'll follow you into the courtrooms and I'll tell them what I know. God help me, if only he had been living with someone *decent*. What have I done that I deserve a trafficker in death? Do you actually kiss her?"

"Look . . . Jesus . . . *Stephanie*," Richard came toward me, arms outstretched.

"Don't touch me."

"You're really getting carried away. Anyway, she's a hell of a lot more decent than you are. I don't know what you're so ashamed of."

"Watch, soon he'll tell you I'm crazy. Just remember, the truth is I was sane until he betrayed me." Richard was standing too close to me and looking at me soft-eyed, hurt, incredulous. I was tiring myself. I summed up. "Oh, Richard, if she had something, like taste, a different name, anything to recommend her, Richard." I let my voice break in sorrow. "Isn't there anything about her we can take pride in? Give us something, darling, so we can forgive the man we love."

He offered me hesitantly and sincerely his something. "She loves me."

I filled my lungs as he backed away. "Out! Get out of here! Get out of this house. This is a decent house with decent people and you don't belong in a decent house with decent people. This is an honest house and you don't belong in an honest house."

"An honest house with honest people," Blossom assisted me. I was getting bored and had lost my flow, structure all off.

171

"I'm going." Richard pushed past me. "Goddammit. I'm going."

"Go, Richard, and if you ever come back to me, you'll have to make a choice, Richard, between Death and Life. Hands that touch bedpans shall never touch mine. Go."

Past his mother, and out. I've always wondered at what point Richard realized I'd thrown him out of his sister's house.

Mark pulled at my sleeve. "I hate sin too, Stephanie."

Pamela kissed my cheek. "You were divine. Just divine."

And Blossom and Richard's mother just stood rubbing my back. "Don't get upset. He'll come back. If not now, later. He'll come back."

Pussycat came to us bearing plates toppling with birthday cake. "Poor son of a bitch, he didn't even get a piece of cake."

"Don't worry," his mother told me, "he'll come back. One thing Richard likes is to be comfortable. All you have to do is make him comfortable." I guessed it was the secret she had been waiting to tell me. It wasn't so extraordinary. But then most secrets like that aren't. "Soft chairs, good lighting, silky sheets, a nice place. Don't worry, sweetheart, we'll fix it. He'll come back. Don't worry."

By the next morning I was on my way back to the city. I wasn't sure if I were totally numbed or simply feeling no pain. Nor did I care to make interpretations. I shared the backseat of Blossom's station wagon with a very ugly four-foot wall-eyed pike who lived in a plastic bag on the floor of the car and sloshed back and forth as we drove to the city. Blossom, Mrs. Slentz and Mark sat up front. About as often as the car hit the expansion joints in the highway, Mark asked to sit in back with the fish. The women ignored him. He continued to ask. I had preferred his Mothra act.

Mrs. Slentz had bought the pike in Southport on the way out. Although I knew the pike was for the gefilte fish she would prepare for the Jewish New Year, I couldn't understand why she'd bought it so early unless they force-feed the fish with herring or capers or something equally exotic from Zabar's so it would be worthy for the holidays. Which meant she intended to keep it alive until then. Mid-September? Was she crazy? I had forgotten the day she stole the crocus plants and threatened to crucify the guard.

Blossom and Mrs. Slentz talked unendingly about Richard. Richard didn't stand any more of a chance than the fish. He and I were going to have a setup, a terrific apartment which Uncle Myron would find and which the ladies would furnish and when Richard came home—Mrs. Slentz clapped her hands together so hard I thought a tire had popped—trapped. The two women prepared lists as we drove. Mrs. Slentz, beetle-browed, pursed lips, scratching into a notebook, was not the same sweet and simple mama she'd been.

There was a new kind of Kali power I'd never noticed before. Both women envisioned empty kitchen drawers and cupboards and efficiently, as if this were the voyage of the *Beagle*, categorized my needs and the evolution of our marriage. But they laughed too often. "An egg slicer. You can't be happy without an egg slicer."

For some reason that was very funny. Blossom added, "And a potato masher. How can she live with Richard without a potato masher?"

"A food mill," threw them both into gales of laughter. I didn't want to get involved at all, but hearing them, I thought there were surely some levels I wasn't operating on. "Thermometers," Blossom giggled. "You forgot the thermometers." Both wiped tears of laughter from their eyes.

"Could you see my son without his Q-tips?" Even Mark paused in his requests to sit with the fish to laugh at the Q-tips. I closed my eyes and leaned my cheek against the cool window. Mrs. Slentz obviously noticed from the back of her head and turned around to reassure me. Her eyes were tearing with laughter.

"Don't you worry, Stephanie. He'll be happy. Just make Richard comfy. That's all he needs. He really wants to get married." The way in which she looked at me that moment, half with fear and half as if I were a Balenciaga she'd found on a bargain table at S. Klein's, I wondered why she was helping me. I couldn't understand why she would want me to marry Richard. She must have known that in two years Richard and I would hate each other. But she also must have known that I wouldn't be a threat to her and that in two years I'd be helping her chop the gefilte fish and anything else she wanted because I would need her to fight with Richard. She must have known. I should have known.

At a rest stop, Mark climbed into the wayback and took the fish with him. He lay on his belly, supporting his chin with the palms of his hands and emulating the fish, every solemn slosh-eyed fish-eyed move, all the way into the city. When the fish rolled, Mark rolled. When the fish swam in his plastic, Mark swam. "Mama, do fish get nervous?"

"Does he make you nervous, darling?"

"No, but do you think *he's* nervous?"

"No, darling, I think he's happy because he's going to be part of our holidays."

"I like him. He has a name. His name is Newton."

"Isn't that nice," Mrs. Slentz commented, annoyed to have her lists interrupted. She was, after all, ordering lifetime supplies in wholesale lots. All of her connections and her relatives would be involved. Washington had far less help supplying the Continental Army. Richard and I would never run out of anything.

"Doesn't he get sick from all the sloshing, up and down?"

"Mark, your mama and I are making lists. We have to *concentrate.*"

But Mrs. Slentz interrupted her lists to tell me about Richard's second cousin Philip, the writer. Philip kept marrying shiksas (her word) because he hated shiksas and as soon as he married one, he set out to destroy her and when she cracked up, wrote a book about her. Five already. Philip, however, was really nuts. Richard, she explained, had no hate in him, not an inch. And he didn't write. A loving boy. I knew then—had really known late the night before, after the fight, after Richard had left— that Mrs. Slentz was well aware there was nothing in me even faintly bordering on the Semitic and that she'd known I'd been lying when I threw my birthday scene. She knew, but she didn't really want to know about my manipulations. I wondered briefly if I were simply a two-year holding device just to get rid of Innocent Marie. But no, the lists were too complete. I was it.

Mark continued to chant up and down, up and down, up and down, until we had to stop at the roadside to clean Mark, my suitcase and the carpet of the car up and down. "Vomiting," he told us from his mother's lap, "makes me *very* nervous."

"Mark," I suggested, "maybe getting nervous makes you vomit."

The grandmother and mother looked at me as if I were the mad one. I shut up and continued to wipe my suitcase up and down with oak leaves.

"Did he get any on the fish?" his grandmother kindly inquired.

"Mother!" Blossom felt Mark's head for fever.

"It's not so kosher, vomit. I'd have to go back and buy another fish."

"Don't make him feel guilty, for God's sake."

Mark started to cry. The women fought most of the way down until they stopped speaking with each other altogether. I managed not to listen, smell, or think.

When I was finally back in my own apartment I was inordinately happy to be rid of them all: the Slentzes, the horrible fish, the kid, the vomit, the whining, the insanity, and, amazingly, Richard. I didn't want to think about any of them. His mother called me often during the next few days. I was polite and noncommittal. She told me about wedding dinners and invitations and getting a setup and mints and nuts and matchbooks with our names on them and then his sister called me and told me not to listen to her mother and then his mother called me and told me not to listen to her daughter and then Uncle Myron called and told me I should apologize to both Blossom and Mrs.

Slentz for making so much trouble between them. I didn't call any of them. And Richard didn't call me for a month —although nobody actually lost touch.

The more I heard from his family, the more I turned off. The more I turned off, the happier I became. I had forgotten how happy I had been without Richard. I felt now like a kid who, trapped and twisted and strangled in her flannel nightgown, suddenly rips it off and sleeps naked. The days were good—hot, pure, cleansing August. Richard, his mother told me, was in the Hamptons and, she added gleefully, it was raining and he was having trouble with his boils. I really didn't care. It was like losing forty pounds.

I threw myself into my work. The exhibition was nearly ready, becoming itself, somehow, in spite of my dysfunctioning. I began functioning again. I took directions from a now very competent Sissy. I prepared the brochure, featuring the Cornwall tailed man on the cover as I had wished. I loved my work and I loved myself and I was not alone. I didn't bite my lip over sad songs about parting lovers nor did I peer wistfully into the windows of the Russian Tea Room where we had once been happy together. We had never been happy together. We had never even been to the Russian Tea Room.

And now I was happy. I met a Lladislaw who taught sculpture at the New School and I loved him for a weekend and a Monday and then forgot him. I adored a grinning smooth investment counselor Uncle Myron brought over to my apartment to discuss my trust funds. I could actually enjoy myself again.

The only flaw in my happiness those days was that I had to move from my apartment to the one Uncle Myron had found for me and which Mrs. Slentz had furnished, obviously with one phone call to Bloomingdale's. "I want everything and everything should match." It was a great, light, sunny apartment but the Bloomingdale's stuff was god-awful. The toilet paper matched the towels matched the shower curtain matched the dishes matched the aprons matched the sheets matched the dust ruffle matched the dinner napkins. Everything was sprinkled with flowers. I shoved as much of it as I could into the cupboards and the closets, which were very deep. I had always wanted very deep closets.

But I loved the apartment and I decided, the hell with it. It was worth the agony I'd gone through and I was rid of Richard and I knew what it felt like to be free and uncommitted without Richard loading up my heart and gut with his elusiveness and his charm and his shit. Someday I'd decide what to do with Bloomingdale's and what to do about the apartment but in the meantime I had a great place to entertain. Jack, Jim, Barry, Robert Redford, anybody. Whomever I wanted. A lot of sexy, willing, amusing, profound men who didn't want to get married. And there were plenty around.

The bed, which horrified me at first—a note was on it assuring me that the bed was temporary and I'd have another one as soon as the warehouse found it—was a hospital bed. An honest-to-God crank-up hospital bed. The upper half and the lower half went up and down. It was most likely the one in which Richard's father had died. It cranked up something vicious in me. I could be evil in that bed. I wrote imaginary ads for the *Barb*: "W/f w. hosp. bed fulfill yr. adult fantasies." Romantic love was death anyway, wasn't it? Good-bye the Armengols. Good-bye the Gothic Chapel and the tears. Good-bye illusions. I would get even with romantic love and get even with the concept of marriage and family and the entire strangling mess Richard had almost led me into. I could even think, with no animosity, of sending all the matching loot to Innocent Marie after she returned from her vacation with Richard. She deserved it. The two of them could eat in the bathroom or crap in the kitchen and still match in good middle-class taste. I was relieved to be free of it all. And I would really decide what to do about the apartment but I didn't have to make any decisions yet, nor did I have to manipulate anything, anyone, any longer. I could just lie back and crank up and enjoy life. Let Innocent Marie suffer. That's what she wanted anyway. That's what they both wanted. Let her be in love. Thank God I wasn't in love anymore. The thicket of the Unicorn is thorny. I was free.

I called Jack. Jack came up. We laughed a great deal. He called me a bitch. I agreed with him and then bit into his shoulder and I realized he was no longer in love with me either and we could have a very good time together. We did. I didn't have to hold my breath anymore until the phone rang. I didn't have to die with every word Richard said or every silence between his words. I could go out to dinner and actually digest. I could spend hours chasing a man around the hospital bed. I was no longer obsessed with marriage. I vowed never again to be obsessed by a man. Never again to be in love. Never again to be trapped by romantic love. All done.

It lasted until the engagement ring arrived in the mail. It could have been the potato masher, it was so big and ugly and Cedarhurst. I was wildly angry with Richard for knowing that I had turned off. That fuck, to figure I had turned off and try to manipulate me this way with the engagement ring. I don't know why I didn't try to reach him in the Hamptons. I simply picked up the phone and dialed his number in the city, quivering with the anticipation of telling him what to do with the ring, when the girl answered.

"Richard?" she questioned, softly, trembling.

"I thought you were with him."

"Oh. I thought . . ."

"Yes . . . ?"

I placed the phone in the cradle. I knew what she was doing there. She was hanging around in case Richard called, in case Richard came home. She would be there to rub his back or take his temperature or whatever had to be taken, given, shared. Clever little lady she was. I knew what she was into because I knew what I would have done. She'd be there for him by accident, sincere, straight, sweet and sorrowful. And that was her winning way. Innocent Marie was no better or worse than I was. She too had a vested interest in winning Richard in her way. And I had a vested interest in winning him in my way. Her way wasn't any less moral than mine. Her vested interest was in being sincere because being sincere had probably worked for her in the past. And my way was to manipulate. That was the way I trusted. I knew exactly what the dance was between us. Her sincerity was just as manipulative as my manipulation. It wasn't even Richard anymore. It was who would win the prize. She was just as convinced that sweetness and innocence would win as I was that manipulation would. If either of us were to back up, start again in a different way, we couldn't. Right or wrong.

I had no idea if I'd chosen the wrong way. It seemed to be working better than her way. People might like Innocent Marie a lot better than they'd like me, but in the long run, it might make her sick, all that sincerity, all that peeling nakedness of soul so she can get what she wants from other people, using innocence as a weapon. She probably made up her own name when she met Richard. My way wouldn't win me any popularity contests. But in the long run, for me, what did it matter? After all, what really matters in life is that you get what you want and I'd be damned, goddamned, if this girl with her sincere little tricks and her innocent breathlessness was going to be a better woman than I. Or if Richard, with his stinking manipulation of me—that ring!—would win. I would win. She was over there thinking right now that she had the magic, that only she could really handle Richard, that only she could really love Richard. I was thinking exactly the same thing: that I was more woman than she'd ever be, that I was the only woman who knew how to make Richard happy. Dumb little Natalie Nurse. At least I was smarter than she was. I'd show her.

I called Blossom. She shrieked at the same pitch as a new Miss America. I took the first train to Westport. Blossom, as in an Olympic race, handed me the keys to the Continental at the train station and I roared off toward the Hamptons. When I stopped for gas, I called Richard. "Don't move. Don't move, darling. I have your ring and I love it and I love you and I'm on my way. Stay right there."

"Stephanie, would you pick up a thermometer? Rectal?"

"Of course, darling." I hated to break my momentum but I stopped at a drugstore and, in the manner of the Slentzes, bought a half dozen matching. I was back into the obsession. The potato masher though was gleaming like a torch on my finger, the Continental purring and speeding toward Richard, and the radio was playing the kind of waltzes one dances with princes. I kept expecting to see Innocent Marie in a VW somehow trying to pass me and get to Richard first. Every time I saw a VW, in fact, I sped up. I should have known then that I wasn't merely breaking the law of the highway, I was denouncing everything civilized within me and responding to my most primitive instincts. Not sexual. Worse. My smile when I greeted Richard was a thoroughly atavistic baring of teeth. Nevertheless he seemed happy to see me and grateful for the many thermometers. I wanted to throw my arms above my head and clench my hands and shout all over the beach: The Winner! Instead I hugged and kissed Richard who allowed me, warning me first that he might have a fever.

Richard and I threw everything from his cottage into black plastic leaf bags, tossed the leaf bags into the back seat of the Lincoln and headed toward the city. Neither of us mentioned exactly where we were going. We were just getting out of the Hamptons and back to the city. My intentions of course were that both of us end up in my apartment. Later, I calculated that I had spent approximately seven minutes kissing Richard and forty-five or more packing his things.

"Tell me when we pass the windmill," Richard requested.

Richard indeed had a boil on his tailbone. He offered to show it to me. I passed. But it was painful for him to sit up and so he curled up, put his head in my lap, drew his knees into a fetal position and I drove. When I announced the windmill at Bridgehampton, Richard announced that he had a deep attachment to windmills and sang "Dream the Impossible Dream." Aah, I thought, today it would be *Man from La Mancha* for our theme. We'd been through enough *Annie Get Your Gun* and I could live happily ever after without ever hearing "The Girl That I Marry" again. Little did I know *Finian's Rainbow* was on the bill.

I had to smile to myself. The Unicorn lay in my lap after all. And the Unicorn ready to share his wisdom with me began finally to reveal himself. Reveal, reveal, reveal. Knowledge is power. Information is energy. I had never known Richard and I was fascinated with all that he was that day and all that he had ever been. Unfortunately there was also to be revealed that day all he would ever be.

We were driving through a rainstorm on the flat road along the ocean although we could see no ocean. Fruit, steaks, baskets, potato fields, Harvey Bellringer Real Estate. I pointed the name out to Richard. He apparently wasn't amused. He didn't respond. Instead he informed me that the tailbone boil was my fault. It was systemic, he insisted. Three times he told me it was systemic because I had altered his life. "In a way," he said, "everything is coming to a head. Here I am with S. Boxwell and we are going to get married. And who is S. Boxwell?"

The boil wasn't precisely my concept of a romantic analogy, but his question was precisely my question. And who is this man with his head in my lap whom I am about to join for life? And who was I that he would tell me his dreams and trust me with them? I wanted to hear his dreams. I prayed he wouldn't get off on Adolf Berle, his regular lunchtime subject. As I had happily anticipated, Richard revealed his treasure, his little pot of gold that held the essential mystery of the man. It wasn't quite what I had hoped for.

"Oh, listen, look at my elbow. Is there something on it? A slight eruption? Jesus, we forgot to take my temperature, didn't we?" He took my hand from the wheel and placed it on his forehead.

"You'll live until we get home."

"Home." He smiled, quite dreamily. Could it be so simple? I had seen Blossom consoling Mark. I hadn't even thought when I'd said "home," and yet, he had acquiesced without a tremble. "I'm ready to go home, Stephanie. I'm ready. I've done a lot of thinking while we were apart, S. Boxwell. And I meditated every morning at six A.M. You know what I concentrate on when I meditate?"

"Mmmm?" I of course wanted him to say me. Richard was not entirely altered however. "Love."

"Oh. How lovely." Well, so what. He was going home with me. I had expected my proposal to be a somewhat memorable cross between the sixth-grade Thanksgiving scene of Pocahontas and a little of the Pope washing the feet of the Cardinal or maybe the Queen of Spain telling Columbus to go ahead. But just a slip of the tongue?

"I'm ready for an equal relationship. That's why I'm going home with you. You know why? You are centered. You know who S. Boxwell is and what she will be and what she means. That's confidence, that's integrity. It's terrifically attractive, Stephanie. I'm very impressed with you. I've watched you for a long time."

Aah, then the confusion and double meaning had simply been his version of *Once Upon a Mattress*, a little princess-and-pea game to drive me mad, the test of a good wife. Think Broadway, you'll understand Richard.

It may have been the boil on his tailbone that kept him turned toward the dashboard. Although he seemed to be speaking to me as he developed, quite interestingly and with nice professional insights, his childhood and his coming into manhood, he was addressing a space on the dashboard, an invisible audience out there, a speech before a mirror. I was vitally interested at that point in his revelations of self and merely noted Richard had what Miriam would refer to as an oblique superego—eyes away at all times.

"There's so much to tell you. Where to begin. A woman has been given to me and I can't misuse her. She is like a precious flower or a beautiful shell. Too rough, too unthinking, I will crush her and lose her. I found that out about you. You are delicate, you feel. God, you feel. You respond to each breeze, to every change of light, like a flower." Richard nuzzled his nose into my belly. "And you are my fine gift so I can free myself. So I can become a man."

Ah so, a bit of *Teahouse of the August Moon*. And this business of my freeing him I've heard before. This man is going to feel so free and good about himself because I've freed him to become what he's always wanted to be, because he can finally relate to a woman, so free that he's going to make neurotically certain he can really relate to every woman in the world. Like a teenybopper going back to junior high with the new breasts she grew over the summer. Jesus. I wish I hadn't freed him so much, whatever that meant. I'd prefer hearing about Adolf Berle, me, Richard as boy scout, anything, but I didn't want to know how free and alive my friend was becoming.

"Well, I *am* jumping ahead. As a kid I never knew enough about anything the other kids knew enough about. I never memorized the records of the guys on the ball teams, or the list of birds in New Jersey. I liked fish. I never knew as much as the other guys in school seemed to know about girls. So I hated ball, hated boy scouts, avoided girls. I think that's why I'm a lawyer today. I could only picture myself as a mediator between people who knew more about life but less about law than I did. Somehow, you know, moving above life, judging, looking into their windows. I'll never forget when the captain of the high-school football team came to me to represent him. I was just out of law school. To me, that was my reward, my justice. But I wasn't at ease yet. I talked too much. Those first days in court I couldn't shut up. I was terrified. You know if you take away the "e" and the "d," terrified is pretty close to terrific. Well, I couldn't stop talking. It was bright talk and impressive and the juries sat drinking it in, every word, but I couldn't stop."

"I understand." I couldn't resist.

He turned swiftly to read my face but he chose not to recognize the nastiness. The jury must have been on the dashboard, little elves from *Finian's Rainbow*, the tiny little jurors all nodding their tiny little heads at Richard and clapping their tiny little hands for him. He turned back to them. How are things in Glocca Morra, Richard, and when do we get to the pot of gold that is your essence?

"Of course you can see that, darling. Because, you, Stephanie . . . I don't have to talk to you. You just understand. I don't feel I have to be "on," prove anything to you.

186

I can relax. I've thought a lot about this. You see, I'm step-ping into a real relationship. You showed me that at the birthday party. You are life. You are in touch with life. You are womb and birth and life. . . ." He turned into my stomach again. Nuzzle, nuzzle, nuzzle. "And you will keep me alive."

While his nose pressed quite warmly into my Eveready belly button, I thought about the fish in the plastic bag and Mark shrieking for his Froot Loops. The rain was heavier, the car steaming up and the rest of the world was going back to the city from the Hamptons. We were making no more than thirty or thirty-five miles per hour. It would be a long drive. The windshield wipers had difficulty keeping the window clear. I had difficulty believ-ing Richard's lines about relationships. I didn't think men wanted equal relationships. I knew Richard didn't want an equal relationship.

"Steve would really like you, Stephanie. He really would."

There wasn't any time now to worry about what I thought or didn't think, what I believed or didn't believe, what Richard really wanted and what Richard was really getting. The Unicorn was disappearing fast and when I stood up my lap would be gone too. But right now, with his head in my lap, his nose against my belly button, the road straight and the windshield wipers steady, I was going to hear the secret I had promised never to ask about: Steve. And perhaps, if I were lucky, I would hear about the chickenstone.

"Who's Steve?"

The question roused him considerably. "You're kid-ding! I can't believe I never told you about Steve!" I'm kidding?

And then I heard about Steve. When Richard was through I didn't even bother asking about the chicken-stone.

"Steve was the guy who turned me on to Adolf Berle.

He was a poet. And we had *some* rapport. Roommates in grad school. He was beautiful. Not that we were into homosexuality, although I've always thought we should have tried it just for the experience. Well, I would have given Steve anything he asked for. We shared clothes, girls, ideas. Hell, we would stay up all night just arguing for the sake of arguing. The Welfare State, The Hero, The New Deal. It didn't matter. And then the next night we'd change sides and stay up again. One day he got a poem into the *Atlantic*. Biggest moment of his life. We took out a couple of girls to celebrate and I made a crack about his date. Not even a crack. I just said I didn't pick up anything on her. And he said, 'You miss a lot of stuff, buddy,' and moved out, moved in with the girl who he had just met and married her. Never saw or heard from him again. Is that something?"

"Wow."

"I wasn't wise enough then to know I should have said something about the poem. But I thought the poem was lousy and I figured if he really loved me, it wouldn't matter what I said, but I wasn't that sure, so I said nothing. He just couldn't let it alone. He couldn't let me be honest or even dishonest by omission. He loved anyone who would believe his own lies. He was a lousy poet. And *that* wasn't my fault, was it?"

Odd that Richard could understand all this and yet he didn't allow himself to understand what I was doing. Sooner or later he would have to. But like myself, he didn't want to face me head on. Too much reality. We both needed the lies.

It was about that point in the drive home that I realized I knew all I really wanted to know about Richard Slentz. End of the rainbow. No gold. On close inspection, here in my lap, no longer mysterious, elusive, charming. No longer an object of love. Just boring. The mate that fate had me created for . . . that old black magic. I had the songs too. You get an empty poke when you trade with the devil for your dreams. Not even a pig in it. And the worst sin is being boring. I had cast him as Jesus and now, stage right, enter the thin, shorter-than-I-remembered, weaker-chinned-than-I-remembered, higher-voiced-than-I-remembered, boils-on-his-tailbone, simple man. Not bad. Bright, hypochondriac, presentable, not handsome. Nothing deep inside, no great secrets, no key. Boring. No wonder men have to go after power externally. They have so little internally. So the Richards cloak themselves in mystery and wrap themselves in illusion and we expect to find in them the depths we know in ourselves. And they, Richard, this man, they just don't have it. It isn't his fault. It isn't theirs. Richard had begun to chat about Adolf Berle.

I passed our turn and had to pull over. When the traffic opened slightly, although I couldn't see well in the rain, I backed up. We were nearly Totaled, Crunched, and Cheerioed. Horns blasted, shocked faces passing us as I reversed slowly toward the turnoff. Richard lost track of Berle's encounters with Rex Tugwell. I don't know why I didn't begin a chain reaction on the highway except that I had my own disaster to contend with. I finally backed up enough to cut over the grass median and take the turn. My hands were wet with fear.

Richard shifted again to how free he felt with me. I was an above-average woman. He asked me if I didn't think women were more interesting when they were dressed. "Last week I saw a woman on the beach at Montauk in a long print dress. I couldn't make out one line of her body but I was absolutely turned on so I followed her . . . and . . . well, you want to hear this?"

Had it been a suicide attempt, backing up on the highway? Make me jealous, Richard. At least it's interesting to be jealous. As I ran down the collection of long gowns I owned, I considered that for an above-average, highly centered mature woman who was in touch with life

I sure was quick to compete with any woman and on the worst levels. Just challenge me and I'm on. I did want to hear it and I didn't want to hear it.

"We went out for dinner and she was really very attractive except this time she had much less on and all I could think of was you. Well, I carried on the most amusing conversation with you while I was with her and I literally had to restrain myself so I wouldn't laugh out loud or call her Stephanie. How I missed you. God, I wished you could have been there."

Maybe the boil was the beginning of a tail, like my Cornwall man. Maybe I had really done a Faustian bit and bought into evil and Richard was growing a tail and Richard was the devil. Sold out to the devil and it would be bad luck all the way from here on. The boil began to swell symbolically for me. I'd known a man whose mother died of dehydration and he found coat hangers all over her house, bent into the form of sea horses with tiny bags of sea water tied at the throats of the coat hangers. The mother lost one hundred pounds in six months and the doctors could find nothing wrong with her. He never goes near a coat hanger unless it's really a straight, untouched coat hanger. I don't blame him. I should stay away from boils and tails and wrong turns. Once you open yourself up, you're vulnerable.

We shouldn't have taken the turn. Somehow I was driving through Hempstead where there should have been a Howard Johnson's because there was so long ago when my parents had taken me there. Twenty-five years? Odd I should remember it. I couldn't find the Howard Johnson's any longer. The Unicorn in my lap was being very stupid, very sentimental, with no sentiment, no awareness that he was hurting me. I wanted an ice cream cone. Richard was a modern Cyrano calling me at midnight: "I just want you to know . . . and I just found out . . . that you are still the best lay in the whole fucking city." And meaning it. That's the sad part. The Richards mean it. "Richard, you know what Miriam says . . . ?" I tried, but he sat up and interrupted.

"Please don't tell me about Miriam."

"Okay, you don't tell me about Adolf Berle."

"Adolf Berle is not a problem in my life the way Miriam is a problem in my life."

"Miriam? You don't even know her."

"I know social workers. I know Jewish mothers."

"Look, Richard, I've been around almost thirty years

and there are parts of my life which are still viable. Miriam isn't like another man. She isn't in competition with you."

"That's what you think. 'Stephanie, you don't let a man *do* that sort of thing. *I* wouldn't take it from *him*.'"

"Christ, Richard, are you *paranoid*."

"Even paranoids can be plotted against. 'What? He hasn't given you a Trashmasher yet? What kind of husband makes you live without a Trashmasher? What? He wants to name his baby after his dead father? Of course you should name it after Nijinsky if you want to.'"

"Richard."

"'It's your *right* to go out every Saturday night. It's his duty to take you out. Does he expect you to stay *home*? What kind of husband keeps his wife home after she's suffered for four hours in a beauty parlor all Friday afternoon?' Stephanie, I don't want her interfering with my marriage."

Richard was not altogether wrong. "Our marriage."

"I don't want you calling her up with would you believe what Richard did to me last night every morning. I certainly don't want her as a social friend or as a professional friend. What more can I say, Stephanie?"

"I couldn't begin to explain it to her. We're best friends."

"You seem to have forgotten something rather basic to our relationship. *I'm* your best friend."

"Oh, God."

"Really? Is that your response? 'Oh, God?' Oh, God, what?"

Now or never, Stephanie. "Oh, God, I forgot to call my mother and tell her. Lord knows what time it is in Munich. Do you know?" How many more now or nevers would there be?

I turned on the radio and almost switched it off at the unmistakable strains of "The Emperor" but Richard was faster and blasted it. "That's the passage!"

"What passage?" Had he really forgotten we'd been through it already?

"You know how I see this? Two primeval creatures like Prometheus with new worlds rising volcanically above them, fighting the last fight. Water, fire, hailstones, red sky and . . ."

"Oh, yes, Richard, and the last fight is meaningless because it's all coming to an end."

"That's right, darling. God, it is so exciting to have a woman to *think* with. Because, because the last fight in reality is producing the new world. Right?"

"Right." I think he'd added the hailstones. I stopped for gas. I stopped for coffee. I stopped for more coffee. I stopped for a hot dog. Richard stayed in the car. I wasn't certain that he was aware I had ever left the car. He was so like the kind of people you find in the audience at a Madame Blavatsky lecture. He ate half my hot dog and went from Rex Tugwell to Harold Ickes laughing wildly at one point about something FDR had said to Ick about dams, bouncing the springs in the rich seat of the Lincoln. I laughed also, marking the vast difference between the prepositions with and at and trying to remember if I was supposed to like Harry Hopkins or Harold Ickes and who did what. I've often wondered since if the plastic surgeon hadn't made an error when he fixed Richard's ears so that Richard couldn't listen when he talked.

How I wished he would stop talking so that I might daydream about my mythic Richard, so that when I seduced him in the apartment, so that then I would at least have built up some amount of anticipation. So that. I'd much rather have daydreamed about him than have been with him. Sooner or later I knew I'd have to forfeit my daydreams and it might be too soon. Too soon, too, he might realize what I am like instead of feeding narcis-sistically off me for his own image. Locked in the car with him for three hours, we'd already bypassed the easy excitement of the first time in bed and, with a little more of his childhood or Rex Tugwell versus Adolf Berle or "The Emperor," we'd miss on the second and third time also. He thinks, I realized, that I've already gone to bed with him anyway. Who is "honey"? Why should he call me honey? I didn't really care. I was abysmally bored. Also he had said he didn't want a hot dog and ate half of mine and I was still hungry.

"Listen, we could have a party. You know, Steve used to crack me up by wrapping candy wrappers around his teeth, blacking them out? You know the little papers you get in boxes of chocolate? I can do it. Really a riot. Always cracked me up. You've got to see it. We could have an engagement party, couldn't we?"

"Don't forget," Miriam had said. "Don't forget," Jack had said. "Once you catch him, you're stuck with him." I couldn't think of anyone I wanted to invite to a party with Richard putting candy wrappers around his teeth and I couldn't think of anything worse than being locked in a car for three hot stuffy hours listening to Richard while he talked about the New Deal and I couldn't think of anything worse except more of the same. Forever. Richard thought of something worse. "We could get one of those recording devices . . . answering things? When the person calls, he hears 'The Emperor.' Just a very few bars, but the right ones." Richard hummed the right bars, over and over, waving his arms for a good mile. I was truly ready to run us both into a ditch.

How he knew at that moment as I eyed a ditch with concrete retainers to say what he did, I shall never know. As I was actually and seriously considering drc ping him, simply slipping the potato masher into his pocket and saying, "I'm sorry, it won't work," Richard rolled over and said, "Don't let me forget. I have to call Innocent Marie as soon as I get back." And then he lifted his head from my lap and put his mouth around my nipple, pulling at it. And then let his head drop back and grinned up at me. If just to rid myself of that curiosity, I really did want to make love. Though the grin was intriguing—a little child who had done something awfully naughty—I hoped he made love more seriously. Grin or not, he had weakened the coils in my springs and somehow he kept quiet, perhaps even slept, and we were what I could safely refer to as "home."

When the car stopped, he woke and looked at me quite directly. Like Mark. He looked at me startled as if he were really seeing the stranger I was and our whole future in one awful naked kaleidoscopic moment. I could only imagine what he saw. I knew what I saw and just as I had refused to look so many times, he let the moment pass, closed his eyes, took my hand and pressed it against his forehead once again.

"Poor baby," I whispered softly not wishing to wake him fully. "Let me take you upstairs and take care of you."

Murmuring, he rolled his head against me and nuzzled. "Mmmm."

"Come up."

"Mmmm."

And we went up and he didn't speak. Luckily he didn't speak except to ask me in the elevator what floor I wanted. Later I'd lock the car up and bring his things up so when he woke up, he'd be all moved in. This time I was going to do it right. Perhaps the only thing any of us have to share is our own emptiness. But dammit, he was more empty than I was. Except, of course, there were still interesting physical areas to explore with him and that could keep us going for a while. We'd have to adjust for the boils.

While I kissed his neck and rubbed his back and rubbed his shoulders, he swiveled his head around and around, entirely preoccupied with the apartment and then, finally, simply slid away from me and walked through the rooms.

"Christ, what a great place. It's so *big*."

He ran his hands along things while I told him not to touch them. But, happily distracted, he didn't notice my nagging. "Oh, yes. Oh, hey, yes," touching his father's hospital bed thoughtfully as if he were visiting the graveyard. "Big bed. Big, big bed. Look at this. My mother's chifforobe." The bed wasn't big at all.

"Look at this." He opened drawers. "God, this is great. I've always wanted this piece. All my clothes. I mean, my new clothes. Isn't this something? Did she get me a towel warmer? She always promised me a towel warmer if I got married."

I took him to the bathroom to see his electric chromium-plated 98-dollar towel warmer. He kissed my head. I reached up to him for more kissing but he was on his way again. Loving him really didn't work. No matter how I needed to love him, no matter how he needed to love me, it didn't work. And so, as he kicked off his shoes and rubbed his eyes with thumb and forefinger, settling into the very soft, down-pillowed sofa, I told him, "Your feet don't smell very good, Richard."

He put his shoes back on and then lay down on the sofa and began to talk.

It was perhaps three hours later. Richard had continued talking. I had learned in agonizing detail of his difficulties at P.S. 104 in Edgemere, Long Island. I had learned about the year his mother was hysterical and how she had never recovered from his father's death and how Richard was sure that somehow she felt he was responsible and how she had suffered ever since even though she stopped complaining and how everyone said he was nuts to put up with her but he felt he owed it to her for the pain. It was exactly ten P.M. and twenty-six minutes into a story about how Richard cheated in seventh-grade Social Studies by sending hand signals to Doug Billington for the answers to the multiple choice questions Mrs. Terrero wrote on the blackboard every day, when Richard remembered, as if an icicle had dropped on his head, that he had to call Innocent Marie. Actually, I was relieved. I had had trouble following the hand signals for a, b, c, d, none of the above, and all of the above. I didn't even question how Richard knew where to call her.

From Richard's face, I could tell how very deeply troubled he was. Most of his responses were a series of "now looks" and "but sweethearts" strung together like so many transparent fish eggs dropping into the silt of his depression. The basic emotion, I was certain from his darting eyes, was one of unremitting guilt. Richard was caught between two women, both of whom had the capacity to scream, both of whom had the capacity to make him feel guilty. I could almost hear her saying, "Where are you? Where are you right now?" And Richard didn't have the magic or the brains to pass through Scylla and Charybdis with one deft stroke of an oar. It never occurred to him there was a way out. He felt he deserved to have his head dashed against one of the rocks. His face dropped farther and farther, the corners of his mouth turning down, his eyes darting faster, left and right, and looking for an escape. Often they landed on me but bounced off very very quickly. I heard him say, "I'm at a friend's house."

It must have taken her exactly four seconds to figure out which friend because from the new look on his face, I could tell she had started to cry. With the sureness of the killer's touch, the way he went directly for my scar the first time we met, he said, "Don't make me feel guilty, Innocent Marie. You want me to be honest? I'm warning you, you won't like it."

Long pause. I knew she was screaming already and I knew by his face that he was happier with a screaming woman than with a sobbing woman because then he knew what to do. Nothing. He was a master at building sentences which would give her absolutely nothing. Neither hope nor solace, neither meaning nor closure. "We'll talk about it tomorrow, cutie. It's a little awkward now."

And he barely had time to hang up the phone when it started to ring. And she called and she called and she called. And he talked and he talked and he talked. Still he said nothing. In between the phone calls he told me he couldn't understand how their relationship had deteriorated to that point. He couldn't understand what he had done to make her think in the way she was thinking. And in between the phone calls, I came to understand the whole relationship between Innocent Marie and Richard. He really did care for her. She reflected back the parts of himself he liked best. She had taken what he had described as his potential and believed in it as his reality. And he both loved her for the belief and hated her for her expectations of him.

I had no expectations. I had expected him to provide

for me and come home in time for dinner at least four times a week. Rather than find fault with the generalities, with the whole man—was he or was he not meeting his potential, was he or was he not an underachiever— I had found fault with the particulars. All those snide comments about shoelaces, the dandruff in his eyelashes, unflushed toilets, the not-so-terrific tie. It would be years before Richard would notice how many of his capillaries were punctured. Innocent Marie, terribly invested in him, was fighting in a very different way. Her kind of honesty went straight for the jugular. She was fighting to keep him. He must hate her because, unconsciously, she knows him too well. He looks at her and, though she doesn't understand it, by her responses to him he can see his own faults and he feels inadequate. He knows she believes in him and he really knows she's wrong. I didn't believe in anything more than what stood before me.

In one of those conversations when Richard was saying nothing and I sat on the couch knowing that the woman on the phone was going berserk, I realized it could just as well be me going berserk. She thought, as I did, that she and Richard had a special relationship, that she was a special woman because he told her his stories. She knew his stories. We all knew his stories. But she didn't know him. She didn't understand that this was his character, unflinching, unchanging, telling the stories because he told stories, not because he wanted to be understood. Richard simply left parts of his emotional life lying around like so many pieces of dog shit on the curbstones. And Richard would always be shocked that the women in his life didn't run after him with enormous gleaming Sheffield Sterling Pooper Scoopers to clean up after him. Actually, at that moment Innocent Marie was shocking him by threatening to rub his nose in it. It aided my case. Up until now she had most likely felt that she knew him completely just by sniffing at the last curbstone. But the stories he'd left around hadn't been by any means a commitment or an unfolding of his soul. They were just something Richard did. What she didn't understand was that Richard had the totally evolved capacity to be a killer. What she still didn't know was that this man with whom she had shared so many intimate hours, whipped so much cream, Windexed so many fish tanks, that this man she thought she knew so well, could turn on her.

It was with these realizations that the other woman was going berserk, that it could have been me going berserk, that she was too stupid to save herself, that I had been misanthropic enough to allow another woman to go off the wall, that Richard with his furtively darting eyes was also out of control and that I, as if all the officers were dead on the battlefield and the lowest recruit were to rise to the heroic moment, I, finally my father's daughter, knew precisely where to strike. I took the phone from Richard, hung it up, took it off the hook and slipped my arms around my man. It was at that moment, in every sense of the word, that I mated Richard.

"Darling," I breathed into his ear. "You know it's that she still has expectations. She still expects. You see, darling, it would only be kind, in all fairness to her, so that she doesn't suffer unduly from her terrible expectations she has obviously led herself to believe, that we make it easy for her and just get married as quickly as possible so she knows it's over. I mean, we'll make a clean break for her sake. She's young. She'll get over it. It's only fair to her, darling, so she doesn't end up as a hysterical woman. We don't want to do that to her. I, for one, couldn't live with myself."

A further realization at the moment was that the phrase hysterical woman might indeed be a redundancy for all of us. I gave it little consideration at the time, for Richard was so relieved to be led out of his guilt and his impasse that he softened inside my arms. Slumped might have been a more accurate word. I had saved him. I could hear him saying to Innocent Marie: "Believe me, Innocent Marie, it's only for your own good. We're getting married to help you, sweetheart. You'll feel so much better once it's over. And you can be grateful to Stephanie. No matter what you think of her, it was her idea. She even agreed to store-bought invitations just to hurry things along. She stayed up all night writing them out for my mother. She was so concerned about your emotional problems." Richard would never understand why Innocent Marie would begin to scream again. I would.

Richard agreed with me. He asked if he could stay the night and I said he could but we would honor our original agreement not to touch each other before we were married. We could sleep next to each other of course. We took his temperature two more times. He told me within a two-hour framework of a girl named Audrey who had blond hair, a trick knee, green eyes, and a maddeningly fascinating habit of sucking her upper lip when they laid out the copy of the yearbook at Syracuse and how she had a deft right hand and never let him touch her. Just as he reached the part of describing the virginal night he once spent in her bed, and I was putting the phone back on the hook and making up the sofa and turning out the lights, the phone rang. This time Richard told Innocent Marie very firmly in my words that we were getting married the week after next and the invitations would be out in a week and it was all over and there was no turning back and then he laid the phone into its cradle, switched out the lamp above the sofa and went into the bedroom. That simple.

Looking back, I think it was Richard's firmness which carried me through those two weeks preparing for the wedding. Convinced that marrying me would make Innocent Marie, his mother, his sister and myself stop screaming, he worked diligently toward that solution. No one could ever say anything to him again about commitment. No one could ever say anything to him about not doing things right. Somehow, the invitations were printed, the matchbooks stamped with our names in gold, a "connection" made with the *Times* so my picture would be on the Society Page. He was so competent and so secure. He must have been very relieved to find a way to keep everyone around him quiet. After a while, even I began to think that the whole thing had been his idea.

Nothing ruffled Richard. He was a rock. He hadn't even shown annoyance when *my* invitation list included only my parents and one spastic cousin who lived in Seattle and couldn't fly. And when we called my folks in Munich, Richard slowly, serenely, spelled out his name three times, very slowly so my mother could pick up the Semitic nuances. I knew my mother. Richard could guess what she wanted to know. Is he Protestant? Is he rich? Is he sane? Nor did Richard display annoyance when my mother gave me the choice of whether they would come to the States to attend the wedding and I said, "Don't bother." Richard didn't even flinch. It was only when we had the *Times* Travel Section spread out before us in the living room one afternoon, that Richard finally flinched.

He had assigned me my pages. I had rattled through them, commenting rather acerbically on the honeymoon specials. Maybe it was the fish tanks already installed in my living room. Maybe it was the blow-up pictures already hanging on my walls. I was itching for a fight. Richard, following lines with his forefinger, was quite oblivious to my itch. " 'Make your dreams come true. Visit Liberty, New York, and find the Good Life in Sullivan County.' Richard, let's go to Grossinger's and find the Good Life. Say, how about Brittany? That would be divine. Oh, Richard, let's go to Brittany."

"Are you skipping pages?"

"Yes, I got bored with Sullivan County."

"Listen, stop dreaming. Let's get this over with. The courts are lousy at Grossinger's."

"A honeymoon is supposed to be a dream," I lamented quite childishly. I didn't like my assignment. "I want to make my dreams come true."

Between his teeth, very nastily, Richard replied, "I told you not to read those pages, didn't I?" He folded his paper in long strips, like a commuter on the Long Island, carefully making knife-sharp edges in the Travel Section and holding up for my benefit the section on the Islands. "How about Bermuda?"

I pouted, enjoying it. "Bermuda is boring."

"All right." He crossed his quarters into eighths and I was faced with a column on St. Thomas. "Is St. Thomas boring?"

"Yes, St. Thomas is boring and so is Aruba. Xanadu is simply bad taste."

"Have you considered the possibility that your boredom is internal?"

I had considered the possibility and I knew it was external and that its name was Richard. Our eyes met like two major electrical storms crossing each other in the night sky. "You know what I feel like, Richard? Like we're at an Interfaith Dance with Jewish Lesbians and the Male Nazi Homosexual League."

"All of this must be terribly boring for you. It is, isn't it?"

I so wanted to fling a lively arc of lightning at him. He asked again when I didn't answer. "It is, isn't it?" But then he lost interest in the answer and returned to reading the ads.

I remembered the first night he'd looked at me as if I were the other half of his Bermuda ad. I didn't mind it then. Now the thought made me ill. I don't think it was because I disliked Bermuda. I'd enjoyed it whenever I had to go there, basically because my father liked the golf course. I've never been picky about where I got my sun and sand. But Bermuda, but Richard, but the whole shmeer of having the *Times* spread out before us as if we were a couple of secretaries with two weeks' vacation, the whole shmeer was so stereotypically dull, not even like a Salem ad, like a Bing Crosby Minute Maid orange juice ad. Actually, looking back, the truth was that anyplace I went with Richard would have been stereotypically dull.

I thumbed laconically through the tabooed pages. He was up to taking notes. "Crete," I read aloud, murmuring, tormenting. He'd already told me that we had to stay on this side of the ocean because what if someone should die and we couldn't get back. I hadn't confronted the logic. I should have.

"I know Greece is perfect now . . . Lesbos, Corfu, around the islands on a steamer." Half needling, half daydreaming. "Lord, and Ireland in early fall, rent a Gypsy wagon and just get lost on the west coast. It's wild. It's gorgeous on the west coast."

From somewhere deep within the folds of his Travel Section Richard advised me that the Irish had stoned the last two Jews out of Limerick three years before.

"So?"

He finally looked up at me.

"Oh."

"I suppose you think that's paranoid of me."

"I'm just playing, Richard. You know." I shrugged. I was feeling little-kid mean. "I've been to Ireland six times in the last two years. I have no desire to go back."

"You're not fooling me, Stephanie. I know you want to go back to Ireland because that's all you ever talked about when we met. Ireland, Ireland, Ireland."

Well, I had won his attention. "Don't bait me, Richard. I don't like being baited."

"Look, I told you to read *those* pages, not those. Get serious and stop daydreaming. I don't have all day and I don't want to go anyplace kooky where I have to eat hair in my coleslaw."

"Jesus," I couldn't help responding, "maybe they have a travel bureau at Bloomingdale's."

"Cute. Very cute. Let's not get started. Because I could really get started with a girl like you. You're really . . . okay, I'm not getting started. How about telling me what's wrong with Bermuda?"

"I'm really what?"

"Skip it. Tell me about Bermuda. What are your objections to Bermuda?"

"It's boring. Four fun-filled nights and five sun-filled days and all the Wedgwood you can eat on the back of a bicycle built for two in colorful and shop in our Free Port."

"Stephanie," Richard tapped his automatic pencil on the sheets of the Islands pages. Then he folded the paper up. The deliberate precision of his activity was directly traceable in style and intent to my father's taking away my toys. "There is a certain lack of emotional

205

validity on your part that I find particularly and increasingly offensive."

"At last, something interesting. That's a new expression, isn't it? Whatever do you mean by that new expression?"

Richard stood up, left the Travel Section somewhere and returned from the same somewhere with his new Yamaha tennis racket and a roll of tape. He sat on the sofa and squeezed the racket, testing the grip, backhand, forehand, full serve, net chop. He spoke at last. I was supposed to have been suffering during the interim. "You can really be a nag. I didn't expect you to be a nag." If Richard were surprised to discover just then I was nagging, the surprise didn't seem to break up his serve.

"What's that? The Bloomingdale's Bon Mot of the Month? What do we get next month? A choice between 'Why Don't You Grow Up and Face Responsibility' and 'Don't You Women Ever Stop Talking?'" I wondered for a fleeting moment what Miriam would have said to all this. And then stopped thinking about Miriam. Miriam had nothing to do with any of this anymore.

"You're all the same. I swear to God." He added tape to the Yamaha. "It's amazing." And then ran through his backhand, forehand and serve again with the new grip.

"That's for sure, Richard. We are, Richard. All the women are the same because you make us that way. You want us that way. Just remember that. You make us what we are. The Richards of the world make us what we are."

"Look, I don't do well with women who manipulate words so don't waste your highly articulate time being clever with me."

"Oh? That's right. I am wasting my time. That's entirely correct. But it's not the words, Richard. It's the real feelings. You who talk so facilely about *my* emotional validity while you caress your tennis racket, you know absolutely nothing about real feelings. But I do, Richard.

I am in touch. And I know you. And I know you can't wait to marry a nag because that's what you have always wanted. You want to be punished because you feel guilty about your *lust*. You're a masochist, Richard, and you're looking for a sadist and you won't be happy until I become one. You need me to be a nag."

"Oh, come off it." He stood to try a full serve, tossing up an imaginary ball.

"The only way," I continued, unhampered by his inattention, "the only way I could get you to marry me was to be a nag, a liar, a stupid dummy, not to ask questions, not to . . . do you think I want to end up screaming like your mother? You think I want to end up in this goddamn set for *Death of a Salesman*? You think what I want from life is two weeks in Bermuda and a house in Scarsdale and a slot in the Jewish Couples Bowling League and fresh gefilte fish and a wacko family and a charge account in Loehmann's?"

Richard maneuvered a backhand, aborted before the follow-through, and returned to his tape and scissors. "Loehmann's only takes cash, sweetie, or a check."

"I don't think it's asking too much of the man I'm going to marry to listen to me, do you?"

"I am listening. I'm all ears." Net return.

"Yes, I've seen your pictures."

"Bitchy, aren't we?"

"It's a matter of goals, Richard. My goal is not to marry a nut who wants to marry his mother so he can really get *even* with women. My goal is not to live without love and die in a hide-a-bed someplace in a lousy Leisure Village apartment. My goal is not to make polite faces at dinner parties and look good in church until I crawl into my hide-a-bed or you get a heart attack in the Lincoln Tunnel. Do you think those are my *goals*, Richard?"

"So shoot me. What am I supposed to do?" Obviously the tape had accomplished *his* goals. He had the proper grip. He swung his Yamaha happily, left the room, returned with his Adidas and a package of new shoelaces and began to restring them. He had so many projects. I think he saved them up for memorable moments such as I was offering.

"Is that your emotionally valid response, Richard? 'So shoot me'? Because if it is, I just want to know so I can recognize it if I ever come across it again. But you shouldn't overdo. It might drain you. A man only has so much."

"Temple." He couldn't get the laces quite even. He pulled one out and began again. "Not church. Temple."

"Oh, you are *so* paranoid."

Richard looked at his laces, slightly cross-eyed, trying to even them up. He began to string them once more, very patiently. "Do you need to fight, Stephanie? What do you want?"

"I want . . . look, church or temple isn't important to either of us. So don't play games with me. What is important is that you're telling me what to read. That you're telling *me* not to dream. That's what's important. That you think you can tell *me* not to dream. If I want to dream about . . . about the Golan Heights, I'll dream about the Golan Heights. What I want is that you just stay out of my head. You don't belong in my head, Richard. Get me?"

"Who wants to get into your head?" He was examining with crossed eyes the second shoelace, dividing it in half before his nose. It was minutely off. "Getting into your head would be like falling into a cement mixer." And he laughed, quite pleased with his line. I would hear it again, I knew. Often.

"Terrific, Richard. Is that the Bonus Bon Mot for joining before September fifteenth?"

He didn't answer. While I talked, Richard finished lacing his sneakers, pulling the laces into very tight, perfect x's.

"Well, Richard, I *am* going to be your mother. Because you made me into your mother. You have to marry me so you can kill me because you've always wanted to cut your mother to pieces. But you're not going to kill me. Somehow I'm going to get a life out of this. Even though I sold out. It's true. I sold out for you."

"A cement mixer. That's funny. Don't you think that's funny?" Richard tucked his sneakers cozily next to each other at the bottom of the sofa and patted his Yamaha in place next to his sneakers. As he walked past me toward the bathroom, I told him my Sabbatai Zevi story. I thought it was quite fitting. He apparently didn't know the reference or care or both.

"I stripped myself, Richard, like all those people waiting for the Messiah. Except I stripped myself of decency and honesty and integrity and I climbed into my white robes and up into my tree and waited for the Messiah. And waited. I thought that's what I was getting. But, thank God, I didn't sell out all the way. There's a little of me left. Enough to get me out of the tree and see you for what you really are. I see you and I know you. Too well."

From his face as he passed me on the way to the bathroom, I could imagine him either cleaning himself or committing suicide. He had a good rigid grip on his face, very much like the young soldier in the war movie pulling the grenade pin with his teeth. We were both on the edge of real violence and I was fascinated. Or maybe real truth. I wanted one or the other very much. Richard slammed the bathroom door. I heard the shower turn on full force and I waited. And finally, drawn inexorably, as if the bathroom were Plato's cave, I flung the door open.

Steam filled the room. Richard's monogrammed deep fleecy bath towel was warming itself on his electrically heated chromium-plated 98-dollar towel stand. "Close the door, honey. It's cold." What happened to the violence? I still had mine and I was gasping the most intoxicating air I had breathed since I met Richard. I tore apart the shower curtain. "I dream about you, Richard. A lot."

He grinned at me, supposing the attack to be sexual.

"Louder, it's hard to hear." And turned, handing me the soap to do his back. I know he had me confused with Innocent Marie or all the other women who had done his back. Or not even confused. Nevertheless, I did his back, methodically, harshly, because he stood still and listened.

"Do you know what I dream about? I dream about both of us lying in that horrible bed like your mother and father, with cobwebs hanging from us. I dream about that every night, Richard."

"I know the scene: *Great Expectations*. Not so hard, honey."

"And when we die, Richard, your mother comes and carries out the bed with us still in it. Every night. And some nights I visit you in a hospital room. You aren't a prince in shining armor anymore. You have a white uniform on all right but it's a hospital robe and you're lying on a shining operating table and there's a marble floor but it has messy organic things on it but no waltzes, no music, no waltzes at all. You are only head and feet. No body. And I reach to touch your hand and you know what the doctor says? He says, 'Mrs. Slentz, don't squeeze his hand. His asshole is under his thumbnail.'"

Richard held out his hand for the soap. "That's funny. You *are* funny today. That's almost as good as my cement mixer." Then he began to scrub his testicles vigorously and lovingly. The soap had a decal on it which matched the wallpaper. I hoped it would transfer itself to his balls.

"That's how I spend my nights with you, Richard. I wanted to marry you and love you and I found I couldn't have it both ways. There's no way to have it both ways. Remember that song? You gave me that song to believe in. 'The Girl That I Marry.' And I tried to be that girl. It was a lie. You . . . you are treacherous."

"Really? Me?" He hummed a few bars. "And I thought you liked my singing. You *have* been dishonest with me."

He then burst forth in full song and I hated finally—him, myself, the song. It was like watching my own death scene. I was immobilized by my hate and mesmerized by his insensitivity. "And in her hair, she'll wear a gardenia, and I'll be there, 'stead of flittin' I'll be sittin'—Next to her and she'll purr like a kitten." At one point, he paused and remarked again, "Odd, isn't it, how everyone blames me for their disillusionments? Tell me, Stephanie, does your mother scream?"

"No."

"And why doesn't your mother scream?"

"Because she's screamed out. Because she had a song, too. Do you know 'One Alone,' Richard? That's my mother's song."

Richard answered me by beginning "The Girl That I Marry" again. I started to yell over his noise and the shower's noise. "Sing, Richard, sing. That's terrific!" Actually I *was* screaming but I considered it an entirely justifiable exchange. Anyway, I couldn't help it. "My daughter isn't going to know radios exist. She's not going to *hear* the songs. My mother sold out to the first kid with hair on his lip for 'One Alone.' One alone, Richard."

Richard was doing his hair now, bubbling with shampoo, quite happily haloed. I'm sure he could hear me. His eyes were closed. He was making believe that he couldn't hear me.

"Because she was in love with the song. You must know the words. You and all the Richards in the world must have *written* the words. 'One alone,'" I screamed, "'to know my caresses. Yours to be eternally . . .'"

He opened one eye. He shut it and wiped the burning soap away with the corner of the towel. "Stephanie," he warned me quite passively, as if he had caught me picking my nose, "don't scream."

"Then turn off the shower so you can hear me."

"I don't want to hear you. I'm washing my hair."

So I screamed. " 'Yours to be eternally the one my worshipping heart caresses.' That's the key word, Richard. Worship." Richard began to sing very loudly again.

"Her nails will be polished and in her hair . . ."

"That's romantic love for you, Richard. It's anti-God, Richard. There's no such thing as love, Richard. It's all a lie, Richard. There's no such thing as the right girl or soul mates. It's the devil's lie. And I made a deal with the devil to get my fantasy, like Faust, and you were my fantasy, Richard, my God-help-me dream man, and I made a deal with the devil for my soul to get you, because you were illusion. And I sold out and you aren't even real. The bag was empty when I got home and looked inside."

We ended together on the same note. He with "marry will be." Me with "looked inside." He smiled. "That's pretty good, Miss MacDonald."

I pushed him against his chest. It wasn't exactly a blow. I had hoped my Nelson Eddy would slip into the abyss under the avalanche. Richard did lose his balance but caught himself on the soap holder. As he recovered himself he smiled crookedly and arrogantly as if he had discovered not only that Jeanette MacDonald picked her nose, but ate of her find and rubbed the rest in King's fur. Very assiduously, Nelson Eddy scrubbed the spoiled spot which I had touched with his bar of decaled soap until the spot was vividly pink. I think he planned to show it to his mother. And all the while he scrubbed and soaped and rinsed and inspected for stray bits of infection, he offered me an incredible overture of the best of Broadway, just lines, significant lines, indicating quite clearly that Richard knew damn well how to use love for his own purposes. He was no innocent. "You're the prize that heaven sent for me. The shadow of your smile. You are love, here in my heart, where you belong, here you will stay. Why do I love you? Why do you love me? How can there be two happy as we? Only make believe I love you. Only make believe you love me too. And if you asked me for the world, I would get it. If I had to sell my soul, I wouldn't regret it. It's just impossible. I'm just a girl who can't say no."

And all the while I screamed because I wanted him to scream, to forget the words, to feel, to hurt. I was beginning then to understand fully what it was I felt: a terrible, irrevocable loss. "Trade off the worship of God for the worship of man and what do you get? You get a jug-eared neurotic, a fake, an illusion, a cheat. Tell Plato his stupid cave's empty. Because now, now, I have nothing to believe in. I believe in nothing and it's your fault, Richard. Your fault."

Richard was just completing "Like the heroes bold in the books I've read." He scratched his scalp, massaging it. "Odd," he repeated thoughtfully. "Awfully odd how everyone blames me. Hell," still scratching his scalp in country boy confusion, but I knew he wasn't confused, that he'd never been confused, "I never told you I was God, did I?"

Then coyly, quite coyly, he pulled the shower curtain around his head, miming someone. He had swung from Robert Goulet to Nelson Eddy to Will Rogers. I was having difficulty following his impersonations. "It's just me. Richard. Just plain Richard." He grinned that crooked grin, like the Cheshire cat, the floating face, the rotten grin.

I turned away, ashamed, everything in me igniting, things which had lain turgid since childhood rising like bile, threatening to choke me, and, as I turned my back on him, Richard grabbed me by the shoulder with one hand, and with the other lifted his testicles rather appealingly to demonstrate, I supposed, his simplicity. "I am but a simple man, Stephanie. Just a plain pair of clean pink balls. That's all. Who the *hell* are you to tell me I'm no good because I'm not God? The Virgin Mary? Woman, let me advise you," he began, with his balls sitting round and pink and small in his hand, "life will be a lot more pleasant for us if you don't scream at me and a lot more bearable for you if you get rid of your illusions and stop dreaming. I am what I am. It is what it is. Face up to reality."

There is no reality as penultimately disillusioning as a handful of pink scrubbed balls or a man who calls you Woman. I don't know if I was more deeply offended by the ugliness of the balls or the arrogance of the word Woman. I wanted to kill Richard. I felt how good it would feel to kill him, to core his head like a head of lettuce, to hull him from the belly button like an overripe strawberry, to literally strangle him in the shower with his warm towel or electrocute him on his electric chromium-plated towel warmer or squash him against the tiles with his Yamaha. Or all at once everything at the same time. And let him drift down the drain into the New York sewer system and meet all the monster alligators that grandmas had sent from Miami Beach and mamas had flushed down toilets. And yet I stood there.

Richard dried himself happily and conscientiously with his warmed towel, whistling his overture of the tunes he'd already presented me with, then dragged the clear Lucite wastebasket over to the side of the tub, unzipped his new Gucci dop kit from Blossom, sat on the edge of the tub with his nail scissors and clipped his fingernails into the wastebasket between his legs.

My anger and pain had focused within me. I knew what it meant. I no longer had to scream. Sanity and quietude washed over me and I could speak softly. "I don't think I can marry a man like you, Richard."

I watched the fingernails drop into the clear Lucite wastebasket and lie there, quite cut off.

"Well." One hadn't been cut deeply enough. He measured and snipped. "Listen, like everything else, it's a challenge. But we can meet it. Together. Just like doubles. You have to get rid of that old ego if you're going to play a good game. Hey, turn off the towel heater like a good girl, will you? I think it gets too hot. Maybe you ought to call the store."

"Richard, you don't seem to understand me. I don't want to marry you."

"You're afraid of the challenge. That's all. Perfectly normal." He found his cuticle scissors in his new Gucci dop kit and concentrated with absolute worshipful intensity on his cuticles. I watched the cuticles drift in on top of the fingernails. They fell exactly. None misbehaved. Richard must have felt good about his clear Lucite wastebasket, his new Gucci dop kit, his richly warmed bath towel, his good aim, and his new grip.

"The only challenge in marriage, Richard, is how not to make a man feel inadequate. The rest is easy."

He looked up. I think I had communicated because a cuticle fell unobserved beyond the confines of the wastebasket. "Are you serious?"

"Yes. I don't want to marry you."

And then he examined the spaces between all of his toes for athlete's foot, found his toenail clippers in his new Gucci dop kit and proceeded to manicure his toes. "I do this once a week. It's a good habit. Do you do it often?"

"No, I rip them out with my teeth. Richard, you aren't listening to me. I'm telling you I don't want to marry you."

I watched Richard clip his toenails. I watched the toenails drop neatly into his clear Lucite wastebasket on top of the fingernails and the cuticles. When he had ten even clippings of toenails in a pile in his clear Lucite wastebasket and he had washed the scissors with hot soapy water, dried them, and put them back into his new Gucci dop kit, zipped up his new Gucci dop kit, rubbed Keri lotion on his cuticles, held them a few inches before my eyes for inspection, slipped into his new monogrammed fleecy LeRon robe, let me follow him to the sofa, tried a few more backhands, forehands, and short net serves with

215

his Yamaha and laid it gently on the sofa, when he had done all that, he turned to me, with a look of true helplessness, and said to me what I realized, looking back, was probably what I would have said to him: "The invitations are out already. It's too late."

What still surprises me is that I never cried.

Much later, I heard him laughing out loud from the bedroom. "What's so fucking funny, Richard?" I yelled at him from the sofa.

"Cement mixer."

"Richard, do you know what the elephant said to the alligator after the alligator bit off his trunk?"

"No, what?" he called.

I held my nose. "Very funny. *Very* funny."

"Good night, Stephanie."

"Good night, Richard."


"Momza! Momza! Am I gonna get you." That had to be Mrs. Slentz. I knew I was dreaming but I couldn't wake up. I was standing in the hallway of Richard's old apartment, right where I had heard the girl singing. The door to the apartment was open. Up and down the hall thin cracks of light showed through discreetly ajar doors. Now Blossom screamed. She was magnificently Wagnerian. "For Christ's sake, Mother, open the drain! Let the fucking blood out. It's the blood that's driving him crazy."

"Newton's nervous, Mama. Gramma, don't do that to Newton. Let's buy filled fish. Gramma, please leave Newton be. Oh, please, Gramma!"

"She's beating him on the head." Innocent Marie sat red-eyed among the warehouse furniture in the living room. She held a dying asparagus plant between her knees.

"Get me more fish. I'll show you, Newton."

We both listened to the noises from the bathroom. God help me, I had walked in at the moment of execution.

I brought Mark an ice cream sundae filled with Richard's strawberries. He took it without looking at me from his seat on the toilet and then, without shifting focus from the bathtub, found his mark and shoveled the ice cream in. Newton was mangled and bloody but very much alive. Mrs. Slentz swung a rolling pin, not well. Blossom came back in with a Maxwell Coffee tin filled with the fish from the fish tanks. She poured them into Newton's blood-red bath with the wonderful manic haughtiness of a Lady Macbeth.

"There, Newton, now you get busy and concentrate on those fish. Shhhh. Everybody quiet. As soon as he forgets." There was a wild thrashing. "Momza! Momza! Get me the tennis racket."

"Mama, why should Newton die? Why can't we just buy filled fish in a bottle?"

"Somebody's got to die to fill the bottle. This way, honey, it's fresher. My grandmother and your father's grandmother always did it this way."

"Did you meet Innocent Marie?" Blossom asked me.

"Yes. She wants to know where the cat is."

"Shhh, Newton's concentrating."

"Aunt Stephanie, they told her Uncle Richard is in Venezuela."

I left the bathroom. Innocent Marie was still on the couch, holding the very dry plant, shaking as the plant shook and lost its leaves. I wanted to sit with her.

"They packed my uniforms and my checkbook and all my things. I know Richard isn't in Venezuela. I just wish I knew where Platypus was. He said I shouldn't stay here. He wanted to save me from this. But I told him I would've stayed as long as it was with him. I didn't mind."

Blossom weaved between the furniture toward the fish tanks and then passed us again with her Maxwell can. "Newton's not stupid," she explained.

"I guess I'm lucky getting out of this. Richard's not

like them. He is sweet and wonderful and sensitive. He's a very sensitive person . . ." Innocent Marie drifted off, lips trembling.

"Zeezagut! There's the cat!" Mrs. Slentz howled.

"Get a shoe box someone. Innocent Marie, do you have a shoe box?"

"I got him! Got him! Look at *that*."

"Mother, for God's sake, open the drain."

"Totsela, Mark, get Gramma a nice big knife."

"Bubby, don't kill Newton. Mama, don't let her kill Newton!"

"He's just sleeping. He won't feel anything. Just hurry."

Blossom came out with a dripping shoe box. Some of the matching flowered towels were tucked into and around the body of the dead cat. "I'm sorry. We tried to get him to stay away from the fish. He wouldn't. He really wouldn't."

"Oh, you mustn't tell Richard. It would break his heart." Innocent Marie peeked into the shoe box. "How many times did I tell you not to play with fish. Poor Puss. Oh, poor poor Puss."

"Bubby, don't do it. Oh, Newton, I'm sorry. I'm sorry, Newton."

As Innocent Marie lifted the shoe box and swung the asparagus plant under one arm, about to leave, Richard burst in through the door. I truly had no place to go except to stand under the doorframe to the living room and watch them. Seeing him at a distance, I was shocked to notice how thin and dry he had become. "Sweetheart," he told her. "Are you all right?"

"It isn't right. It just isn't right, Richard. It's not right." She clutched the shoe box to her breast.

Blossom started to shout from the bathroom. "Richard, come quick. Mama's fainted."

"It isn't fair, Richard. Richard, I'm not trying to hurt you, Richard. I would never hurt you." Innocent Marie's voice was clear, bell-like through the insanity and the shouting, steady and sane and loving and comforting and I could understand how Richard loved her and needed her. I wished somewhere there would be a voice like that for me. "It's not going to work anymore. I would hurt you more if I stayed."

"Richard, don't you have a fucking *conscience*? Your mother's on the floor," Blossom yelled.

"Stephanie, go help them, will you?"

I didn't. I couldn't. It was the first time the girl knew who I was. I was ashamed.

"Sweetheart, what are you going to do with . . . with that, that box, sweetheart?"

"I'll bury him someplace nice. With sunshine and mice. In Bermuda."

"I don't ask much from you, Stephanie, but I am asking you to go in and help my mother. NOW!"

He turned back to Innocent Marie. "Look, let me just throw it in the incinerator."

"Good-bye, Richard."

"Just a goddamn minute, Innocent Marie, don't go."

She turned to leave. If only I had the strength to leave with her. Richard closed the door after her but there was one moment when she turned around and looked at him, that last horrible moment, and her face looked the way mine felt that day in the taxi when he closed the door on me and said we'd do it right. Hurt, shock, confusion. But she was getting away with more than her dying asparagus plant and her dead cat. She still had her integrity. And she was getting away. Richard and I stood very still. Then he walked by me and looked upon me with glaring hatred. I shrank away from him. Then another Richard ran past me in tennis whites, ran back and forth, weaving between all the women, trying to clean his mother and lift her from the bathroom floor. I at last found a box of Q-tips and began to clean the grout in the bathroom tile of the blood and fish scales and cat hair.

Richard simply stepped over me again and again. Wine, ice cubes, tea, smelling salts. His mother finally groaned, stood, and leaning on that Richard, stumbled to the living room.

"So, now, Richard? That's over. We'll have to buy the gefilte fish." She was heaving. "Do me a favor. Settle down now. Another time like this would kill me."

"I didn't ask you to do it. Don't blame it on me that you don't bounce."

"Richard, don't get her upset, for Christ's sake. Leave her alone."

"She used my tennis racket. My stainless steel tennis racket. Nice?" His temples pulsed incredibly. I returned to the bathroom. I wiped the walls down. I scrubbed the golden cat hair and the scales and blood, but I did not look in the tub. I was numb. The Richard in the bathroom with me was too quiet, almost automatic. I hoped both of us didn't come alive at the same time. We'd destroy each other. I cleaned every line of grout slowly and painstakingly and used all the Q-tips. I was trapped in the bathroom. And I couldn't stand the smell and then I looked into the tub and began to scream. I filled the small bathroom with my scream. I slung my scream into the grout like Newton's blood. I screamed long and well for Harry Truman to get me out of the bathroom.

Richard looked in and exclaimed simply, "Jesus, another one." And shut the door on my scream.